Praise for *Such a Lovely Afternoon*

"Flather writes with a fearless honesty that makes you wince with recognition and weep with relief that there's someone who can put the complexity of living into words. These stories are soaked in the light and darkness of Canadian intergenerational experiences. Flather takes us north, west, and to the far east, right into the hearts of characters trying to get out from under their own lives, whether they're travellers, adolescents, parents, or political refugees. Her captivating, lively, and heartrending stories are peopled with characters as troubling, provocative, and lovable as our own friends, families, and acquaintances can be. You'll find yourself buying extra copies of this book because, as much as you want others to read it, you can't bear to give your copy away."

—**Joanna Lilley,** author of *Endlings*

Such a Lovely Afternoon

Such a Lovely Afternoon

STORIES

PATTI FLATHER

INANNA poetry & fiction

Toronto, Ontario, Canada
www.inanna.ca

We gratefully acknowledge the support of the Canada Council for the Arts and the Ontario Arts Council for our publishing program. We also acknowledge the financial support of the Government of Canada.

Cover design: Val Fullard

Such a Lovely Afternoon is a work of fiction. All names, characters, businesses, places, events and incidents in this book are either the product of the author's imagination or used in a fictitious manner.

All trademarks and copyrights mentioned within the work are included for literary effect only and are the property of their respective owners.

Library and Archives Canada Cataloguing in Publication

Title: Such a lovely afternoon : stories / Patti Flather.
Names: Flather, Patti, author.
Series: Inanna poetry & fiction series.
Description: Series statement: Inanna poetry & fiction series
Identifiers: Canadiana (print) 20220284865 | Canadiana (ebook) 20220284873 | ISBN 9781771338844 (softcover) | ISBN 9781771338851 (HTML) | ISBN 9781771338868 (PDF)
Subjects: LCGFT: Short stories.
Classification: LCC PS8561.L34 S88 2022 | DDC C813/.54—dc23

Printed and bound in Canada

Inanna Publications and Education Inc.
210 Founders College, York University
4700 Keele Street, Toronto, Ontario, Canada M3J 1P3
Telephone: (416) 736-5356 Fax: (416) 736-5765
Email: inanna.publications@inanna.ca   Website: www.inanna.ca

For Leonard

Contents

Penis Envy

MARCH IS WHEN TRACY LEARNS about her best friend Amanda getting her Dot. Code name for period. Amanda taps her finger on the wall in the open area between the grade fours and fives. It's their code action, with no words required. Tracy takes eight days considering, and checking her dad's human body book, to believe it might just be possible to get your period if you're ten. Then comes word from Amanda that their other best friend Katherine's next for her Dot because she's already getting hair down there. "That has *nothing* to do with it, okay?" Tracy says. She's never been more sure of anything in her life.

Katherine gets four stretchy pink Training Bras at her birthday party the day before St. Patrick's. Training for what? At the party Tracy feels sorry for her friend. She would slit her throat and die if that happened to her. (Tracy got one Training Bra, girly and scratchy, for her tenth birthday last fall. She hid it in the bottom of the kitchen trash.) Katherine apparently loves Training Bras, though, because she's tracing the sucky flower pattern on the lace and then folding each bra carefully instead of hucking them in the pile with the okay and dumb presents. Tracy does not get it.

Back at school the next Monday, Tracy and Katherine lean against the brick wall at recess watching Amanda play tetherball. Amanda's a soft-round teddy bear, so maybe her boobs aren't real boobs. She's the best at tetherball in the school, for girls and boys, cupping her hand on that ball and sending it swinging on its rope, wrapping all the way around the pole. Other girls play stupid four-square with a bouncy ball the colour of liver. Tracy and Katherine are talking about a rumour that Amanda swore was true about Bobby McIntyre, who Tracy has her biggest crush on, but who likes Katherine. The rumour is Bobby walked out of the can this morning with his fly open and no underwear. They're debating whether it really happened or not, because Amanda loves to gossip. And if it did, was it on purpose or accidental? No way does Tracy believe it's on purpose, Bobby's not creepy like some other boys.

"I wonder what they look like," Katherine says, kicking the asphalt with her runner.

Tracy's mouth must have been hanging open for eternity because Katherine goes, "What? What?!" and shakes Tracy's shoulders.

"You've never seen one?" That is basic.

"Tracy, I can't help it if I don't have brothers like you."

"I only have one," Tracy says. "Don't you see your dad?"

Katherine's hand flies to her mouth. "You saw your dad's thingy?"

Doubt creeps into Tracy's voice. "Yeah." Don't all moms and dads have their pee naked in the morning? "Only a coupla times."

"No way. My dad would never..." Katherine's mom and dad are from England and they're super nice. She's an only child. When Tracy goes to her house they play hide-and-seek in the yard and board games, but not on the days when Tracy has swim club and Katherine has catechism, because she's a Catholic like Bobby McIntyre. They go to the same church on Mountain Highway that the prime minister of Canada had his secret wedding in. Tracy's mom is a Lutheran and her dad is an atheist, but he likes church music and drawing cartoons on napkins in the pews.

Tracy looks up the dirt bank dotted with lumps of sulphur to the mucky gravel field where Bobby and the other boys play soccer. Maybe she'll play tomorrow, she thinks, pulling up her turquoise hip-huggers.

"Well?" Katherine says, sticking her face right into Tracy's.

"Well, what?" It can't be that weird to go pee naked in your family. At swim club the girls shower without their suits on and get changed together.

"What does it *look* like?" Katherine looks like she might wet herself.

Tracy steps back and breathes in spring air with a thrill of power. "Okay," she says. "Ugly like an earthworm but way bigger."

"What colour is it?"

"Pinkish."

"That's it?" Katherine frowns like she doesn't believe it, twisting the ends of her hair round her finger. She has cute brown bangs that curl under and two long braids.

"Interesting in a way. Then boring." Her dad's job is sitting around helping grownups with their problems. Tracy read in one of his psychology books that little girls got jealous of penises and wanted to stand up and pee too. Penis envy. Which made no sense because why would you want to stand up and spray it all over, maybe on your pants and the floor, when you could sit very comfortably and get it all done at once in one place, especially if you needed to do the other stuff too. B.M., her dad said. For Bowel Movement.

Tracy's teacher Miss McDougall encourages research. "Hey Katherine," says Tracy. "Do you have penis envy?"

"How can I envy about something I never even saw?"

Tracy considers—Katherine has a point. The bell rings. Amanda joins them, her forehead dripping sweat.

The boys race down the bank, Bobby in the lead, and rush through the girls playing four-square. Andre is small and mean and always last. He pushes Kuldip. She falls down. He shouts a cruel word that Tracy doesn't understand, not exactly, but she somehow knows it's about Kuldip's thick black braid and her dark brown skin. Kuldip's the only one in their grade who looks like that. Kuldip gets up, grabs the ball, and hurries into the school. Tracy wants to sock Andre in the mouth, except she doesn't.

The only thing Tracy can do, because it's her duty, because Katherine is her best friend (well, it's a tie with Amanda), is educate her. Otherwise, Katherine could travel without basic knowledge through the end of grade five and possibly the rest of elementary school.

With Miss McDougall, who wears jeans most days, T-shirts, dangly bead earrings and zero makeup, they work at their own speed, trying to think above the racket in the open area with four classes all together. It's easy to slip a clean sheet of paper into her arithmetic workbook and start the pencil sketch. (After the first parent-teacher interview Tracy's mom told her dad that Miss McDougall was a flaky hippie, and that was before she found out about drama three times a week.)

When Tracy moved to the neighbourhood and started at Valleyview Community School in grade two, everyone else already knew each other from grade one. She printed so lightly with her pencil that it was almost invisible and hardly spoke in class for grades two and three. She actually wet herself not once but twice, too shy to put up her hand to ask permission for the bathroom, ashamed as she waited for her mom to bring clean clothes. Now she has friends. Now people always ask her to sign her name for them or draw horses or deer and the pencil marks are dark enough.

A few minutes before lunch, Tracy has to admit it is a good penis. The balls are well done too, quite wrinkly. A song jumps into her head naturally in her dad's silly voice.

> There once was a man from Leeds
> who swallowed a package of seeds.
> Great tufts of grass sprouted out of his ass
> and his balls were covered in wee-eeds.

She smiles and hums the last line to herself, examining the hair, which she finished last. Frizzled. Thick. She hasn't seen her dad's thingy up close of course, that would be weird, but she's studied his human body book and used her imagination. Miss McDougall gives her a strange look, lifting her eyebrows. Tracy stops humming. Katherine, two desks up in the next row, is... no way. She's touching her back... with her finger... No way. She's probably wearing one of her four Training Bras. She is! Tracy can see the outline under Katherine's stretchy shirt. She's tracing the sucky lace that feels like sandpaper. In school, where everyone can see. Tracy hucks her eraser at her friend to make her stop but misses, hitting Andre a desk ahead. He scowls and she buries her head in her hands.

After the bell Tracy passes her workbook to Katherine, whispers, "Look inside," and waits. The others are in the cloakroom excavating lunch when Katherine opens the workbook, gasps, and shuts it. Tracy looks around and of course Miss McDougall stares with eyebrow question marks because Katherine just has to be loud. Amanda peeks out of the cloakroom. Katherine rushes over to Amanda, grabs her arm, and races towards the bathroom with the workbook.

Tracy sits back down at her desk and eats her cheese and pickle sandwich. Meanwhile, she observes, then imprints Bobby McIntyre's meal choices in her brain. White bread. Some kind of meat inside. An apple. Luck-ee—a Hostess Twinkie, vanilla cream filling inside soft yellow cake.

A scream comes from the hall just outside the bathroom, followed by numerous giggles. Almost every girl in their class is huddled around Katherine. She's whispering something. The girls jump and squeal, covering their wide-open mouths, excited, then descend on Bobby and the other boys eating their lunches. Katherine is at the front of the pack. Katherine! A few minutes ago she never even saw the thing. Now she's lead boy-dragger, enticing them towards the hall. As if they don't know what's what. Only Ross, the boy with no arms, whose mom got given a horrible medicine when she was pregnant, stays behind, eating with his bare feet. Watching the mob leave, Tracy savours sweet bread-and-butter pickle against mayonnaise and cheese slice, a sandwich she made herself. She feels puffed out in her chest like a school principal. Also as if she's floating deep in a pool, her goggles pressed to the glass bottom, watching her friends watching her picture of a penis.

She would never have ended up in the office missing the entire drama class if it was only Miss McDougall. Tracy swears her teacher is smiling as she looks at the work of art. Miss McDougall puts on a strict teacher face before passing the paper back across the desk to the principal, Mr. Buttons, with his baby moustache and double chin. It's too bad that Mr. Buttons had to find it first, as the gang of grade five girls and boys poured out of the boys' can screaming and somebody tripped when they were all supposed to be playing outside at lunch. Mr. Buttons tells her, "I'm very disappointed in you, Tracy," which probably is not because she did such an excellent drawing, which she did. She can't help wondering if his penis looks the same as her dad's or the ones in the book, or puny like his moustache. In her head she pictures his thing under his slacks and then tries not to because it's gross. This is possibly why she doesn't hear Mr. Buttons until he raises his voice. "Tracy. I'm talking to you. Do you have anything to say for yourself?"

About what? "No."

"Are you sure?" She nods. The principal sits straight like he's in a picture frame, head glued to the top, both chins struggling to reach his chest. "If that's the case, I'll have to call your mom and have a little chat about her young lady."

I'm not a lady, Tracy thinks. I don't want to be.

Before Miss McDougall leaves, she touches Tracy on her shoulder, gives it a little squeeze. And winks. Her earrings tinkle. Suddenly Tracy knows. Her teacher's not a lady either. She's a hippie, which is better.

"Miss McDougall," he calls to her. "I'll speak with you later."

You have legs like tree trunks.

That's what Tracy's coach says. After school, at swim practice, on the pool deck of the rec centre.

Tracy knows she's fat. Fatter than Katherine, nearly as fat as Amanda, who wears long baggy shirts to hide it and has chub-boobs but no Training Bra. (Many years later, scrutinizing photos of herself in a bathing suit, circa age ten, she realizes that her swim coach was full of shit. Suspects that her coach was fatter. Many years later.)

If she has legs like tree trunks, then Eddie must despise her. Eddie in Red Group, who is eleven, with brown eyes mostly hidden by greenish-brown chlorine hair, and who says hi to her sometimes. Eddie is her second major crush besides Bobby.

Coach Nelson tells Tracy, "I'm moving you down to Blue Group next month. It'll be better for you, okay?" That's it, before he turns away, screaming for everyone to get their butts in the water. She slides in. Time for another glass bottom pool moment. Floating. Sinking. DOWN TO BLUE GROUP. She can't keep up anymore, not with her freestyle or flutter kick or anything. Stacy from their carpool beats her. Eddie's little brother, who's eight and wears underwear under his suit and it shows, beats her. Freestyle, fifty metres, Nelson yelling GO! What is wrong with her? Her dad pees naked. Nobody else's dad does. She drew a good penis but probably everyone's talking now, rumours about how she knew how to draw one that good. Ten seconds apart, Nelson yells GO! She's never done *anything* with a penis. The closest she got was in grade two on the slide at recess, Andre behind her pushing something at her bum over her skirt so she froze. Finally she went down the slide, him behind her laughing, then ran away to the dirt bank by the field to look for sulphur chunks, small and yellow, smelling like egg yolk. Remember your flip turns. Nelson yells GO! She's pulling as hard as she can with her arms, flutter kicking, breathing every three strokes like her coach said, not moving anywhere, fat, stupid, slow. Chlorine streamlines her tears away.

Barbi Benton doesn't have legs like tree trunks.

But she's not skinny. She's a Twinkie. Delicious.

Playboy Bunny.

Playmate of the Year.

In her bedroom Tracy sometimes draws horses and deer. Other times she draws ladies. Curvy ones with tiny waists and big boobs.

Tracy sits on her bed before dinner with a pile of their dad's old *Playboy* magazines. With her younger brother Curtis, her next door neighbour Sam and his sister Cindy. It's okay. Tracy's dad lets them and her mom doesn't exactly say no. Before their baby sister was born, their parents took Tracy and Curtis to prenatal class to watch a birth movie. There was a vagina and mostly a lot of blood. Tracy knows *Playboy* is not okay in other families. Otherwise, why would it be such a hit when friends come over? She keeps a stash in her cupboard below her art stuff. It's okay, sort of. It still better be. Tracy suspects her penis art could threaten this.

She and Sam look at one together while Curtis and Cindy check out another one, all of them silent. Sam tilts his head up and breathes. She knows it's time to turn the page. It's not weird them close together here, sitting side by side on her bed, the magazine in her lap. It's not boyfriend-girlfriend, okay? Sam's younger anyway so of course it's not that. He's skinny and blond just like his sister and has never said a mean thing to her that she can remember.

Barbi Benton is in a lot of *Playboys*. Barbi Benton is the most luscious person Tracy has ever seen. Tracy's mom is nightlight-glow in red lipstick, a blonde wig with a curl and a dress without any straps in that picture on their upstairs wall. It's from a fancy New Year's Eve party at a big hotel downtown. Her mom looks like a movie star. Except her mom doesn't look like that every day, not in her jogging shorts and baggy T-shirts. Barbi is soft and perfect all over, in every issue. By the California pool. Indoors. Anywhere.

When her mom calls her down to set the table and Sam goes home, Tracy writes Twinkies on the grocery list.

At dinner that night, it's boring hamburger patties and Kraft Dinner and her mom seems grumpier than usual. She lets out a giant sigh so everyone knows she's not pleased when Tracy's dad slathers mayonnaise on his patty like always. Her mom orders Tracy, "Get your elbows off the table and show some manners." Afterwards her mom tells her, "Go and clean up that room of yours, Tracy Elizabeth." Tracy stands by the dishwasher. Her mom glares and says, "Now."

As Tracy moves to the hallway, she hears her mom say, "The principal, Mr. Buttons, called me today about that daughter of yours."

Whoa, hang on, principal, Mr. Buttons. Tracy stops near the stairs, just out of sight of the open doorway.

"*My* daughter?" Now her dad sounds grouchy.

"Drawing penises and testicles and handing them out all around the school."

Tracy isn't sure but she thinks she heard her dad laugh.

"Don't you dare snigger about this, Allan." Her mom. Yup, her dad really did laugh.

"Come on, Bev, what's the harm? Fifty per cent of the population has them." He starts singing, "Do your balls hang low, do they wobble to and fro?"

Tracy smiles even though she knows her mom must be super mad with being made fun of.

"Stop it. She doesn't know what's normal for a young lady and you and I know bloody well where she gets that. All your *Playboy*s and your silly songs."

Tracy tries to guess what is "normal" for ladies. Looking beautiful? Making dinner for your husband and kids? Working at the bank? Sometimes her mom seems so happy like when she comes home with a full paper bag from the bakery and they all pig out on flaky sausage rolls together. Not other times, like when her dad walks in the door and her mom says, "You better pick up dinner from McDonald's if you want anything to eat because I'm bloody well not cooking tonight."

"Easy, Bev." Her dad's calm voice now. That's good.

"We need to talk to her. People will think she's some sort of—"

Of what? Her mom thinks she's a sicko?

"Our Tracy's all right. I'll handle it."

Whewf. That's better than her mom on this one. Probably this won't be a case for the usual grounding with no TV, no playing outside or seeing friends. Tracy heads upstairs, puts her *Playboy*s inside her art box, and hides it under her bed.

Later her dad comes up to say good night. He sits on the end of her bed and clears his throat. "I heard about your latest artwork."

Tracy doesn't know what to say. She's still sort of proud but also feeling strange with all the fuss.

"Maybe in future, keep those kinds of pictures, well, you know."

"Yeah," Tracy says.

Her dad pats her leg. "Good stuff."

A shipwreck. A deserted tropical island with Gilligan, the Skipper, and the other wacky castaways. Lying in bed, Tracy sings the theme song to *Gilligan's Island*, her favourite television show. She knows it by heart. After she finishes, she also knows. She will quit swim club. Rather than go DOWN TO BLUE GROUP. She will play soccer instead. She will not look if her dad pees naked. She won't even go in the bathroom when he's there to ask him if he wants to play outside or anything. She will keep her *Playboy* stash. She will not get boobs or a Dot for many years. If ever.

Closing her eyes, she watches TV in her head, conjuring the Professor and Mary Ann on the Deserted Desert Isle. Mary Ann has braids like Katherine, and they're almost the same colour too. It's obvious the Professor is older than Mary Ann in her gingham dress. In Tracy's lying-in-bed version, he's not too old to ask her for a stroll along the beach. Gilligan and the others are… hmmm. She decides they are chasing pirates on the other side of the island. Tracy replays the instant the Professor's lips touch Mary Ann's on Gilligan's Isle. And replays it again.

First Katherine wears her Training Bra to school, now she won't play soccer anymore like they always do. Well, just about every other day. "It's dumb," Katherine says. What is going on with her? Amanda sticks to tetherball or making forts in the woods but Tracy asks her anyways. It's no surprise when Amanda says no. So who's going to go to the field with Tracy at lunch? It has to be another girl. Monica? Hardly will the four-square queen get mud on her from all the puddles. Kuldip? She's never played before, usually she sticks to hopscotch or four-square, plus Kuldip generally hangs around with girls in the other grade five class. So who?

Unreal. Tracy, floating above herself, walks up the bank to the field. Alone. Without any other girls. Bobby and Andre and all the other boys are there, everyone except Ross, who stays indoors sitting on the floor to draw with his feet. Not penis pictures, but Ross's art is excellent. They're still picking teams. She joins the unpicked. The boys stop picking. Tracy waits. Bobby juggles the ball on his thigh, loses it, then pops it back onto his thigh with his foot. Tracy waits.

Andre steps forward. "No girls."

"I always play. Me and Katherine."

He folds his arms across his chest and moves closer. "It's democratic. We voted." Nobody else says anything.

They can't do this. She does always play, all year she played. Katherine too. Tracy doesn't move. The boys don't move. Bobby looks away when she looks at him. She looks down and draws a toe line in the gravel, making a stream for a puddle to flow into.

"Hey, Tracy." Andre takes another step. "Draw us a cunt."

"A what?"

"She can draw a wiener. But she don't even know her own pisser."

The boys laugh as one blob.

"I do so," Tracy says quietly. The blob doesn't hear. It races after the ball, each mini-wiener, still hairless, jiggling up and down inside underwear inside jeans.

Tracy walks to the bottom of the bank to hunt for lumps of sulphur. She's not going to play stupid four-square with the other girls, that's the last thing she'll do.

"Oh no, you're not," says her mom. She's at the kitchen door with her coat.

"I am so quitting." It's Saturday morning and time for swim practice. Except somebody hasn't packed their swim stuff, and it's somebody's parents' turn to do the carpool. And somebody isn't even dressed yet.

Her dad looks up from his *Time* magazine. Doesn't he EVER get bored of reading about President Nixon? "Get your swim trunks ready," he says.

"I'm quitting." (And they're not trunks.)

Her mom wants to know why she's quitting. Why should she care?

"Boring." (She hasn't told them about getting moved DOWN TO BLUE GROUP. She. Won't. Tell. Anyone.)

"That's not a good enough reason," her mom says.

"I said get your swim trunks ready," her dad says. He's missing President Nixon.

"I hate swim club." (They're not trunks.)

Her dad puts President Nixon down on the kitchen table. To explain the family rule. "If you quit swimming, you have to do another sport instead. For exercise."

"Soccer."

Her dad says, "All right."

ALL RIGHT!

Her mom gives her dad a not friendly look. That makes him say in his strict voice, "If your mom has to do the carpool today, you have to go to swimming this last time."

All right! This last time!

In the car Tracy is held captive by pirates on Gilligan's Island, tied up by her seatbelt under the coconut tree. Even though her dad already talked to Tracy, her mom seizes the moment before the first carpool pickup to talk about Mr. Buttons and "appropriate versus inappropriate drawings" and "causing a school disruption." Tracy stares out the window counting trees. "*Playboy*s," her mom says, "are not suitable for a ten-year-old young lady." There are a lot of trees.

There is no soccer for girls on the north shore. Her mom just phoned. Tracy heard her. So let's see. She could work on her tetherball, stay late after school. Get Amanda to show her some tricks. Would that count?

Would it count to play soccer with her brother and her dad in the yard before bed? Like they usually do because he gets home late from work. And maybe her mom would stop shouting out the front door, "Allan, get those kids in. It's past bedtime again."

How can there be no soccer for girls on the entire north shore.

Her walkie-talkie is cutting out. She's in the cedar hideout beside their banged-up fence next to the Austins' house. This particular location has a little arch entrance, and the boughs hang nicely from a few feet up as it's a pretty old tree. Sam is huddled with her. It's not weird them being cramped together in the damp dirt, leaning against the fence. It's not boyfriend-girlfriend, okay? It's their gang. They've played together every weekend and summer holiday since Tracy's family moved here three years ago. No Training Bras. No boys only play soccer, girls play four-square.

The other walkie-talkie is with Curtis and Cindy who are assigned to be located behind the garage, also near the fence but a bit higher up in their yard. It's not a major distance for their voices to transmit, so what's up with the walkie-talkies? They have new batteries so it's not that. How are they supposed to complete their mission? Both commando groups are by the west fence because they are spying on the Austins today. Admittedly this isn't the most exciting plan as the Austins are both about eighty, but they can be cranky and they usually do yard work, so there is some danger.

Tracy shakes her walkie-talkie and tries again. "Do you read me, Unit Two?"

Static. "Do you read me?" A door creaks open, then bangs shut. Mr. Austin in his plaid shirt and wool pants is out on the deck. If she talks much louder Mr. Austin will hear. It's Mrs. Austin who has the hearing aid. Tracy looks at Sam. He nods, ready for the next move. Crouching low by the fence, they sneak through the salal and prickly Oregon grape bushes towards the garage and Unit Two.

The mission has to be spoiled by Tracy's mom telling them to come inside and watch Kelly while she cleans up. *Babysitting.* They are forced to go from spying in the wilderness to being cooped up in Curtis's room, with the door closed to block escape because if their baby sister crawls out and down the stairs both Tracy and Curtis would be decapitated by guillotine. Also probably grounded for a week.

With pillows and a chair, they erect a fortress in the corner as a prison for Kelly.

This frees them up to wrestle in the middle of the floor, taking turns to guard Kelly against breakouts. She's graduated from rolling to crawling to walking around chairs and the coffee table. They wrestle and she cries for freedom.

Of course they get sweaty and have to take some clothes off. Will it be pants or shirts? They decide on pants as they seem to be doing more leg-wrestling. Tracy's not sure how they move from wrestling on the carpet to wrestling on Curtis's bed, two at a time. Tracy and Cindy go first. Cindy's two years younger, puny and easy for Tracy to beat, but Tracy goes easy on her to give her a chance, stretch it out a little. Next is Curtis and Sam, which is a more even match. Rest break. Round Three is Sam and Tracy. It's not boyfriend-girlfriend, okay?

There's no laughing whatsoever because this is a serious battle, this is Round Three. Tracy pulls the covers over them. She's not sure why this round seems better with the bed covers up but it does, their T-shirt chests pressed together, her bare leg wrapping round Sam's blue underwear hip to try and lock him. She's clammy. Both of them are breathing hard. Now he's on top of her, hands on her arms, pinning them. Breath, she needs more. Panting, this is hard work. Got to… breathe… get free… another breath… get on top of him instead. It's boiling hot in here. Sticky skin. Round Three never ends. No smiling, no talking, this is combat to the death. Tracy gets Sam's T-shirt and whips it round. Oops, wait, that's not his T-shirt, it's elastic and cotton. Something soft and loose and floppy… attached to… Gross. She should move her fingers away. Sam's not moving. She can't move either, she can't even breathe. This is the longest Round Three in history. Poison ivy prickles burn down her arms into her fingers. Maybe Sam feels it too. Somebody, it could be her mom, shouts her name from far off on a deserted isle. Kelly cries. Her fingers tighten. Sam screams. She can't let go of that pinkish earthworm. What is she doing? She doesn't know. She *touched* it. And can't let go.

"Ow," Sam says quietly, his body still.

Her mind dives deep down under water. She holds her breath and presses her goggles and fat belly onto the pool bottom. It's clear glass. She watches Sam, who's never mean, getting... squashed for no good reason.

"Ow, Tracy." He sounds ready to cry.

She's going to burst. Swimming to the surface, she gulps in air and releases her fingers. Round Three is over. She runs to the bathroom, her cheeks pinker than a Training Bra. At the sink she scrubs her hands with soap and hot water for ages, trying to wash it away, but it's not working.

Curtis wants Round Four but, not surprisingly, Sam is unenthusiastic and the same goes for Tracy. After Sam and his sister go home, Tracy curls up on top of her bed for a long time. It's hard to explain but she can feel those magazines right underneath, *Playboy* Bunny Barbi Benton and her luscious curves and her ready-to-please smile, tempting and alive and suddenly not okay.

She finds a plastic bag downstairs, hauls her stash from under the bed, and stuffs each and every magazine inside. Checking that the coast is clear, no parents in sight, she makes her way from her room downstairs through the hall and kitchen, out the back door, and up the back driveway to the garbage cans. In they go. She closes the lid.

After dinner she sits on their front steps while her dad and Curtis play soccer in the grass. They ask her three times if she wants to play and she finally says, "I said no, quit asking me." Their "soccer" means a bit of dribbling and passing and a lot of rolling around, wrestling and tickling, and sometimes hucking the ball at each other. Curtis breaks free from a ground-rolling session and staggers, giggling, before running towards her.

"Tracy, come on! Help me defeat him."

"Who dares to face the legendary Pelé?" her dad says.

"Bug off, you guys," she says.

Her dad holds the soccer ball above his head. "Pelé is unstoppable."

"Tracy, I need you." Curtis grabs her hand. "For real."

She lets out a big sigh. "Okay, fine. Just for a minute."

Tracy and Curtis face their dad with the ball. Tracy passes to Curtis. Her dad lunges towards him. Curtis passes back to Tracy on the left. She dribbles along the grass next to the shrubs. She glances back. Yup, her dad's closing in on her.

"Shoot!" her brother screeches. "Shoot now!" She aims for the space between the two windbreaker-jacket goalposts, fires with her left foot, and sends the ball through the far corner and into the cedar trees as her dad tries a diving save.

Curtis rushes over and leaps on her, knocking her down. "We did it!" he says. "We beat him."

"Nice goal," her dad says. "Left-footer too."

She lays on the grass next to her brother and smiles.

Scotch Pine

MELVIN OUTLINES THE CHRISTMAS tree options as he guides the family station wagon out of the driveway. "We can go with a balsam fir again. It's got a lovely scent and doesn't drop its needles if we remember to water. The Scotch pines have that bluish-green tinge." The garden centre over the bridge has the best selection in the city but it charges an arm and a leg. The trees the Scouts sell in the parking lot across from Melvin's school are perfectly good, grown right in the Fraser Valley, but it's a fundraiser and not much less of a bargain. Artificial, that's out of the question.

Next to him in the front seat, Phyllis peruses homemade candles in one of those ladies' magazines, making notes with her pen and paper. Last year she sewed reindeer and other tree ornaments with their daughters, teaching them how to, now what did the gals call it? Sewing on eyes and smiles with thread, anyways.

All three girls are in the back. "Gang, the trees have gone up in price this year," he explains, "so we're going to have to think about this."

Her dad's voice is so serious, it's hilarious. Lisa, sitting behind him, lobs back, "We're going to have to think about this." Attempting, mocking his deep voice.

He cranes his neck around. "Don't be facetious, Lisa." His eldest daughter tosses limp brown bangs that her curling iron barely flipped. Lisa looks just like her mother when she pouts her lips.

"Maybe we should hold a bingo," Lisa says.

His wife hmmphs. This is the first weekend in a month Phyllis hasn't been at the Legion to all hours, coming home reeking of cigarettes, to raise money for Lisa's skating club.

The windshield wipers swoosh on top speed but can't keep up with the pelting rain. Melvin's eyes barely penetrate the wet grey gloom. He was awake half the night after the latest call from that deranged mother. He checks the mirror. In the middle of the back seat, Sarah, the youngest, sails her pink pony through the air, neighing. Tammy slouches against the other door. What's she doing—skimming yet again through that stamp collection of hers?

"Hang on there. Let's discuss this." Melvin firmly believes in giving family members a say. Lisa named their black cat Middy—short for Midnight. Tammy chose Doodles for their hyperactive standard poodle. Melvin himself wants balsam fir. It's the most fragrant and he loves the way the tree lights glow on its conical form, angling down in pleasing lines from the angel's perch. Melvin lying on the area rug next to the fireplace, listening to Bing Crosby's classics like "White Christmas," although knowing Vancouver, it'll be rain and slush outside. Closing his eyes for "Silent Night." A rum and eggnog and some of Phyllis's sugar cookies, maybe rolled out by Lisa this year.

"Quit that, you pest," Tammy says. In the mirror Melvin catches Tammy swatting her little sister. Sarah howls.

His wife slaps her magazine down and pivots to the back seat. "Tammy, now what did you do to her?"

"Nothing, Mom. She keeps kicking me."

Melvin twists around. A kink jabs his lower back. "Can't you kids stop fighting for one weekend of the year?" He turns back to face the road.

"Tammy, you're older than her, act like it," Phyllis says. "You touch her one more time and your father's giving you the carpet beater."

Melvin, merging the station wagon onto the main road, glimpses Phyllis's lipstick mouth fire out the words. He noticed his wife's tight beige turtleneck before she put her coat on.

"But Mom," Tammy whines.

"You heard what I said. Grandma's rug whip." Phyllis's tone now is anything but comforting.

He almost failed his final semester at university when they were dating. After Jimmy's motorbike accident. Phyllis kept him going that spring. She called him every day. Long walks. Their bench on campus tucked away under the oaks. Crimson lips and green eyes against her short red hair. The way she stroked his hand and held it in hers next to her warm cheek.

"You always take Sarah's side," Tammy grouses. Melvin glances back again. Tammy, the sulking twit, tosses her stamp book at her feet.

"Tammy, don't let your stamps get soaked."

She mumbles, "Who cares?" but picks the book up. "Baby," she tells Sarah under her breath.

Melvin smiles, knowing Sarah will badger her sister again when their mother's not looking and Tammy might snitch her pony in retaliation. That's how he and his big brother were, bickering back and forth, but Jimmy would save that last scoop of chocolate ice cream for him, no matter what. Good old Jimmy.

"We got balsam last year. I want a Scotch pine," says Lisa. "A gigantic one with room for lots of lights." Has that tomboy put eyeshadow on? You can barely see her eyes most days under those ridiculous bangs but when you do—the clear green of his wife's eyes but Lisa's are wider, more stunning.

That girl's vacant face, eyes on the floor, as she sat in his office, arms folded across her chest. With her hysterical mother sobbing, berating him about "that sick monster." Their high school's music teacher had built a program renowned throughout the city. Students flocked to it. They adored the teacher. He had a wife and kids. Barbara wasn't exactly a Doris Day; she probably got knocked up with one of the older boys, stupid girl. What was he supposed to do? He was the principal, not God.

"The tallest tree in the lot," Lisa said. "Majestic."

"You kids might have to pitch in." They don't know how lucky they are. Their own bedrooms. Downhill ski passes every winter.

The lakefront cabin in the Cariboo. Melvin could use a holiday right now, out on the boat with a cooler full of beer. That mother was out of control.

"I don't get why you can't just buy the tree this year," Lisa says.

Did Lisa not hear her mother this morning? His wife knew he'd barely slept but the first thing Phyllis said when he walked into the kitchen was, "There's no money in the bank again, Melvin." Like mother, like daughter—the best of everything for those two, no matter what the cost. Lisa's figure skates, her competition suits, the extra coaching, it was endless. School sports were good enough for him growing up and barely cost a cent. At least Lisa worked that paper route, never complained or asked for a ride in the pouring rain.

"I want a Charlie Brown tree," Tammy says. "Lonely and sweet." Tammy's much less demanding.

"No, Tammy, not a puny sad one," Lisa counters.

"Well, gang, I think it's fair for me to pay for a regular tree, but if the family really wants a more expensive one, then we all need to contribute," Melvin says.

"Yeah, fair," Lisa says. "Like the puppies." Tammy snorts in agreement. Lisa smirks and pokes Melvin's arm. "Right Dad?"

Lisa remembers Doodles' litter. It was an accident. Doodles took off out the back door while she was in heat, right before she was supposed to get spayed. Lisa and Tammy helped take care of the puppies for weeks. They were adorable, some with curly apricot hair like their mom. It was Dad's idea to sell them through an ad in the newspaper. He pocketed most of the cash "for the household." Sarah cried when each pup went to its new home.

"Don't poke me while I'm driving. And don't get flippant." Melvin's head throbs from lack of sleep. The girl doesn't have to go ahead with it. She can get it taken care of at the hospital like other girls do. But her family is Catholic. Forget it for now. You're getting a tree with your family, Melvin.

They're nearly at the tree lot. He guides the station wagon around an ambulance, lights flashing, parked near a crosswalk. There's a motorcycle on its side. He slams on the brakes.

"Melvin!" Phyllis braces herself on the dash.

"Sorry, gang." Rattled, Melvin drives on by.

Lisa takes another plunge. "Sarah should really start pulling her weight."

Tammy pipes in, "Better get a paper route, peanut."

"I'm only in grade three," Sarah says. "I'm not a peanut."

Melvin wants to reach back and swat the ungrateful lot of them. "Cut it out or you're all getting the carpet beater instead of a tree."

"How much would we have to pay?" Lisa wonders what will be left over for Christmas presents—a flowered scarf from the ritzy westside mall for Mom. And for Dad, well, she's not sure yet.

"Let's see," Melvin says. "Maybe ten dollars for you, Lisa, and seven or eight for Tammy now that she's got her own route."

Ten dollars. There go half the Christmas tips from her paper route customers. She doesn't babysit; changing diapers is as dumb as cheerleading. But a blue-tinged tree reaching up to the ceiling, better than ordinary. Much more than everyday. She loves tucking each light under each branch, almost planting it in the greenery as she weaves the lights in gentle near-horizontal spirals.

"Dad's such a stinge," she whispers, leaning across Sarah to Tammy, who nods.

"What, Lisa?" Sarah asks. Tammy ignores her.

"Let's take a vote, kids," Melvin says as he turns into the tree-filled parking lot, lit up with strings of holiday lights. Back in university he was on student council.

"Tammy? How about you?" Melvin parks the station wagon.

In the window's condensation Tammy traces a tree, then smudges it gone. "I already told you."

Sarah proclaims, "I want balsam. It's really green and has a lovely scent."

"Me too, Sarah," his wife says. She reaches to the floor, picks up another magazine, the latest from the teachers' federation, and flips it open.

"All right," Melvin says. Hammers slam at his temples. "That's two for balsam."

"I want Scotch pine," Lisa says. "Don't you, Tammy?" She leans across again. "I'll pay your share."

Tammy twists her lip, considering.

"Come on," says Lisa. "Please?"

"Okay," says Tammy. "Scotch pine."

"I don't believe it. My dip of a classmate is a math prof now in the education department," Phyllis says to no one in particular. "He couldn't teach arithmetic if his life depended on it."

Melvin could make Lisa happy. "Well, let's try something new. I'll vote for Scotch pine," says Melvin. "So that's three for Scotch pine, two for balsam." He looks back at the kids. He wishes he could capture Lisa's tiny smile on camera. She doesn't like him taking her picture anymore. But Sarah looks like she's going to cry. He glances over at his wife. She's immersed in that magazine. Melvin rests his head on the steering wheel.

Lisa helps her dad carry the tree from the car to the living room, her sisters lagging. Her mom clucks her tongue and scowls at their dirty shoes on the hardwood. "I'm not your maid," she announces and struts off. She is anal about cleaning, always wanting Lisa to make her bed, which is utterly pointless—it's just going to get unmade at night again.

At the living room's large front window, they lay the tree on its side underneath her dad's orchids. They're like his babies. They need special dirt that's not actually dirt and no one else is allowed to water them. Only one is in a delicate snowy bloom right now.

Sarah sits with her pink pony and sniffles by the fireplace. Lisa catches Tammy's eye. Connection.

"Pony says she loves this tree colour," Tammy says, standing over her sister.

"No, she never."

"Bluish-green goes best with Pony's pink coat and mane," Lisa adds.

Sarah's eyes widen. "You think so?"

"See," Tammy says, giving Sarah a gentle punch this time. "It's not so bad."

"I'll vote for balsam next year. I promise," Lisa says.

Their dad walks over and tousles Sarah's hair. "Come on, squirt. All of you. Let's get this tree up."

Sarah gets up slowly, rubs her eyes, and joins them. They raise the tree together in the corner.

"It's a beauty," her dad says.

"Yeah," Lisa says.

The rain has stopped. Melvin plants the stepladder in the sodden grass at the base of their largest holly, sprawling twenty-five feet up and out next to the fence. Lisa spots while he climbs with the pruners, finding a step two-thirds of the way up close to berry-laden branches. He lets them fall as he cuts. He's feeling better out here in the moist air. The aspirin didn't hurt either. Neither of them speaks for several minutes.

Then Lisa says, "Dad, this one's got tons of berries!" Not a hint of teen surliness.

"There's some nice ones this year." Snip. Each Christmas he delivers holly in cardboard boxes across the city to his parents and mother-in-law.

"Can we save this one for us?" she asks, holding up a branch. He turns to look. There she is, two years old, fistful of dirt, saying, "See? See?"

"You bet," he says. Anything you say, Lisa.

Now she's down on hands and knees examining each branch. Complete concentration, her fingers touching at berries, tracing the prickly curve of a leaf. Her jeans must be soaked at the knees.

"Can I cut some?" she asks.

"Sure, Lisa," he says.

She climbs the ladder until she's next to him, then keeps going.

"Careful."

"I know, Dad." Up here, Lisa basks in holly all round her. She visualizes leaves and berry clusters she will paint in watercolour on Christmas cards for Dad, Mom, and her sisters. It's misty and nearing dusk. The berries turn darker. The mucky wet patches on her new painter jeans give her goosebumps. Across the inlet at Stanley Park the foghorn blows. She does not want to come down.

"How was skating this morning?" Melvin asks.

"I landed my double salchow twice in a row. And my free skate's almost done. We finally figured out the first jump combination. I just couldn't get my transition into the loop jump. I'm going to end with a lutz now. It's so much better. I can't wait to show you, Dad."

Her words leap out, energetic, as strong as her legs propelling her into the air.

She takes a breath and looks down at her dad. Something about his expression is sad to her, though she doesn't know why. Fog puffs out of her dad's mouth in heart bursts, vanishing in the mist.

Melvin sniffs the warm kitchen air. "Mmm, something smells good."

Sarah's eating crackers. "Dad, you always say that."

"It's sausages and instant potatoes," Phyllis snaps without turning from the stove.

His mouth waters. Melvin doesn't mind sausages and he's hungry now. He almost trips over a cardboard box on his way to forage in the fridge. "That woman. Someone needs to settle her down."

"What woman?" Phyllis asks. The sausage fat sizzles and pops.

"The one causing the big fuss about her poor darling." He finds a jar of Cheez Whiz.

"The school board is advertising for teachers again." More fat flies up. Phyllis slaps at her arm. "I found out from Nancy," Phyllis says. "Why didn't you mention it?"

"For chrissake, Phyllis." She's already helping out in the library at their younger girls' elementary school and with the constituency office. Then there's driving the kids to and from their activities. Tammy's in gymnastics now. At least twice a week his wife sends him for takeout, saying she doesn't have time to cook. And she wants *another* job? "Let's not discuss this today."

His wife stabs the fork into a sausage, sliding the pan off the burner.

"Ready to destroy a good teacher's reputation." Checking that his wife's not watching, he dips a finger in the jar. "That selfish woman."

"Who?" Lisa asks. Melvin hadn't seen her walk in. Her hands are full of cedar boughs.

"A difficult parent," says Melvin. The girl, Barbara, not much older than Lisa.

"I got cedar for the mantle, Mom." Lisa holds up the branches, then presses her nose to them and takes a deep breath in. Cedar smells tangy and fresh. She puts the boughs on the table.

"Oh, good!" Her mom looks happy. "Thanks, honey. Should we put it up after dinner?"

"Yeah!" Kneeling by the cardboard box, Lisa delves in and pulls out an object covered in tissue paper. She unwraps it to reveal a carved wooden figure—a chickadee perched on burnished wood, its smart black cap and white-streaked cheeks painted on. Lisa holds the bird in her palm. Sarah "oohs" and reaches out. "Careful," Lisa says as she lets her sister touch it.

Her mother's eyes are glued to the chickadee. "My dad made that for me when I was little. Gosh, I wish he was still here."

"I know, Phyllis," her dad says.

"Yeah, Mom. Me too." Lisa's grandpa died a few years ago. He collapsed with a massive heart attack at his kitchen table and was gone before the ambulance got there. Lisa sort of remembers him giving her toffees but he feels like he's fading. She stands up, cradling the chickadee.

Noticing Lisa's dirty jeans, her mom parks her hands on her hips. "Lisa Elizabeth, I just bought you those. It's time you did the laundry."

Her face drops. "Sorry, Mom."

"Yeah, everybody's sorry. But I'm the one telling Safeway and the bank there's no money because your father had to have a speed boat at the cabin."

"Oh-kaaay," Lisa says.

Melvin catches her eye and smiles, throwing his arms up to say: That's your mother. Phyllis cannot grasp investment concepts the way he does. He took economics courses at university.

"Did you put money in the account, Melvin?"

"I will," he retorts.

"Maybe I'll apply for one of those teaching jobs. Better than relying on you."

Lisa puts the chickadee back in the box and mimics her mother in her head. Your father this, your father that, blah blah, shut up, you cow. She slams the kitchen door on her way out.

Phyllis flinches. A clump of orange Cheez Whiz sticks to Melvin's finger. Sighing, his wife checks the clock. "Melvin, it's almost six."

"All right, all right." He almost forgot the liquor store.

It's after two in the morning. Phyllis is in the kitchen in her bare feet and faded nightie, fixing another drink. Although Melvin's only had a couple to wind down, he can't sleep either. "That's enough, Phyllis." He grabs the tumbler from her. Down the sink with the gin and tonic.

"You prick," she says.

Her eyes look but they don't see him. It doesn't matter what he does. She always asks for more.

How did she grab another glass so quickly? "Oh no, you don't." He doesn't mean to wrench the glass out of her hand like that. It crashes to the floor and shatters. Christ, Phyllis. Now she's gone and tripped. Definitely had enough.

"Ouch, Melvin!"

He didn't really do anything but her knees hit the broken glass. Great. She stands herself up and makes a beeline out of the kitchen and up the stairs before he can grab her.

"No, Phyllis, stay away from the girls' rooms." He follows and finds her seated on the upstairs toilet. She's hunched over. Blood trickles down her shins and drips onto the yellow bathmat.

"Don't lock the door, Melvin. Please."

He locks the bathroom door behind him. This is the only way. In a confined space where she can't throw anything or get more alcohol into her.

"Goddamn it, Melvin."

"You're going to wake the kids," Melvin says.

"Open the fucking door."

"Not until you learn how to listen."

She stands up and makes for the door. He blocks her but she won't give up, driving her fists at his ribs. "You monster." She's surprisingly strong. He has to grab her wrists and make her sit. Last time in here she grabbed the mouth wash, screwed off the cap, and threw it in his face. He has to make her sit and listen. That's all.

In the hall it's dark except for that glowing sliver below the bathroom door. Lisa flicks on the hall light and sits inside the door of her sisters' bedroom, a few feet from their bunks. She knows they're awake because they're stiff and deader than sleep. People don't breathe when they're frightened. She covers her knees with her nightie and wraps her arms round.

Her mom just completed her "yelling act" as her dad calls it. It was the first time in a while. She marched up and down the stairs shouting things at her dad like "I'm getting a job, mister, just try and stop me" and "you stay home and cook supper, see how you like it." Maybe her mom could choreograph this performance to the angry Tchaikovsky that Lisa's coach picked for her short program. Lisa can't stand the strident score.

Their father's school principal lecture voice carries down and across the short dip of stairs on the other half of the second floor. "You're my wife. You need to keep your end of the bargain."

Lisa feels like throwing up. She doubts that Sarah understands what their dad means although Tammy might. It's more than cooking sausages for supper. Marriage is so stupid. Lisa is never ever doing it.

Mom is into the crying phase now, trying to say something. The muffling tells Lisa that her father's hands are on her mother's mouth again. Tammy stares at the ceiling. Sarah clutches her pony to her chest and watches her big sister like Lisa is the angel on the tree. Freaking Lisa out with her baby sister eyes. Jeez Sarah, stop it. Like she's supposed to know what to do, because she doesn't, okay?

Lisa gets up. Her heart in triple time, she pounds on the bathroom door. "I'm going to call the police, Dad. I'm really going to this time."

"We're just having a talk, Lisa."

"How come I can't hear her, Dad?"

"Because it's my turn to talk."

A little-girl voice breaks through. "Lisa? Lisa?" Your mom's not supposed to sound younger than your littlest sister.

"Mom?"

Melvin really wishes Phyllis would cut the "poor me" crap. "She cut her own bloody knees on the glass she broke, okay? Now go back to bed."

"If she's not okay, Dad, I'm calling the police." The thought terrifies her. Lisa doesn't really want to. But she's not sure Mom's okay.

More firmly now. Take charge. "Your mother's fine."

"Really?"

"Yes. Goodnight, Lisa." He hears the stairs creak. One, two, three. Now up the other side. Good girl, Lisa. He turns to his wife.

"This really wasn't a good night for one of your shows."

The next morning Lisa watches her dad by the fridge guzzling orange juice straight from the container. Doodles mooches beside Tammy's chair as she places toasted waffle bits in the dog's mouth, keeping an eye on her dad. Sarah digs her fist into a cereal box, picks out the crunchy pink sugar balls, and eats them straight up, one after the other. At last, her mom in her nightie baby-steps into the kitchen. Lisa looks up from corn flakes loaded with sugar. The cuts on her mom's knees are no surprise but her wrists have purple bracelets under the flesh. She keeps her head lowered but can't hide the dark swollen cheek. Half-chewed cereal sits in Lisa's mouth, refusing to go further. Doodles barks for more food. Lisa spits her cereal out and leaves the kitchen.

Minutes later Lisa returns holding her turquoise competition suit with the sparkly sequins that her mom sewed on one by one. She walks calmly out the back door.

What the hell? Melvin thought she didn't have skating this morning. He follows his daughter, still in her pajamas and in bare feet.

She stands in the cold wet dirt of the flower bed below the kitchen window. Her hands twist and crumple the nylon. This could break the sequins, silver and white, that she helped choose with her mom. A special trip downtown. "I'm quitting."

"Don't be silly." He's getting cold on the stairs. "Get inside."

"No."

"Come out here, Phyllis," Melvin says. "Come see what your daughter's doing with her outfit."

Lisa rolls her eyes. He is so clued out. "It's not an outfit." She picks up dirt in her hand, holding it over the suit.

His wife walks out on the porch, the girls following. She peers over. "Lisa! What's got into you?" This satisfies Melvin. See what your antics have brought on.

"That's enough, Lisa," he says. "You can buy yourself a new one."

She turns around. "Is Mom gonna make you give me the carpet beater?" This is almost fun for her now.

That's it. If that's what she wants. He reaches from the stairs and grabs her arm. "Come on, young lady."

She juts her chin out. For a second, he hesitates. Lisa's face blurs. That girl, Barbara, emptied of emotion, sitting in his office. A bright student in fact, but clearly not bright enough. She'll likely drop out of school, have the baby, and give it up. His Lisa's too smart to end up like that.

Lisa pounces on his doubt. "Make me."

He pulls her in towards him. She digs her heels in and leans back. She's an athletic girl. But he's stronger.

"Melvin?" Phyllis squeaks. "Don't."

"Get out of the way," he says sternly, seizing both wrists, yanking, hauling Lisa up the porch stairs and into the kitchen. Her feet trail mud. She's glaring, contemptuous, disrespecting his authority. He tightens his grip. "Get the carpet beater, Phyllis."

"Melvin, no." Her mom doesn't move.

"Do as you're told. Now."

Her mom hesitates, then reaches up to the ledge above the oven and delivers the wicker carpet beater, with its long handle, to her dad. "Don't hurt her, Melvin," her mother says. Lisa laughs out loud. Mom's not a cow, she's a sheep. Baaa.

Lisa grabs hold of his wrists. They will dance. "I'm too old for the carpet beater."

"No, you're not, as long as you live in this house," he says. She drops the outfit, knees him in the groin and wriggles free. There she goes, racing through the front hall. He catches her again in the living room near the undecorated tree, rooted in its stand. Her wild legs shake needles from the low branches. She seizes the top, where the angel will go, tearing the tree down with her onto orchids, hardwood. She gets up again and runs across the floor where he gave the kids horsey rides.

At the French doors that no one uses, Lisa struggles with the knob. It rattles. With the first touch of his hand on her shoulder, she propels her muscled leg through the glass. Her mother screams as it shatters. Melvin looks back. Tammy's face is a mask. Clutching her pony, Sarah huddles into her mother's nightie.

"Dear God, she's bleeding, Melvin." Her mom's voice thinned with fear.

His daughter's leg is cut. Melvin did not do this. He was pushed. Phyllis handed him the carpet beater.

Lisa lets her dad examine her ankle. The lacerated skin is a pinprick in her lingering adrenalin buzz. Like more than a hundred perfect double salchows in front of a thousand rink side judges. Taking off from her back inside edge instead of her toe pick, swinging her right leg forward in coordination with her arms, launching into the air, vertical, tall as a tree, spiralling once, twice, her arms in tight. Then arms out, perfect landing on the back outside edge of her opposite skate.

Although the cuts seem minor, he takes his time examining them with gentle hands. When he faces Lisa finally, briefly, her green eyes are not animal terror. They are bright and high after the chase but without the cornered prey's fear. A woman's eyes, matching his, unrelenting, defiant. Melvin's chest trembles. His arms drop limp. He's no monster.

"Let's move you out of here and get you a Band-Aid," he says, picking up larger shards of glass. Lisa tiptoes past. Crisp wind from the patio nips his cheeks. "How about splitting the cost of the window?" Melvin says. "You and me."

Lisa stops, her back facing him. "Okay," she says evenly. She raises her eyebrows and turns her head. "That's fair," she says over her shoulder.

Tramp

LOUNGING IN HER CHAIR, Janice sipped her mug of Berry Cup, a tradition at the Beach Grove Motel and Resort. The sweet red wine was cheap, local and came in jugs—everything her husband bought was cheap, really, but she had never been a connoisseur in drinking. The bonfire crackled in the firepit on the sand, the flames quivering, reflecting in the lake water nudged by a hint of a wind. An almost-round moon illuminated the silhouettes of the walkout and floating docks. The women were drinking on the grass near the cottonwood trees. The men were on the beach watching the kids. Just as it should be on holidays, she thought smugly. There was no rest for the wicked when they were home, her husband Dick at the law office to all hours, evenings and weekends.

Dick had the marshmallows. Stan Stapleton used his pocketknife to sharpen cottonwood branches into roasting sticks. Eddy Carlson, Budweiser in hand, well, he was being Eddy: loud, confident, gregarious. Jan's three children and a gaggle of others, all in bare feet, held their sticks over the fire, wieners and marshmallows browning deliciously.

It was quite something really. Since the early seventies their Beach Grove gang had been coming to this Okanagan resort, its lake flanked by vineyards and sage brush hills. Dick and Jan and Ted and Carol-Ann from Vancouver, Stan and Sally from out in the valley, Eddy and Kathy and their friends from Washington state.

Sally Stapleton had her double martini resting on the arm of the wooden lawn chair, her sandaled feet up on one of those nylon-strapped folding chairs. She wore extravagant glazed earrings, hoops inside hoops, a green kaftan and matching scarf which covered most of her tinted blonde curls. Sally, with her slim tennis body, came from old money, didn't work, and shopped at Saks on jaunts to Arizona. Carol-Ann wore a flowered Hawaiian muumuu with ruffled neckline and nursed her rye and Coke. Her husband worked at the same firm with Janice's back in North Vancouver. All three women were smoking, tapping the ashes onto the lawn. Eddy's wife Kathy was the only one missing. She suffered from migraines and didn't socialize much.

Janice noticed Sally's eyes settle on Eddy's six-foot-three bulk as he doled out wieners from a large package. Sally chuckled and elbowed Carol-Ann. "Look-see what our big boy Eddy's handing out."

Janice complied. Carol-Ann giggled, tried to stop, then snorted.

"They're the thick kind," Sally said, letting her tongue linger on "thick."

"Sally," Janice half-scolded. Sally was nothing like her friends from the elementary school where she worked, or her old high school classmates.

"The big... beefy... kind," Sally said in a throaty voice.

"Oh cripes, Sally. You're just down in the gutter, you really are." Carol-Ann snickered.

Sally lit another cigarette. "He's so puffed up and American." She was enjoying herself. "There's so much of Eddy, he has to spread it around."

Carol-Ann blurted, "Spread the love!" then covered her mouth at her naughtiness. She couldn't stop laughing.

Janice had an inkling she was not fully in the loop. "What do you mean?"

Sally dangled her olive. "Our Eddy," she whispered, "has a room at the Belleview."

"Downtown? Why?" Janice wondered.

Sally leaned over and kissed her cheek. "You are a sweet sugar doll, I just can't corrupt you, and that's why I love seeing you here every single year."

"A room for..." Carol-Ann's giggles were getting out of control. Oh. The light went on for Janice. No. "But he's..."

"Uh-huh," Sally replied.

"Poor Kathy. Does she know?" Janice asked.

"She's a ninny if she doesn't," Sally said.

Nobody Janice knew personally had ever told her they had cheated. Or were cheated on. There were rumours back home about a couple down the block, and Dick's senior partner at the firm with a paralegal. She was dying to ask. "With who?"

"That snooty doctor who thinks she knows it all," Carol-Ann said.

Janice stared blankly.

"The redhead tramp in unit eight," Sally added.

Janice skipped a beat. She was a redhead too. She hated her freckles. "How do you know?"

"Well, everybody knows about Eddy and the Belleview," Sally said. "That's been going on a few years."

"Oh," Janice said, deflated. No wonder Kathy had migraines.

Sally inhaled and blew the smoke out slowly. "I couldn't sleep last night. Two in the morning. I brought my blanket out and got comfortable. First Eddy pulls out in his big fat Oldsmobile. Bonnie from unit eight's peeping out the door at him. Soon as he leaves, she's in her car skedaddling."

"She has a toddler. What in God's name is she doing?" Janice said.

"I have a pretty good idea!" Carol-Ann said gleefully.

"I can tell you one thing, though," Sally said. "If I was Eddy's wife and caught him with that uppity bitch, there'd be more than feathers flying."

Carol-Ann sniggered. Janice wondered what kind of damage Sally could do. She was small-boned, not much meat on her. Janice hesitated. She wanted to ask her friends if they had. Of course they hadn't. She wouldn't either. But if she asked, they might think she wanted to. Although sometimes she was curious. She had been nineteen, second-year university, when she and Dick, well, fumbling around in his junker car soon after their blind date. By the following year they were married, and she missed out on any sixties "free

love" to be had. Although she'd been shocked, Janice could relate
to the latest escapades of Margaret Trudeau, the prime minister's
wife. Marrying young and in North Vancouver too. Leaving her
handsome older husband and young kids behind and running off
to New York on her "ultimate freedom trip"—that's what she
called it. Spending nights with Mick Jagger and the Rolling Stones.
Telling reporters, everyone, about not wearing a bra and her strong
sexual energies.

Janice came out with it. "Have you ever...?"

Sally twirled her martini glass.

"I wanted to last year," Carol-Ann admitted. "I was smoking a,
um, a marijuana cigarette with the gardener out behind our condo
in Kihei. Makoa, a big, strapping Hawaiian guy. In his fifties but,
you know, good shape."

"You're kidding." Janice was shocked, more about the
marijuana, though she knew Carol-Ann and her husband were a bit
unconventional, even soft, whishy. They were the 'social programs'
sort of Liberals, their car had a "No Nukes" bumper sticker, and
Carol-Ann didn't eat meat.

Carol-Ann touched Janice's arm. "Nothing happened. But I did
get the giggles."

"I don't do drugs, I never have," Sally said evenly, "and if my kids
touch it I will kill them."

Janice regarded Sally with surprise. She was loads of fun in a
spoiled, irreverent way, how Janice imagined the sorority girls
would have been if she'd joined, if she hadn't got pregnant, dropped
out, and become a teacher's aide instead of a real teacher.

"Your Cheryl wouldn't," Janice reassured Sally. "She's a good
girl." Janice knew her own daughter Debbie, just turned fourteen,
wouldn't either.

"We've all got good girls," said Carol-Ann. Her eyes drifted back
to the men at the fire. "Don't you ever wonder? What someone else
would be like in bed?"

Yes, Janice thought, am I bad? Sally jumped in. "Oh, I imagine
one cock would be as disappointing as the next."

"You're awful," Carol-Ann said.

"I know." Sally gave a deep lusty laugh.

Janice wanted to tell Sally she was wrong, it couldn't be that bleak, even though she didn't really know for sure. Instead, she laughed along with her.

"British Bull..." Debbie shouted, standing barefoot in the hot sand in her flowered bikini. The gang of children and teenagers in the lake water prepared to bolt. She felt all-powerful, savouring their tensed bodies waiting for her command. "British... Bull-farts." Her little sister and a few others ran into the sand towards her. Debbie hooted. "False start. Get back," she ordered. Two of the boys grumbled.

"Hurry up, Debbie," challenged Cheryl, her best friend at Beach Grove for the past five summers, in her surly new tone.

Debbie silently chose her target—Cheryl's younger brother Buster. He was almost twelve, sun-scorched blond like his sister, easy-going and easy prey. "British Bulldog!" The stampede began, the kids kicking up water, reaching sand, ducking underneath the volleyball net and sprinting the last few metres to safety—the low concrete wall dividing the beach from the grass above. Debbie ignored Cheryl as she barrelled past in her string bikini. Just beyond the net, Debbie dove and wrapped her arms around sluggish Buster's knees, bringing him down hard.

After two more rounds, Debbie's feisty friend was the last one left, as usual. Debbie advised the huddle, "Cheryl's a kicker. You gotta grab her feet." Philip Carlson, the same age as Debbie and Cheryl, pug-nosed and stocky, clapped his hands eagerly. As Debbie expected, Cheryl put up a vicious fight. Her legs were lethal. Cheryl was a synchronized swimmer, although she said she was quitting. Philip seized one leg, Debbie the other, her experience with eighth grade basketball proving helpful, but it wasn't enough— it took other kids pitching in, two pairs of hands on each leg, to subdue Cheryl before everyone dog-piled her. Even then, she kept writhing.

Debbie and Cheryl had both always loved the games at Beach Grove: British Bulldog and hide-and-seek and beach volleyball. But Debbie thought her friend was going overboard on BB, far more this summer than before. She had a restless air about her. More hyper. More makeup. A sense she had to stir things up.

Debbie stepped off the mound of kids and glanced up at the parents in lawn chairs on the grass. Her mom was talking to Cheryl's dad, Mr. Stapleton. He always told Debbie to "call me Stan" but Mr. Stapleton was old and she just couldn't. His skimpy Speedo suit was hilarious. Her mom looked weirdly excited.

Suddenly Debbie felt something coarse chafe her chest. Philip had grabbed a fistful of sand and was rubbing it into her blossoming cleavage, an unwelcome development in the past year. The sand scraped her skin. His fingers wriggled in under one of her polyester cups—revolting. In a split second she noticed Cheryl watching, fascinated. Debbie broke free and elbowed Philip hard in the gut. He grunted. She stepped away and leaned over to brush the sand out. When she stood up, she saw Mr. Stapleton and Philip's dad, Mr. Carlson, standing at the wall's edge, watching her, oh God, watching her there. She blushed, turned, ran, and then dove into the lake. She stayed under as she lifted her top, letting the water free the sand. She jumped up and filled her lungs with air, facing out across the lake, away from those old guys. Dads. It was disgusting that they were looking there. Why did she feel such a thrill?

Oiled up for the day, Janice sat next to the cottonwoods, smoking her du Maurier King Size and reading a paperback copy of Gail Sheehy's book *Passages*. She had skipped the twenties and thirties and zeroed in on the Deadline Decade, thirty-five to forty-five. Although it was only noon, Dick was having a nap. The kids were on the beach below playing British Bulldog yet again. It was fine for her younger two but she thought Debbie was getting too old for prancing around in her bikini like that. It had been a monumental effort to pick out a bra with her last spring after an entire year of arguments and refusals and the girl was not flat as a pancake, no sir, she was like her mom in that department.

A tall, bronzed figure sauntered along the grass. Stan Stapleton in his tight yellow racing trunks displaying his ample natural attributes—muscular legs, a taut torso. And that hair. Brushed back, sleek, and wavy. Long sideburns, dark bushy eyebrows, and a carpet of chest hair. In all her summers coming to Beach Grove with Dick and the kids, Janice always thought Stan was something. A stud. He really was. And a catch too—he was a dentist in the Fraser Valley and took Sally to Scottsdale every January while the kids had a sitter.

"Janice," Stan crooned in his sonorous voice. "Don't you look fantastic today."

Fantastic. She hadn't heard that in a while. She couldn't seem to lose the pounds from her last pregnancy six years ago—Lori, her youngest, who started grade one in the fall. "So do you, Stan."

Stan stood there for several seconds eyeing her up and down with a lazy grin. He lingered on her breasts. She liked her breasts, they didn't sag, she hadn't breastfed, but still, broad daylight, she was thirty-five years old now. Stan asked, "Is that a new suit?"

Janice touched her Hawaiian-patterned bikini self-consciously. The kids were right below. "Maui this winter."

"Sexy." Stan added a little growl at the end, like a tiger.

That did it. Janice wanted to burst out laughing. He was too much.

Stan winked. "Barbecue at our place Friday night." Stan, Sally, and their two children had a larger motel unit with an enclosed patio. "I'm making my spicy hot sauce. It's got my secret ingredient."

"What's that?"

He raised his index finger and pointed it at her. "If I told you then it wouldn't be secret, would it?"

"I guess not," Janice said, playfully touching his finger. What was the harm? It was only Stan. Still, she scanned the beach quickly for his wife but didn't see her.

"It's so hot you're not going to know how to cool down."

Janice giggled in spite of herself. She paused and looked him right in the eye. "I don't know if I'm ready for something that hot, Stan."

"You fiery redheads know how to handle that," he said.

She blushed. Her freckles, multiplying with each sunny day, cried out for attention.

"Well, I am ready to burn right up." He tipped his glass towards her. "Time to go buy some thick bloody steaks. And some olives for those martinis."

Just then Janice heard a scream. She looked to the beach and gasped. One of the American boys, that cheeky Philip Carlson, had his hand in Debbie's top. Janice leaped up. "Hey!" she cried. But her tomboy daughter elbowed the boy and backed away. Janice watched Debbie bend over to clear the sand out, giving anyone on the grass at Beach Grove a view of her cleavage. "Debbie!" she shouted, but it was too late. Stan and Eddy stood there ogling her girl. And then, as if they remembered that she was there or her daughter was jailbait, they both averted their eyes. She wanted to kick the creeps in the balls. Her daughter sprinted towards the lake. Debbie had the beginnings of hips and those long slim legs and her brown hair with a sparkle of red. Janice knew her daughter was beautiful. She felt proud. And she felt envious just a little.

A six-foot wood fence separated the Beach Grove Motel from the private property next door but that didn't keep Debbie out. She simply waded through the shallow water to the other side, her grasshopper hunting ground, ambling barefoot through the sand, tufts of dry grass, and twigs below the haunted house. It was silent there except for the chirruping of grasshoppers. She had never actually seen anyone in the dilapidated house with its faded white paint, its porch and turrets, set back from the lake, a far cry from the mansions they spied from the motel's pedal boats as they tootled along the shorefront. But the house's presence made the hunt for grasshoppers more menacing, with the risk that she would be caught trespassing, stealing insects. Whether by humans or ghouls, she did not know. She moved softly, following the clicketing song, crouching down and cupping her hands over a creature. She stood up with it contained in her enclosed palms. She liked the feel of it, those powerful legs leaping against her trying to escape. Her younger brother Graham, swimming, spotted her and glided in. Without saying a word, he joined her in the hunt. Catch and release, catch and release. She could do this all day.

Cheryl peered over the fence. "Come on," she said. "Mr. Carlson's taking us skiing."

All the Americans at Beach Grove had speed boats but Philip's dad, Mr. Carlson, had the grandest, with luxurious leather seats and drink holders, slick stripes in metallic blue down the sides. He was tall with a grand belly to match. He sold cars in Puyallup. He hauled the boat from Washington state with a black Oldsmobile.

Minutes later they were crowded in the boat, idling towards the floating dock, Debbie, her brother, Philip, Cheryl and Jeffrey, another one of the Americans—he was fifteen with brown eyes, dark wavy hair, and lips like Mick Jagger, and suddenly not interested in British Bulldog or hide-and-seek. When Jeffrey stood near Debbie in the boat she couldn't breathe, so she couldn't really talk to him. She detected a hint of booze and remembered Mr. Carlson with a beer earlier. Debbie's dad wouldn't approve but he was out of sight, luckily.

They all climbed out at the dock except Debbie's brother who was going to spot. Jeffrey was the first to ski. He jumped in the water, put his skis on, and got up easily. Debbie watched furtively, trying not to be obvious, as Jeffrey jumped the wake and then flew back across it while the boat sped down the lake.

Debbie and Philip and Cheryl all laid down on the dock. Debbie fixed on the lone cloud in the otherwise clear sky. It was a crocodile's head. The water lapped gently. The crocodile turned into a Tyrannosaurus Rex. Suddenly Debbie saw Cheryl roll over onto her stomach and pull at the elastic on the front of Philip's swim shorts, get her fingers under there, lift it up into the air and let it snap back. She did this a couple of times, right in the front part, the second time letting even more air in. What was she doing? Debbie didn't mean to look but she saw something pale down there. Philip retaliated—he yanked Cheryl's bottom down so her bum was exposed. Debbie's mouth dropped. She sat up. "Whoo-hooo!" he cackled, pinning Cheryl's bikini down her legs with both hands while Cheryl, still on her belly, tried to reach behind and stop him. This went on for a good while before Cheryl rolled away from him, laughing, then got up and dove into the water. Philip turned to Debbie. She froze, struck with horror as his hands reached for the ties on her bikini top. She yelped and backed up until her feet met air and she toppled backwards into the water, her heart pounding out into the lake.

She and Cheryl dog-paddled away from the dock. Debbie asked, "Do you like Philip or something?"

"He's... amusing. A little young and inexperienced."

"He's the same age as us."

"Jeez, Debbie. You act like you haven't had a boyfriend yet."

Debbie hadn't—she slow-danced and kissed one geeky guy to a Bee Gees song at the last school dance even though she hated disco music, then turned him down when he asked her out—and a few hours ago she might have admitted this to Cheryl. "Of course I've had a boyfriend. Gawd."

"What are the guys like in Vancouver anyways? How are they with their tongues?"

Their tongues! She had only kissed on the lips and when he pushed his mouth onto hers so urgently—eugh. "They're good with their tongues. Yeah. Really good."

"Do you think Philip has a clue how to French kiss?" Cheryl giggled.

"No way," Debbie said without hesitation, chortling at dumb Philip in spite of the fact she had no clue either.

Between spasms of laughter, they floated on their backs and kicked languidly back to the dock. By the time Mr. Carlson eased down on the motor and nudged up to the dock, Debbie and Cheryl together had pulled Philip's shorts down twice. Philip had untied Debbie's top and tickled her and slipped his hand down Cheryl's behind. When Debbie looked at Jeffrey, who barely noticed her as far as she could tell, she felt strangely guilty. She didn't even think Philip was cute.

Janice was making lemonade in their unit's kitchen when she felt a hand on her buttocks. Her husband Dick was frisky again. God, that man. He either wanted to sleep, or he wanted to do it, or he wanted to play tennis. That was a holiday for Dick. She stirred the lemonade with a wooden spoon. Debbie was out skiing. The younger two had gone to Pitch 'n' Putt with their friends. Dick's other hand was stroking her belly. She stirred absent-mindedly, thinking, he's off tomorrow. Flying back to North Van early for work, what time will he leave? His hands. He had gentle hands, long delicate fingers. On their first date, pizza-to-go and a movie, she had approved. Stirring the lemonade, his hands still stroking. Who would have thought lemonade crystals needed so much attention? She'd have the bed to herself and extra space and quiet in the unit. She wouldn't cook. She and the kids would get burgers from the Tastee Freez and eat at the park. She responded to those hands, if not enthusiastically, then at least with moderate signs of enjoyment, enough of a green light for him to lead her by the bikini straps to the bedroom door, which she locked. Dick never thought to lock it. She realized, not for the first time and not resentfully, that men didn't think of those things. They lived in a charmed world where kids didn't need snacks or bedtimes and hot dinners miraculously appeared, every single day.

Afterwards they lay in bed and cuddled and really, if truth be told, this was Janice's favourite part. It was fine, she didn't often, well, get aroused enough to reach—not like Dick, it seemed effortless for him, zero to sixty and then, bang it was over and he was happy as a clam—so she didn't feel disappointed. He stroked her forehead. "Jan," he said breathlessly. "That was great." He stared at the ceiling, smiling softly. He had lovely blue eyes, so dark she had thought they were brown at first. And that gentle smile. The kids adored him.

Janice placed her hand on his chest. He did work hard. Why shouldn't he have sex and tennis? Oh shoot, if he was leaving early tomorrow—"Did you put the money in?"

He groaned. "Can't it wait?"

"Dick, I have to get another week's groceries."

He sighed.

"The kids want to do Go-Karts. And pick cherries." How quickly she switched her tone. She didn't mean to but they had to eat. She only worked part-time at the school for not much pay and not in summer. Her money went to extras like Debbie's piano. Dick was supposed to put money into their household account every two weeks.

"All right." He sounded peeved. "I'll go to the bank." He rolled over. "I could use another week."

Janice got up and threw a sundress on. She unlocked and opened the door. "There were men looking at Debbie's chest today."

"You're a mother. You're imagining things."

"She has no idea, Dick, thirty-eight-C bra and horsing around, bending over on the beach."

"She's a kid," he said fondly.

Janice felt her voice rising. "She's a developed young lady now, and she's going to get herself in trouble putting everything on display."

Debbie appeared outside their bedroom door with a glass of lemonade. "Mom, what are you talking about?"

Janice's heart plummeted. "Oh Debbie, you're back."

"Don't ever talk about me again." Her daughter spit out the words. She put the lemonade down on the table and grabbed her purse.

"Debbie honey, I'm sorry." Janice touched Debbie's arm. Her daughter jerked it free. "I just don't want people thinking you're some kind of tramp."

"Jan, stop it," Dick said.

"A tramp," Debbie repeated.

"Debbie, wait," Dick called from the bedroom, but she ignored him, walked out the door, and slammed it. He turned to his wife. "Now look what you've done."

Janice planted her hands on her hips. "What *I've* done?"

"You're making things worse. You always do."

Her husband worked, slept, screwed, and ate. He wasn't there buying that bra with her. He didn't have a clue what happened to girls at this age, what could happen. "If you had your way, she'd be galumphing around with no bra till she's eighteen, all hours of the night. A boy groped her today. How do you like that? Just felt her up right on the beach. She's fourteen."

"Come on, Jan."

"Philip Carlson. If she hadn't elbowed him."

Dick laughed. He laughed. "Good old Deb."

Janice grabbed the glass of lemonade, marched back into the bedroom, and poured it on Dick's head. He wiped his brow and gazed up at her with that goddamn beatific smile so that she felt, once again, that it was all her fault.

Stupid cow, stupid cow, Debbie recited in her head, striding away from their unit. She despised her mother for talking about those things. And what were her parents doing in the bedroom? She felt like throwing up. She folded her arms across her chest and banished all thoughts of boobs, old-man eyes, groping, and the dock. It was repulsive. She had her purse, she had money in her purse, she was meeting her friend, and that was good. Beach Grove meant treats from the ice cream truck, cherry soda and lemon-lime and all the neat different flavours of pop the Americans brought, fresh Okanagan cherries and cider from the fruit stands, and the Tastee Freez with banana splits and ten kinds of shakes and chocolate-dipped cones covered in nuts. This was what six months of allowance was for, and now she earned babysitting money too. Even so, she felt self-conscious as she walked, exposed in a way she hadn't felt only yesterday. She blamed her mother a hundred and fifty per cent.

Over in Cheryl's big bathroom on the other side of the motel, it took almost an hour for the girls to get ready. Cheryl was lucky, her blonde hair was thick with a bit of wave—when she used the curling iron her feathered bangs flipped back obediently and stayed there like Farrah Fawcett on *Charlie's Angels*. Debbie's thin brown hair just hung.

Cheryl's mom, Mrs. Stapleton, sat in the living room with the curtains drawn watching TV, a scarf on her head and a drink in her hand. Mrs. Stapleton was glamorous, perfumed, ultra-thin, her high-heel sandals with a fancy flower at the toe, the prettiest plum nail polish, and the way she walked with her cigarette held out like the models in those magazine ads. You've Come a Long Way, Baby. She was probably gorgeous once too, way back, but now her tanned brown face was wrinkled leather. It was late in the afternoon to be wearing a bathrobe, but Debbie figured Mrs. Stapleton just had a shower. She didn't even look up when Cheryl told her they were getting ice cream. "That better be all you're doing," Mrs. Stapleton said in an icy voice.

"Well, actually, after the Tastee Freez we planned a couple hits of acid and then maybe some heroin, Mom. Some really good smack."

That got Mrs. Stapleton on her feet. Her eyes blazed.

"Just like *Go Ask Alice*," Cheryl said. Every girl Debbie knew had read that book about the evils of drug addiction. "I just can't get enough drugs, Mom. Where are the drugs?" Cheryl opened her arms for emphasis.

Mrs. Stapleton paused, doubt in her eyes. It was so obvious Cheryl was joking but her mom was totally sucked in. "You're not—I don't believe you."

This was getting intense. Debbie never realized before how paranoid Mrs. Stapleton was.

"You're going dressed like that?" Cheryl's mom said, switching subjects.

"Dressed like what?" Cheryl asked.

"Like you know what. A little tramp."

Déjà vu. Were their moms talking or what? It was such an old-biddy word. What was it with their mothers all of a sudden? Debbie didn't get it. The girls were wearing what they always wore at Beach Grove—their bathing suits, halter tops, and faded jean shorts. Cut-offs. That was the style. Didn't Mrs. Stapleton know that?

"Mom." This time Cheryl's toughness was gone, she sounded hurt. Not for long. "Who's calling who a tramp?"

"What is that supposed to mean, missy?"

"At least I have a life of my own. Outside of shopping and drinking and waiting for my husband to come home."

Mrs. Stapleton, still holding her drink, lunged towards Cheryl, who hustled Debbie out the door. They scuttled away between the motel rows, their flip-flops crunching on the gravel drive. Debbie glanced back, fearing pursuit.

"What's with her?" Debbie asked.

Cheryl shrugged. "She freaks at everything now." She laughed but it felt false to Debbie. "The hosebag's mid-life crisis."

"Tramp," Debbie repeated. "My mom said the exact same thing today. All because I have boobs now. I'm sorry, what am I supposed to do, chop them off?"

Cheryl looked stunned. Then she started to laugh. Debbie, flattered at the response to her joke, made chopping motions at her bikini top with her hands. "Look Mom, no more boobs. You happy?"

Cheryl joined in. "Kung Fu!" she yelled as her hands flew. "Tits gone!"

"Tits gone!" they chanted, right in the motel driveway. "Chop, tits gone!" They managed to synchronize their motions with the words, mimicking a Chinese accent. "Tits gone. Tit-tees gone." A small boy with a sand pail stared at them before his mother picked him up. We're a bad influence, Debbie thought with satisfaction.

"They want to lock us in chains until we're twenty-five 'cause that's what they had to do," Cheryl said.

"Those fucking old bags can go to hell," Debbie said. It felt excellent saying that. "Because I'm gonna dress how I want and do what I want, and if anyone calls me a tramp or a slut, well, just screw them."

"Yeah, screw them," Cheryl said, looking at Debbie with new respect. "Let's get some ice cream."

As they walked back from the Tastee Freez along the busy main street, Debbie felt older, and braver. She licked the chocolate dip on her large soft cone, the ice cream oozing out and dripping in the heat. And she strutted in her cut-offs, pushing her 38C chest out as far as she could.

A car slowed down. Cheryl started swinging her hips, saying "Ba-boom, ba-boom" in rhythm. One of the guys stuck his head out the window to watch her. They honked and drove on. Cheryl tossed her plastic sundae cup on the sidewalk and started singing Aerosmith's "Walk This Way" all on her own, getting louder and louder.

Debbie joined in on the chorus. Cheryl put her arm around her and they zig-zagged down the sidewalk. People stared. Debbie felt crazy and potent. This was better than British Bulldog. There was a honk from a red convertible that kept on going. Cheryl waved and blew them a kiss.

Another car slowed down. Wait, it was that first green car again, a Valiant or something. There were two guys inside, bare-chested. Cheryl stuck out her thumb. The guys pulled over. Now what? Debbie tossed her head up, acting like this happened every day, while her heart thumped harder than when Philip came after her on the dock.

Cheryl jogged over to the car. Debbie edged closer. She heard Cheryl talking about Beach Grove, the end unit, the guys saying something about a "shit-kicker" Friday night in the park. Cheryl leaned into the car. Her laugh was high-pitched.

"Who's your friend?" the driver asked, catching Debbie's eye. "She's looking good."

A bullfrog in her throat. "Debbie," she said at last, blushing.

"See you, Debbie." The car burned rubber as it drove off towards downtown. Cheryl waved again. Debbie was amazed that any sound had squeaked out of her.

Cheryl grabbed Debbie's arm. "You and me are going to have fun this weekend."

An exhilarating tingle rose through Debbie's body, a collision of panic and joy at what lay ahead.

The moon was out and so were the Mai Tais. Stan had strung lights all around his cement patio and rounded up three more small Hibachi barbecues. One picnic table had a fruit platter, potato and macaroni and tossed salads with iceberg lettuce, garlic bread. The other table held hard liquor, lots of it, and pineapple juice, Coke,

Clamato, all the mixers. It was fairly loose, the liquor and who had some. Dick would have cared but he wasn't there. Janice and the rest of the parents weren't hung up with the teens having a little of this or that, half a glass of wine or beer. A taster.

Janice wore a new yellow cotton dress with spaghetti straps and a snug bodice; she bought it that afternoon with some of the grocery money. Taking a cue from Sally, she had yellow earrings and sandals to match. Debbie was keeping an eye on her little sister with the promise of ten dollars. The kids didn't have to do Go-Karts.

"Bloody-rare, sweetie." Eddy deposited a thick steak on Janice's paper plate. His hand lingered on her shoulder. "No Dick anymore. What's our Janice going to do?" She could not believe it. Eddy's floozy doctor from unit eight was there with her husband. Eddy's wife Kathy was only a few feet from them, making what for her was an uncommon social appearance.

"I'm going to have a whole lot of fun, Eddy," Janice said mischievously.

"That's my girl," Eddy said, caressing her bare skin. His wife was facing the other way.

Janice heard Stan's voice, low and soft at the open patio door. "Come on, Sally."

"This 'production' was your idea. Get more ice yourself," Sally snapped at her husband from inside. Stan turned, grinning like everything was top-notch, and glided away from her. Janice realized she didn't often see Stan and Sally together at Beach Grove.

Stan sidled over. His pale blue golf shirt was unbuttoned, his chest hair curling out. "Need a top-up?"

"Yup. Top me up, Stan. Make it a double top-me-up." She giggled at her brazenness, not just now but especially now, her general feeling of freedom. Dick was back home slogging away and she had an entire week to go.

"If I get you a top-me-up, can we make that top go down?" Stan asked.

She giggled again like a young virgin, then something let go and her laughter turned deeper, more carnal. She almost lost her balance, that was comical too. She wasn't drunk, just not used to her new heels, and she grabbed Stan for a firm athletic pillar.

"Mom." It was Debbie, dismay in her voice. Janice turned. Her daughter stared. Sally too, standing in the doorway. Janice straightened herself up.

Debbie told her some of the girls were coming over to their motel room to watch TV. "I hope that's okay. Don't worry, Mom. I'm still watching Lori. With my eyes glued." That was a Dick saying.

"Sure honey," Janice said, not sure why her daughter was telling her all this. Although it was thoughtful of her. It wasn't that strict at Beach Grove.

"Good." Debbie vanished.

The moon was coming up nicely over the lake and Eddy began to howl.

"Eddy, cut it," his wife drawled, to no effect. Kathy had a puffy face, everything about her felt heavy and bored.

"Anybody for a moonlit cruise? Ar-oooooo," Eddy crooned like a soulful wolf, head to the sky.

Janice, Carol-Ann, and the others whooped and cheered. Kathy was clearly outnumbered. Sally was nowhere in sight, the party-pooper. It took several minutes to get both passengers and additional alcohol into Eddy's boat.

Kathy stayed behind. Carol-Ann's husband Ted told her not to go.

"I'm going in that boat," Carol-Ann told him matter-of-factly, "and I'm not wearing a life jacket, and there's nothing you can do about it so shut your trap."

The warm wind felt fantastic on Janice's bare chest and shoulders. She stood up front next to Eddy. Putt-putt, nice and easy and then vroom, off they went into the middle of the lake. "Ar-roooo!" Eddy howled this time. "Ogopogo here we come!" he yelled, summoning the fabled lake monster. Janice drank in the speed, those bodies crammed close together, jostling, bumping, you pretty well had to put a hand on someone's hip or their back or their broad shoulders, just for support.

Eddy cut the motor and they drifted way out, far from the twinkles of the vineyards and orchard homes in the rolling hills, Beach Grove and the other lakeside holiday getaways. Someone passed around a bottle of rum—no Mai Tais now, only straight gulps. "Down the hatch," Carol-Ann ordered after her turn. Janice took the bottle and drank. The rum burned. She sputtered and felt like a lightweight. Carol-Ann laughed so Janice clutched the bottle for another go, willing herself to pour it down smoothly, no flinching. "Down the hatch," Janice echoed and passed the bottle on.

The water was calm and mysterious, the alcohol glowing in her belly, Eddy's warm, pudgy skin against her arm, scents of sweat and perfume and alcohol and sweet night air. She squeezed her way to the back of the boat, took off her dress and placed it on a cushion, climbed on the stern, bent over and dove. She tucked her head down, extended her arms—one hand neatly folded over the other, and sliced into the water. She did a couple of underwater breaststrokes before emerging to meet the moon's light.

"Janice? Are you all right?" Carol-Ann's voice. Janice couldn't quite make out her face.

"Fantastic." The water caressed her free breasts. She pulled her panties off and balled them in her hand to expand the experience, doing the eggbeater she had learned in her lifesaving course.

Soon Eddy, Carol-Ann, and two other water-babies joined her. They had a splashing session until Eddy became the lake monster. "Ogopogo!" he said before disappearing under water, nibbling at whatever flesh he could find. His bite on her thigh was painful and titillating.

As they returned to shore, Janice back in her dress, shivering under a beach towel, the shadows of Beach Grove came into view, the yellow lights at the party unit, moving shapes on the patio. Suddenly Janice felt a jolt and heard a splintering crash. There was a second's silence, except for creaking—no one knew what had happened—and then recognition and an eruption of laughter. Eddy had plowed his speedboat straight into the floating dock. Revellers slapped Eddy's back. Someone cried, "Do it again!" It was Carol-

Ann, for goodness sake. They all slapped the sides of the boat, chanting, "Again, again!" Janice's voice was one of the loudest. The dock was broken already, wasn't it? "Again. Smash it to bits!"

"Smash it to smithereens!" Carol-Ann piped in.

"Only if I get a kiss from all the ladies." That Eddy. The women lined up eagerly to pucker and smooch the horny giant. Janice couldn't remember when she'd had so much fun.

The public park was just past the haunted house. Debbie and Cheryl walked along the road and into the parking lot full of cars and a cacophony of music, The Eagles's "Hotel California" from one boom box, a DJ from a rock station, Fleetwood Mac from another direction. Although the night was cooling down, Debbie felt warm all over thanks to the Berry Cup at the barbecue, two mugs full. Debbie's little sister would be fine with the TV on and her brother checking in on the promise of a deluxe sundae. Cheryl stopped beside the biggest weeping willow and pulled the bottle of vodka out of her purse—she'd snuck it from the table at the barbecue. Cheryl opened it, chugged, and handed the bottle to Debbie. "I can't see anything. How are we gonna find those guys?" Cheryl asked.

Debbie hesitated, then took the bottle.

"We have to find them," Cheryl said.

It wasn't that Debbie was frightened, but the darkness, the buzzing of voices. "We don't have to."

"Yeah, we do. They were really cute."

"It's gonna be kind of hard."

"Are you gonna drink that or just keep it for a flipping souvenir?"

Debbie tipped and drank. She wanted to spit it out, her first hard alcohol and straight up no ice. She got it down before she coughed, almost retching. "Harsh," she croaked.

"Come on." Cheryl took her arm and pulled her towards the beach.

Bob Seger's "Night Moves" blared from a ghetto blaster near the bonfire, which was much larger than the ones at Beach Grove and expanding with each wooden crate hurled onto it. "Right on!" a long-haired guy yelled, holding a huge bottle up to the sky.

Cheryl sang, rocking gently to the beat.

"Party hearty!" someone else hollered as he hurled his beer bottle into the fire. A girl had her hands on a boy's bum over his jeans. More crates on the blaze. People lighting up, smoking. Flicking ashes away. A girl chased another and dumped beer on her. "You fucking cow!" the doused girl shouted. A much older guy looked Debbie over, up and down, and grinned wickedly. So much wildness. She forgot her little sister and brother, and her mom weirding her out at the barbecue, all dolled up with those other guys and her dad gone. Everything here was dangerous and new. Another swig of vodka for Debbie. That was all she could do just now.

"That's them." Cheryl pointed to the other side of the bonfire, then pushed her way over, dragging Debbie by her forearm.

Greg and Pete. Eighteen and nineteen. She and Cheryl were "sixteen." They passed a new bottle round. Southern Comfort. Then one of them, Pete with the skinny moustache, brought out a joint. A "toke." Debbie had seen it and smelled it before, skunky and rank, girls at the school dance in the bathroom stalls, kids in the trails. Even with the vodka inside her she felt nervous, but she did not want to look stupid so she watched them suck it in, pucker their lips, and puff their chests up until they could take no more. Cheryl did it too, like a pro. And then Debbie's turn. It burned, searing her throat, down into her chest. She hacked. The next time the joint came around she barely inhaled, she just pretended she did.

Cheryl's prize had his arm around her. They were necking. A lot. When they came up for air Cheryl said, "Let's go somewhere." He said, "Sure, baby."

"I know where we can go," Debbie piped up without thinking. "Take off your shoes." As Debbie led them wading through the water and over to the sleeping grasshoppers, she stopped and saw the moon over the lake and spun, her head orbiting the moon as it circled the earth. She tried to stay with that moon but she teetered and Pete laughed and caught her and held her tight. She asked herself, for a second, why, why this. And then she said, "Almost there."

"Top go down," Stan whispered, trying to yank down Janice's snug bodice. He changed tactics. "Bottoms it is."

This was not really Janice down in the weeds and shrubs and dirt on the narrow path behind the row of units along the wooden fence at the far edge of the property. Janice didn't mix her drinks or smoke pot, which she just did with Stan for the first time moments ago. She didn't dive off party-boats and swim topless and get nibbled by an Ogopogo, or let married dentists gnaw her neck and ruin her new yellow sundress rolling in the dust and thistles. Janice was home with the kids or servicing Dick or supervising the girls at the elementary school during lunch-hour bucket ball, laying out the garbage pails on the school's gravel field. The person whose body Stan roamed with greed and abandon was beyond her recognition and completely free. She had no panties on, not since the boat. Lori was fine, she was with Debbie, and her son was eleven, he was a boy, she didn't have to worry about him. It wasn't that late. There was a bathroom light on in a unit down the row, enough to see the outline of this dark panting shape.

She found to her surprise that she didn't want to look, to try to find his eyes. She had to feel and move and smell and listen and record every detail. He felt different than Dick. He was not gentle, he was rough and urgent. He smelled strongly of musk and the laundry soap on his shirt was not what she used for Dick. And his mouth inside tasted like that funny cigarette, not her du Maurier King Size or breath-mints like Dick who never smoked. Strange that Dick was so present while Janice had vanished. That curling carpet of hair on this backside and chest, so unlike Dick. And this heavy breathing, it drowned out the voices in the distance, the party going strong. Every cock is not the same. Stan. That's who this stranger was. "Stan." Was she speaking now? Whose voice was that? "Stan, you bastard!" It was familiar but the light had gone out and she couldn't see except for a blurred shape in the moonlight, glowing, and then the sensation, hands grabbing flesh, claws scraping her cheek, a chunk of hair ripped from her scalp, powerful arms wrenching her, the night air on her skin. She cried out, not knowing anything but shock and pain. "Slut, you whore!" Barbs raining down on her like spit. The new not-Janice moaned and rolled onto her stomach, arms shielding her head, as brutal kicks landed on her chest and back.

The assault on her ended as quickly as it was launched. She heard a slap and then another. Male curse words. "You crazy bitch!"

Female. "This is the last time, I've had it with you and your cock!"

Male again. Ruthless. "Get out of here! Do as you're told." Sounds of exertion, pushing.

A woman's cry. "You're hurting me!"

The man. "I don't fucking care!"

A light blinked on again. She laid in the dust with her head turned, watching the figures fade. She whimpered. It was too much effort to touch her clawed cheek, her bruised ribs, the tears in her yellow dress.

And then other voices. "There she is." A hand caressing her forehead. "Janice, Jan, it's Carol-Ann."

Janice opened her eyes. She could see the outline of Carol-Ann's face with someone behind her.

"You waltzed yourself into a hornet's nest," Carol-Ann said.

"Don't tell Dick. Oh God. It was a mistake. Please don't tell him."

"We won't, dear. We won't tell a soul," Carol-Ann said. "Let's get you cleaned up, good as new."

"Thank you." Arms lifted her up. She felt too dirty to cry.

Debbie ran barefoot through the shallow water, hastily pulling her tube-top down to cover her breasts, lifting her legs against the drag, away from the haunted house, those bodies on the sand, fourth base, home run, it's what Cheryl wanted. That other stranger unzipping his pants and beckoning to Debbie. She froze, then she ran, her flip-flops left lonely next to him. Was he coming after her? Around the fence jutting out into the lake, back to shore on the Beach Grove side, tripping in the sand and up again, sprinting faster than she had in the regionals track meet, stubbing her left big toe on the cement sidewalk. Home to unit six, her brother and sister and newly strange mother who called her a tramp. Locked. She pounded on the door, half expecting him to track her down, dripping wet, jeans around his ankles. "Mom!" Her knuckles hurt. Pounding. Looking. Checking.

And then—what about Cheryl? Would she make it home okay?

Her mother opened the door and stood there in her short nightie. Debbie stood panting, full of frightened adrenalin, winded from her exodus but also fierce. She took in her mom's red eyes and scratched, bandaged cheek.

Janice caught Debbie's quick breaths. The fear in her daughter's face flipped to shock. She struggled to hold the girl's gaze and looked down. What happened to Debbie's sandals? Janice caught a whiff of liquor but could not say if it floated from her own breath or her daughter's. Debbie trembled. Janice felt overwhelming relief that her child was home.

"I'm not a tramp," Debbie said finally.

"No, you're not." I'm the tramp, she thought. Her shame flickered and burned from her toes up to her flaming hair.

Janice put her arm around her daughter and led her inside. "I'm not going to use that ugly word ever again," Janice said. "I promise. Okay?"

"What happened to you, Mom?"

"Never mind." She would never speak of this to Debbie or to anyone.

"I can't help it if I have boobs," Debbie said.

Janice laughed, deep and loud and wild, surprising herself.

"Mom!" But Debbie joined in the laughter.

The younger ones emerged from their bedroom to check on the foofaraw, hovering, as Janice hugged her daughter close and Debbie let her and together their breathing calmed. Little Lori wrapped herself round them.

None of this happened. This is what Janice knows. In a few hours she will tell the kids to pack up, they're leaving early—she hasn't figured out her excuse yet. The younger two will whine and plead and there will be tears as they load the station wagon. She'll drive them home in sweltering midday heat along the winding Hope-Princeton highway, treating them to milkshakes as many times as they want. She will never set foot at Beach Grove again, whether Carol-Ann keeps her lips zipped or not, and Dick won't understand and that's just too bad. She'll remain close with Carol-Ann, who was there for her, a true friend.

This is what Janice has no clue about. How to raise her daughter to be a strong, independent woman, to keep elbowing the boys, and stay safe and live her life with strong sexual energy and without shame, for Debbie to remain free to make her own choices, be who she wants, and not rely on any man.

All Janice knows is she'll try her best.

Typhoon

THIS MORNING AT SIX, like each day but Sunday, my tiny island is bustling alive in the winter dark. Hawkers beside the ferry terminal sell steaming congee in takeaway bowls for people hurrying to work in Hong Kong. Others cook rice noodles from carts, spooning runny white dough over heated metal trays. The vendors dot the dough with shrimp, roll it deftly into long tubes, cut them in segments, douse the pieces in oil and soy. Heaven.

Across the main thoroughfare near the terminal, Jonathon and I sit perched on rickety chairs outside my favourite dim sum restaurant, drinking jasmine tea. Watching the world. Eating. Smelling. The tea's fragrance is ecstasy. My mom has a saying about the things she loves, "I wouldn't trade it for all the tea in China." She doesn't know how precious this tea is, equal to the rosebud china cups she gave me when I was a girl.

Not everyone's in a hurry here. I sneak glances at old men sipping whiskey. Drinking so early. Wiry children carry bamboo trays suspended from leather straps around their necks. Trays for me to choose from. Har gau, shrimp dumplings. Siu mai, dumplings with pork. Sticky rice with chunks of chicken. Char sui bao, steam buns with that sweet, red-brown barbecued pork hot inside pasty white dough. Peel the paper off the bottom. Sip my tea and smell tangy bowls of chicken feet in black bean sauce, breathe and sip and watch.

Poor Jonathon. He gobbles his sponge cake. He has to get on that ferry, arrive in Hong Kong, and catch a double-decker bus halfway round the main island to his job. That red Brit bus careens around the curves next to the sea. One day it's going to tip and flatten some Rolls Royce. I know. I took that bus with him to see where he spends his days working as a copy editor. I saw office girls flutter round him, red-lipped with impossibly tiny waists. It made me smile. It made me nervous. Lots of gweilos, foreigners, walk round our island with young Chinese wives and Eurasian babies.

I would sit here happily every single morning if only I could convince Jonathon. Today he didn't want to come but he gave in because we skipped yesterday. Instead, we had white bread and peanut butter. He ate it in big bites standing over our kitchen counter. This morning I cajoled. I cuddled. I whispered behind his ears where he's ticklish and it makes him giggle.

"Jen, it's too heavy," he told me. "I can't eat that much meat every morning."

"Please?" I said. "Eat the shrimp. And the sponge cake. It's light." I lifted up his shirt and wriggled my fingers up his belly.

"All right," he said and shivered. He always does in our unheated flat.

At dim sum this morning he leaves half his cake. I reach for it. He's looking into space. He's boyish and handsome, sensitive and small-boned with delicate skin almost the colour of steam buns, blond curls falling round black-lashed hazel eyes. The young women notice him. But he's mine.

He looks tired and sad, half-eaten like his cake. I'm in our flat all day freelancing newspaper articles home to Canada for a hundred bucks here and there. Going out to interviews with inspiring people like Portia at the women's centre and maybe soon landing a job with a Hong Kong paper before my tourist visa runs out. He's carrying us. Jonathon. He's got his work visa, that and falling asleep at his desk by the South China Sea, editing deadly trade magazines about widgets six days a week. I touch his hand. He stands up and pecks me goodbye. He walks onto the ferry in his cotton shirt and tie and dress pants and away off my island. I eat the last of his yellow cake. It's springy and light.

From the ferry dock I meander home at dawn. I can walk my whole island in two hours. I love that. I'm from the West Coast where mountains and evergreens climb forever; even walking to high school was thirty minutes each way. I have never been somewhere so contained in miniature. No cars. Just two hilly chunks of land joined by a skinny neck, as if a giant had throttled the island in his fist, stealing its breath. The ferry, fish boats, bank, and shops are clustered on one side of the strangled neck. I take a detour to the other side curved along the channel, only five minutes away, and amble along the white-sand beach fit for a picture postcard. In my letters I describe it to my parents and little sister. Their last note back was before Christmas. It said *Merry Christmas*, nothing more, as if they're bewildered by Asia and me leaving or maybe not interested at all.

I turn off at a narrow cement walkway which slopes and curves in switchbacks up to higher ground. I pass an elderly woman with her hair knotted in a bun.

"Jo san," I say.

She smiles, returns the greeting, and squeezes by.

Nobody says good morning to you in Vancouver.

Puppy greets me outside our flat on the second floor. After I open my door the shepherd-cross shimmies inside on her tummy. She's a black-and-tan pup from next door who wriggles up whenever she sees me. She's my buddy. Her short tail wags so furiously her entire rear end sways back and forth. I scoop her up. She licks my hands and face. She doesn't have dog breath. Her slobber doesn't bother me, even though I have to look good for a job interview this morning at the *Hong Kong Standard*, a real English-language newspaper. All right, it's not with the *South China Morning Post*, not with *Asiaweek* magazine and certainly not with the *Far Eastern Economic Review*. But I have to get this job. I have to I have to.

I had a plan and it failed, costing us nearly two hundred dollars in the bargain. Last weekend we went to the Portuguese colony of Macao on the hydroplane. We wandered in the cemetery reading old gravestones of sailors and babies and young women dead a century ago from influenza or consumption. From wide boulevards we gawked at the crumbling elegance of Portuguese buildings with plants nudging up the cracks. Decay. We ate chicken and drank cheap wine. We didn't go near those giant gambling halls by the dock.

It was a grand day's fun until we returned to Hong Kong on the hydroplane and walked through customs, me half-drunk and loose in the knees, facing the prospect of not getting my visa extended, with Jonathon's hand on my elbow. The customs officer stamped my passport with a one-month extension. One month! That was it. Expats said they always gave you three. One month is nothing. One is going back to Vancouver with my tail between my legs.

Sure, not everyone will see it that way. My grandpa will be relieved to see Asia spit me back alive. I can take my sister to that music festival she wants to check out in the States. But what's Geoffrey going to think? Geoffrey and the other British guys from the newspaper back home. They seemed thrilled for me, as if they were reliving their own Hong Kong adventures and it was up to me to keep that quest going. You know, hanging out at the Foreign Correspondents' Club, writing for the *South China Morning Post.* How could you not love a rag with a name like that?

While I nuzzle up to Puppy, a man outside the flat calls in Cantonese. My neighbour Winson, a bulky man in his thirties, appears in the doorway. A cowlick seems to fly from his head. "Sorry. So sorry."

"It's okay," I say. "Your puppy is adorable."

He laughs shyly. "She never listen to me. I told her, 'Come.'"

"Hey, why are you here today?" Winson has a wife and kids and job in Kowloon on the mainland. He usually brings Puppy to our island on weekends. Today is Monday.

"I stay too long." He grins. "Last night with friends." He makes a drinking motion.

"Oh, you were bad."

"A little," he says.

I try to recall the last time I was remotely bad. Not since Geoffrey visited last fall. He invited us out on his friend's junk for the afternoon. We putted the boat over to the largest island, Lantau, and feasted on seafood and too much beer. I let him flirt with me even though he's far older, but sweet and harmless, he could be my father. Jonathon didn't seem to mind. It was the happiest I'd seen him since we returned from our month backpacking in China, where he'd battled a horrendous cold and I got food poisoning.

Winson says, "I have to go to work now."

He takes Puppy from me firmly. She cries out, looking up at me with her black eyes. I hesitate before I close the door.

The phone rings. It's my friend Mercy. She and her husband Peter live in a larger furnished flat up the hill. The *Standard*'s news editor, Jimmy Wah, hired her two weeks back. "What time are you coming to see him?" she demands.

"Ten. I'm not even dressed for it."

"Act like you know everything," Mercy nearly yells into the phone. "Remember, Jen, you're an asset to this shitty rag."

"You're not at work, are you?" Mercy is brazen. Petite, dark-haired, and mouthy as hell. She told me Mr. Wah got sold on her last name—she married Chinese Canadian Peter Chan in the Maritimes—plus her white skin, fluent English, and tight blouse.

"Of course I'm at work," she says. "Wear something sexy. Oh, here he comes. Gotta go."

Sexy. Hah. All I've got is my two-piece, wrinkle-free polyester dress in a plaid as white, black, and grey as the Hong Kong skyscrapers. Formal enough for all the suits and ties downtown, great for the humidity, but uh-uh, not sexy. I put on my camisole and half-slip dotted with grey mildew. We can't afford a dehumidifier. Then the dress and a braid down one side for my dirty-blonde hair, done without benefit of a mirror. A maroon silk scarf from Shanghai around my hair elastic. Voilà. Foreign correspondent leaps out door of unheated, unfurnished flat (except for Lilliputian table, two plastic chairs, and one manual typewriter) into waiting arms of destiny.

Bliss is coffee with milk and sugar in a paper cup and the latest *Far Eastern Economic Review*. Reading what the *Review*'s Hong Kong correspondent Emily Lau has written about 1997 and Martin Lee's campaign to protect rights. That's all you hear about. The Basic Law Drafting Committee, which Lee sits on, writing the constitution for Hong Kong's handover from Britain to China. 1997. Eleven years from now. "One country, two systems," proclaims China's leader Deng Xiaoping; many here don't trust that promise and are already shopping for Vancouver real estate. Lau is obviously pro-democracy and human rights, and brave.

I feel a light tap on my shoulder as I carry my coffee towards a seat on the ferry. Peter towers over me, beaming. Long-limbed with a regal nose and gentle, near-whispering voice, he always has a smile, though he hasn't found a job, not even teaching English. The Hong Kong Chinese don't want Asian-looking teachers. Even if Peter's roots in Canada go back further than mine.

We grab a table. He opens his briefcase. "Check this out," he says. He has a business degree but inventing is his passion. I examine the tiny silver contraption, trying to decipher its purpose.

"Cuff links with a pen holder attached," Peter offers.

"Oh. I get it." I giggle, then stop myself.

"It's faster than putting your pen back in your pocket. I timed it."

"Really?" I mimic taking a pen out from a shirt pocket and then from an imaginary cuff link. Not much difference to me. Peter watches expectantly. "It's great," I say.

"I'm dropping by a couple of manufacturers today. Give them the prototype and my card. Hey, have you seen it?" Peter proudly flashes a business card with his name and address embossed in English and Chinese. "And hey, don't tell anyone," he says, "but I've got a guaranteed concept for glow-in-the-dark jewellery. Earrings, necklaces. I've got a line on a couple of designers in Kowloon."

His eyes are hopeful. No, desperate. Maybe I'm reading that in because I've got a make-or-break chance in an hour.

"I've got an interview at the *Standard*," I tell him. "I'm already nervous. If I don't get this, I'm gone in a month."

Peter squeezes my hand. "You'll do great." His long fingers are soft, gentle.

"Thanks," I tell him. "So will you. Knock those capitalists dead."

My feet feel stuck to the sidewalk. Five to ten. I'm staring up at this ugly grey box in the sea of Kowloon warehouses. The *Standard*. It occurs to me as I stand planted in cement that Mercy doesn't get paid much, works long hours, and barely catches the last ferry home in the dark. Peter meets her each evening at the terminal. I see myself walking from the Star Ferry exit on Hong Kong Island to our island ferry in pitch black. I feel frightened. It will be fine; Mercy and I will walk together. A man bumps into me. "Oh!" I say and manage to move my feet.

In his fourth-floor office Jimmy Wah reads over my puny résumé. I remember to cross my legs. My sweating fingers are locked together to stop the shaking. He is short. His cheeks sag. His hair is unkempt. He tosses the résumé like a soiled tissue to the side of his desk littered with papers and a full ashtray. "You don't have much experience."

Geoffrey's watching from his newspaper desk back home. Jump on it. *Want it bad.* "I'm good." Lame. "They wanted me to stay at the newspaper in Vancouver." This was true. I wrote about suntanners sizzling on Kitsilano Beach and trick Super Dogs at the Pacific National Exhibition. So much for being an "agent of social change" on the university newspaper.

"Is that so?" He raises his bushy eyebrows and smirks. "You're a modest one, Miss Jennifer."

He's making fun of me. *Don't smirk*, my father said. Am I ridiculous? I give my best modest smile while my fingers throttle each other.

From Jimmy Wah, curt newspaper editor, to Martin Lee, distinguished pro-democracy activist. I can't believe I'm sitting in Martin Lee's law office to interview him. It took a month to set up but I'm here. Me, some unknown freelancer, no Foreign

Correspondents' Club member, promising I'll try to sell the story to the Vancouver papers. I'm drawn to his high cheekbones. He is impeccably dressed in a dusky-grey tailored suit. Eloquently explaining *to me* his crusade to expand the limited political rights Britain has conceded to its colony, to enshrine more rights into China's Basic Law for Hong Kong after 1997.

An hour later, my right hand cramped from scrawling notes, I shake his hand. I waft down the elevator (I shook his hand) and burst into the street (I shook his hand). A woman hawks redolent meatballs floating in oil from her cart. My nose devours them. Down steep streets I skip towards the sea. Porsches and Jaguars compete with racing buses and trams. People swarm in this steamy sardine can. Down to Statue Square where Filipina women sit and laugh, speaking Tagalog as they eat box lunches. Martin Lee stands up for these people. He makes a difference.

Back on my island that afternoon, I wander towards the open-air market near the Taoist temple dedicated to the island's deity. Wooden fishing boats rock gently a few yards offshore, some with bright laundry hanging. I grocery-shop every other day because our flat doesn't have a refrigerator. At a pungent fish stall, I point to white fillets. "This one, please," I tell the woman, and then, "That's enough," after she selects two small fillets.

The woman wraps them, then holds out four fingers outstretched.

"Sei," I say. I can count to six in Cantonese. I take four Hong Kong dollars out of my wallet and hand them to her. The customer next to me, a woman in her thirties holding a round, flat, dried fish, says something in Cantonese to the fishmonger. They both laugh. I smile. They glance at me. My ears feel hot. Maybe I got charged extra and they're laughing at my expense.

I stop next at the bakery for bread. I love how they put loaves in white plastic bags with the ends turned over and knotted. Mangy dogs pick through a garbage pile nearby. Sprigs of magenta bougainvillea arch languidly down the concrete wall above the refuse. How does mange spread? I hope Puppy doesn't get it.

At the foot of the stairs to my flat, I buy two cheap Filipino beers from the tiny man with a bad leg. "Doh je," I say.

"M goi," he replies, adjusting the cigarette in his mouth.

There's mail waiting. Mail from Canada! Queen Liz on the stamps. Letters from my dad and Jonathon's mother. I want to open mine now but I'll wait. We'll do ours together.

It's nearly five when the phone rings. Jimmy Wah from the *Standard*. "Can you start next week?"

A stomach blip leaps to my chest. "I think so."

"You think so."

A job, a visa, yes. Why is my heart racing and not in a good way? "I have an assignment to wrap up." Why am I saying this? I typed up the story this afternoon about the kindly Sikh gentleman I interviewed last week. He has daughters. He's a civil servant. He could be my dad. After 1997 he's a nowhere citizen because Britain won't take him and he's not Chinese.

"You want this job or not?" Jimmy asks.

How long was I holding my breath? "I can't wait to start. Next week. Monday's great."

"All right. Nine o'clock." He chuckles. "We'll see how good you are, Miss Jennifer."

I hang up, lean against the wall, slide down, and count twenty-six grey flecks in the white wall facing me. I want Puppy to snuggle but I know Winson took her.

Jonathon surprises me in the kitchen; he wraps his arms around my waist from behind. I turn and kiss him. "Seems you get home later every day." I didn't mean it to come out like that.

He looks hurt. "No later than usual."

I'm chopping coriander. He wrinkles his nose.

"Hey," he says. "Typhoon coming. By the weekend maybe."

"Seriously! A real typhoon!" I jump up and down like a kid, then remember. "It can't come on Saturday. We're going to Lantau with Mercy and Peter."

"Tell the South China Sea to hang onto its farts for a day," he says, grabbing the bread bag.

At dinner he asks, "How'd your job interview go?"

"I got it." I say the words but don't believe them.

"Great. Maybe I can do some articles now and you can support me."

I put my spoon down. "Where did that plan bubble up from?"

"Hey, you don't have to snap."

"I didn't snap."

He stirs fish stew around in his bowl. "Right now you're getting all the glory."

"What's that supposed to mean?"

He says, "Getting your stories published all over."

"Yeah right," I say, "three stories to Vancouver and two to Seattle. Whoop-dee-doo."

"Goes a lot further than saying you work at some trade magazine."

He's glaring, beating one tight fist's bony knuckles against his open palm. I can't believe it. He never gets mad. "Don't be silly," I say. "Sounds like you're jealous."

"I never said that. It's just, the job sucks. I had a migraine by lunch. Anyways I thought we were going to Thailand after this."

"What's the hurry? It's not going anywhere."

"I almost wish we were back home," he says. "It sure would be nice to have hot showers again."

This is all fine. I miss things too. My sister, her high school graduation. "Canada's not going anywhere either."

But he carries on. "Cold milk in the fridge. Five-day work weeks without half your weekend shot."

Obviously, I get annoyed. It's like he's bailing before we're done. "Don't." I take a breath to simmer down. "I mean, not yet. Okay? Please, Jonathon."

He won't look at me. He concentrates on liberating every green fleck of coriander from his stew. I don't say anything about my next article on Martin Lee.

After an hour I say, "I'm sorry, I didn't mean to snap." Later we lie in our two single beds pushed together—one bed higher than the other—drinking beer, reading our letters, and trying to avoid the gap in the middle. Jonathon wears his sweater to keep warm.

My father's handwriting is almost illegible. *Your mother wants to downsize...not the best time to sell and move...wish you could have a word with her.* And almost as an afterthought, *Laura broke her leg in a car accident.* He doesn't ask how I'm doing.

"Fuck," Jonathon says.

"What?"

He shields his eyes with his hands. "'Don't worry,' she says. 'Don't worry about us.'"

"I don't understand."

"He had a heart attack." He clenches his fist. "Triple bypass. And his sick leave's almost run out."

I put my arm around him.

"After twenty-five years with the company, hauling us to every crappy logging town they told him to." He's crunched up now with hands wrapped around his legs.

It's only the letters. We'll be better tomorrow, back to normal. Jonathon will come home with stories about other expats from Australia and England. He'll crack me up with the day's grammatical goof-ups in articles and ad copy. "Our micro-chips has to shove into your newest hard-drive." My favourite was "This screwdriver really turns tricks for you."

My bum rides the split between the beds the way it always does, the way it has for five months, the way that just this second has become intolerable. I stand up naked clutching my beer can. "I hate this fucking bed!"

"So do I," he says.

I grab him and pull him up. "Come on."

We bounce on the mattress yelling, "Fucking bed!" over and over.

On Friday after supper, the mahjong tiles start their clacking from the flat upstairs. Jonathon and I give each other a look. The neighbours will play long into the night.

"I mailed my article on that old Sikh gentleman," I tell him.

"Good."

"I forgot to take my pill yesterday."

He kisses my nose. "That would be okay with me."

"I'll take two pills tonight to make it up."

He pulls away.

I want to love Jonathon. He's good. He didn't want to come here, not as fiercely as me, but he did, because he loves me. The pollution in China, his sinus migraines and hacking cough, left him thin and weak. When we returned to Hong Kong, he could barely walk up the path to check out our flat. I yelled at him to hurry up. I did that. I never loved a guy before. It's awkward; it means effort and embarrassment, opening yourself wide and exposed, seeing another person that way too and loving them harder. I keep a hard kernel hidden for no one to touch—not trading it for all the tea in China.

Jonathon will be a patient father, teaching his children how to ride a bike or put their face in the water. My dad did that with us. I was never the kind of girl who liked kids automatically. Kittens were easy, especially calico. Puppies also. My little sister Laura was a cutie, her fine hair standing up straight as if her finger was permanently stuck in an electric socket—but changing her diapers? No, not for me. Other babies were terrifying. The first one I babysat, just six weeks old, cried all night. The next, a toddler, spread shit on her legs and crib. I left her in her mess until her mother came home. My children? They'll be hideous.

Jonathon says his muscles are tight from hours at the computer and asks for a massage in bed. Sitting on his bum, I work my fingers gently into his back. I hear Puppy bark and I squeeze Jonathon's flesh sharply. That's how I like it, having the tension ripped from my muscles, but Jonathon cries out in pain. "Sorry," I say without meaning it. Sometimes I want to sink my fingers into the scruff of his neck, just shake him to toughen him up.

Puppy barks over and over, her sweet baby yaps. There's a man's voice low. Puppy barks again, squeals in bursts, stops, then squeals once more. My thumbs jab into Jonathon's shoulder blades. He moans and rolls over to escape me.

"He's hitting her." I grab his arm, then burrow my face into his bare back. It's quiet now except for the mahjong tiles and us breathing.

Jonathon works half-days on Saturdays. He's home by one to change for our outing with Mercy and Peter. The sky is cloudy and the wind's up a bit but it's hardly a monsoon.

"I saw Puppy this morning," I tell him. "She wagged herself up to me as usual."

"Winson probably stepped on Puppy's tail by accident last night," he says.

"Yeah."

"It'll be good for you to work again. And get your visa."

"It'll be good not to eat lunch all by myself." I'm getting tired of instant noodles.

Mercy marches next to me down the path to the ferry, with the guys behind. "The *Standard*'s no worse than the Chronically Horrid," she says. That's what she calls her hometown newspaper, the *Chronicle-Herald*. Economically depressed Halifax is "Calcutta on the Saint Lawrence" in Mercy's books. "I'm gonna get a helluva lot of mileage on my résumé back in Canada from good old Jimmy Wah and the *Hong Kong Standard*. You will too, sweetie."

"That's what Jonathon said." I look back. He's out of earshot. "I think he's jealous."

"Of course he is. So's Peter, though he'd never admit it. Just leaves empty milk cartons in the fridge. Little acts of rebellion." She laughs.

I glance back again at the guys walking. Peter, almost a head taller than Jonathon, gives him a playful elbow. They're both laughing. Peter catches me looking. He winks and I smile. Jonathon, noticing, seems to miss a breath.

Nearby Lantau is larger than my island and Hong Kong Island put together but far less developed. The ferry chugs along Lantau's shoreline, approaching an isolated collection of plain white boxes passing for buildings. As we get closer, I see barbed wire around what look like oversized chicken coops.

"What's that?" I ask.

"It's for boat people," Peter explains. "Refugees from Vietnam."

"They're *not* refugees," Mercy cuts in.

I read about those camps with thousands of people that no country wants. "I bet their lives were tough in Vietnam," Jonathon says. Our ferry is next to the camp now. The barren dirt yard is deserted.

"They left to make money," Mercy says. "Now they have to go back."

"They'll be persecuted if they're sent back," Peter says.

"They should have thought of that when they hopped on a bloody raft," Mercy says. "There's people way worse off than they are."

Peter speaks softly to his wife but his words carry conviction. "We hopped off some sort of raft, didn't we? Coming to Canada?"

"It's not remotely the same, Peter," Mercy says, as if talking to a child. "Our grandparents worked their butts off, wood-cutting, chambermaid, washing dishes, no handouts. There was nothing but trees and a few Indians when they landed."

"And what about now. Us coming here?" Peter asks.

"Don't be ridiculous."

Peter doesn't reply. I wonder at this moment why he stays with Mercy.

Jonathon looks at me and rolls his eyes. "It's not their fault," I say forcefully, surprising myself. "They didn't know what they were coming to, only what they left behind." I suddenly want to cry.

Peter stares. He's not smiling. He turns to Mercy. "Sometimes you're so heartless." He hesitates, then takes her hand. "We don't know how lucky we are."

"Lucky my ass, Peter. Nobody takes one look at you as an English teacher here. Canadian-born, don't speak a whit of Cantonese, and they treat you like dirt. It's more racist than Halifax, for God's sake."

Peter's mouth drops. Jonathon seems to wince in solidarity. It's not fair that I have a job and Peter doesn't. His graceful fingers flutter at his sides. He retrieves his smile. "Come on, Mercy."

I watch the receding prison for a proof of life. Is that a child peering from a window? I want to believe yes.

Light rain sprinkles us as we walk over the hills, through a village with chickens, ducks, and dogs roaming freely, to a sprawling burial area in wild grasses. Stone markers face the ocean next to a steep drop-off. "It's a wild place," I say, though I know the markers weren't cast randomly but with careful feng shui. I have an urge to be alone with these battered spirits gazing out to sea, but I don't know why they're calling to me.

"This is eerie," Mercy pronounces. The wind picks up, adding to the drizzle.

Peter stretches his long arms upwards and twirls. "Lantau is one of Hong Kong's last bastions of space." He stops. "Did you know Hong Kong's so crowded that bodies get dug up after six years and cremated?"

Mercy says, "They should get cremated in the first place."

"They're taking chunks out of the harbour for more development," says Jonathon. "Stealing land from the ocean."

I barely hear them over the melancholy wind. Waves crash on the rocks. There's something gnawing at my hard kernel. I'm not sure why I came. I turned down the newspaper job in Vancouver, everyone from my grandpa to Jonathon asking me why. Something about being different and tough and not needing that iron rice bowl—a union job. A family you can count on. About creating oceans of distance. "Why did we come?"

I didn't mean to say that out loud. Jonathon's face is a stunned silent question—*You don't even know why?* Mercy answers, "To get rich."

That's not it. Is it? This city oozes money from its pores. Peter's hand rests on my shoulder. It feels safe, heat pulsing to my doubting heart.

"They didn't know what they were coming to," Peter says, "only what they left behind."

I turn to look at him. "And now they know."

"Yes," he says. "Now they know."

His face is soft and wise. I want to hold it in my palms. But I don't. Jonathon plants himself next to me.

The rain comes, along with more wind. Let it come, drenching us clean as we tear down the dirt path to the terminal, muck and water coursing with us. "Last ferry," says the man at the dock. "Hurry!" Stand-by Signal Number One hoisted minutes before. Typhoon.

Our ferry rocks in the gale. We giggle and whoop with the swells. The swaying intensifies. My stomach is in turmoil. My hands grip the table for support. We're going so far over we're going to tip. Oh no, back to the other side. My pack slides along the floor. Nobody's talking now.

This is not how I want to end up, capsized in the dirty South China Sea. I find Jonathon's hand. He squeezes. Where's the lifeboat storage? I don't see it. I can swim if I have to, I think, I hope. Remember from lifesaving to kick your shoes off. Jonathon will sink, he's not a strong swimmer. I can be mean to him and I know it's not right but I won't let him drown. My old boss Sam Leung at the Chinese restaurant escaped from China when he was only sixteen. He swam to Hong Kong through the sharks. He wanted it bad. What was it like to want something that much? I was a spoiled kid who could see the ocean from my bedroom. We tip further. A collective "ohhh" of fright ripples through us and the other group. I want my sister with her broken limb and my mother's bread pudding and my complaining father, even if they don't ask about me. I want them now.

"I'm scared," I tell Jonathon.

He wraps his arms around me. "It'll be okay."

My island, I see its grey form through rain-stung windows. The ferry slams into the dock.

Through the downpour we run to our flat first and stuff dry clothes in a plastic bag. Puppy whimpers from behind her door but we don't stop. All four of us race up the hill to Mercy and Peter's for refuge and the spaghetti and sauce with the Chinese beer Peter bought that morning. We shut the door on the typhoon, all of us wild-eyed, giddy, dripping wet and panting, stripping off our soaked shirts and pants together. The others seem excited, even Jonathon, at the clamour of tree branches crashing, wind and rain. I conceal my fears about what a typhoon might do. It might not let us go back.

We watch a spaghetti western with our typhoon spaghetti. I haven't watched TV since we left Vancouver but I'm not watching really. *I'm not sure why I came.* To be a foreign correspondent? To escape what was known? The ground-floor flat starts to flood. I help Mercy put towels at the front door. The rain keeps on. Peter, ever hopeful, says he has a lead on a marketing job with a Canadian company. Mercy tells me we can commute home from the *Standard* together.

"I'm not taking the job," I say brightly.

"Of course you are, sweetie," Mercy says.

Jonathon looks up from the TV.

"I want to go home," I say.

"Let's just watch the end of the movie," says Jonathon.

"That's not what I mean." I smile at him.

Jonathon opens his mouth to speak, then stops. His shoulders relax as he breathes out. "Okay," he says.

Mercy and Peter stare at us. "You're just getting cold feet," she says. "You can't pull out now."

"Yes, she can," Peter says.

Mercy gives a disgusted snort.

I turn back to the TV and take a bite of spaghetti.

Jonathon and I saw Thailand and Malaysia and India. When we got home, skinny and full of parasites, my mom was preparing to move to a condo, with or without my dad. Her packing boxes overwhelmed my old room above the sea. Displaced, I crashed with Jonathon on foamies in the living room. The newspaper hired me for casual shifts which dried up fast. I saw Expo '86 with my dad that summer. My parents sold the house and rented their own places, with my sister floating between them. Jonathon's dad returned to work with his patched-up heart. Jonathon and I, both unemployed and drifting, broke up the following spring. My parents got back together in the end, and bought a condo.

Hong Kong residents consumed with Communist fear kept gobbling up Vancouver property, sending prices further up and fuelling racist resentment from anglo-white people. My people. Martin C.M. Lee was expelled from the Basic Law Drafting Committee after he spoke out against China's brutal crackdown on Tiananmen Square protesters. He became the founding chairman of the Democracy Party. I don't know what happened to the Sikh gentleman. Or Puppy.

I told myself I would be back for midnight December 31, 1996, and the handover from Britain to China. I could almost smell the steamed pork dumplings and rotting garbage, taste the shrimp-filled rice noodles covered in oil and soy.

To not believe this meant admitting the truth. Those battles weren't mine to pick up, hold and carry. That island never belonged to me—a searching, privileged interloper. It wasn't mine for the taking.

I needed to return home, whatever that was, to learn what I wanted, no, what I cared about and how badly. Getting on that flight was a step on the way.

Piss and Vinegar

ONE. THE CHEMICAL TOILET in the A-frame cabin was not working. In fact, the chemical toilet had not worked since day one. Two. The water dribbled out of the sink tap and shower head. Wendy had taken to hoarding rainwater outside in a plastic bucket, dipping a cup in, using that to wash her hair. Unfortunately, there'd been no rain in a week, her island maintaining its reputation in "Canada's Banana Belt," the Mediterranean of the West Coast. Three. Wendy could barely scrabble together the rent.

The islands in the Salish Sea were coveted summer destinations; rentals were scarce, overpriced to gouge tourists from Vancouver and Victoria. When she rented the cabin the previous month, she'd been desperate. There was the house-and-dog-sit in the spring for her older friend who baked and sold puppy treats, two ill-advised weeks crashing with her ex-husband in his yurt on a communal organic farm (they were not *technically* divorced and were trying to remain friends), and an apartment sublet that had cleaned out her meagre savings. She spent much of August tenting in the provincial campground, driving her rusting station wagon to the Saturday markets in town to sell her knitted sweaters and socks, and to her waitressing shifts at the restaurant, until a campground warden twigged and told her it was time to move on. Anyways, by then, the Labour Day weekend around the corner, she could see her breath in the ocean air and the dew on the wild grasses above the tidal pools. She felt the chill in her fingers as she crawled out of her tent, watched the ferries, and boiled water for tea. This summer she turned thirty-six. Her wispy chestnut hair was tinged with grey; suddenly she felt old.

The ad in the *Islander* described a "quaint, rustic cabin, ocean view, $750/month, available immediately." Wendy's cell phone needed charging so she called from a payphone in town. "This is Dr. Larsen," a brusque, deep voice answered. Yes, the cabin was available. Wendy asked when she could she see it. "Come right now. Turn right before the school. Left on Blackberry Drive. Just past the flower stand."

She parked in the lane behind an ancient orange Volkswagen van. Blocking the sun, Douglas fir and cedar trees towered above untamed blackberry brambles and broom, which she'd learned were coastal intruders like her, and native honeysuckle. A narrow unpaved driveway sloped down. She got out of the car wearing her typical fall attire—one of her ex's undershirts and a flowing paisley shirt under a grey fisherman's sweater from the thrift store, calf-length purple layered skirt, cozy leggings with a hole in the crotch that needed mending (a bit of wool would do nicely), and rubber boots, ubiquitous on the island. A lanky white woman, easily six feet tall, strode up the drive, her free-flowing red hair needing a comb. She looked to be in her late forties. Able to scale mountains in her outdoor pants and battered hikers. And distracted.

"I'm Astrid." Her tone was abrupt.

"Wendy. I thought for sure this place would be rented already. Everywhere I phone it's the same. Locals can't even find a decent place to live on the island anymore." She figured local was a minor stretch. She had moved here with her husband two years ago; they broke up and reunited twice in that time before the final split.

Astrid bounced slightly, continuously. It seemed an effort for her to listen. "Right. Okay."

Maybe Astrid was not local and she'd offended her, or Wendy's combination of words and appearance screamed "hippie," though she wasn't meaning to be *that*, not really. And Astrid's van was a clue that she could be an old hippie herself. She was peculiar, though. Her pale-blue eyes darted to and fro. Her plaid shirt had lost two buttons and she had flecks of yellow food—egg yolk?—on her chin. She didn't seem like a rich city interloper.

"This way." She motioned for Wendy to follow. "I have to get back." Astrid appeared in quite the rush.

They descended a hundred metres or so. The cabin came into view. Someone a long time ago had painted the A-frame's wood trim in green and red, now washed out and peeling. They came closer. Out front was a porch with a bleached wooden chair and a derelict barbecue. Through Arbutus and Garry oak trees, Wendy saw sunlight on a calm bay and, further away, the faded blue mass of Vancouver Island. Astrid said, "There's a trail down to the water."

A speck on the water—it just could be a loon. "It's stunning."

Astrid showed her inside. "It comes with electricity, running water."

"Hot water?" Wendy said.

Astrid nodded curtly. "Of course."

Wendy already felt rivulets of blistering water soaking her head, becoming a virtual monsoon down her face, breasts, and legs to her toes.

The cooking area was in a cramped corner with one tiny window. Astrid tapped twice on the precarious plywood counter, nearly tipping it, and informed her "the whole entire kitchen's being redone," as if it was a grandiose scheme never the likes seen before. "The carpenter's just finishing another job."

She led Wendy into the bathroom with no tub, just a miniscule shower. And a squat, beige, plastic contraption with a rubber valve on a top rear corner. Wendy's brow furrowed. "What—?"

"It's a chemical toilet. Completely odourless," Astrid said. "Works like a dream."

"How does it work?"

Astrid demonstrated. "All you do is pull the handle up to open up the waste tank and push down once or twice on this rubber valve when you do your business. Then pour a bit of the blue chemical solution into the bottom tank every few weeks. I've got oodles in a bin behind the cabin. Presto."

"Presto. I can do that."

In the doorway between the bathroom and the main (and only) room, Wendy took it all in—mildewed linoleum, shower curtain missing three hooks, sagging couch, small round kitchen table, stools with ripped upholstery, chipped enamel sink, two-burner stove, gaps in the well-worn hardwood, bookshelf, propane lantern. A framed photograph. She stepped closer. It was of an athletic man with windswept blond hair and a child in a sunhat on a small sailboat in brilliant sunshine. On the nearby bay? Next to the frame sat a homemade candleholder—a stub of green candle firmly melted into a base decorated with pebbles and clam shells.

Wendy envisioned knitting rainbow socks during winter storms. Reading by candlelight. Drinking wine and smoking cigarettes, lots of them, while on the deck bundled in sweaters.

She picked up the candleholder and caressed hardened runnels of wax.

Astrid gave a nervous laugh. "My daughter made that."

"It's so sweet." Wendy put it down. "How come you're renting this place?"

Astrid glanced at her for a split second before twisting away and mumbling almost to herself and the dusty shelves. "It's no longer practical, is it? Someone decided to do their PhD on Beowulf and it wasn't me but here we are five years later. The kid's got youth symphony, part-time jobs. Things change, that's just the way it is, and we forge ahead, don't we?"

"I suppose. Yes."

Astrid stared out the window. "Enough nonsense. It's not important."

"Do you have lots of other people interested?"

"The ad just came out. You're first on the scene as it were."

"I'll take it. I have references."

Astrid brushed off this notion with her hand as if at a wasp circling red meat. "Just give me the damage deposit and the first month's rent. Fifteen-hundred dollars."

Wendy felt boulders sink into her gut. "I'm a perfect tenant. Quiet. Mature. I really want this place but my restaurant shifts are only three times a week now. And my car just needed new brakes. You know how steep these island roads are." (The first and third parts were true.) "Can you give me a break on the damage deposit? Please?" Then with a panicking heart-flutter as she realized Astrid might well question her ability to pay rent at all, she said, "I've got tons of markets coming up. I sell out of my socks and sweaters every time. I'm just a bit short temporarily. Because of the brakes."

Astrid's shoulders sagged. Her mouth soured. "All right, fine."

Wendy's stomach rocks vapourized. She wrote Astrid a cheque for the first month's rent, praying her tips would be decent this weekend so she could top up her account and the cheque wouldn't bounce. Astrid didn't have a formal rental agreement, saying she forgot it at her clinic back in the city, but she scribbled her name and contact information on a ripped-out page from the newspaper.

On the deck Astrid handed her the keys. "Good then." She shook Wendy's hand with a rapid, crushing jerk. Astrid's grip was impressive.

It was only then that Wendy noticed the outhouse. Seconds later, a petite figure peered over the other side of the fence. "Astrid. Hellooo! Can I have a word with you?"

"Gotta run, Inez. Catching the ferry. I'm on call tonight." Astrid tucked her head down and hurried down the wooden steps off the deck.

The woman's voice had an edge. "I really need to talk to you about this septic field."

"No time." Astrid practically bolted up the drive. Mountains would mean nothing to this woman. The neighbour—Inez—pursued along the fence but she was barely five feet tall and couldn't keep up with Astrid's endless legs. A small furry creature—a squirrel?—scuttered low along the fence.

"You need to make time," the neighbour insisted. "This outhouse is not up to code. It's draining into my garden and it's a health hazard." A sharp bark. The mini-beast was a scruffy black-and-tan dog.

Astrid swivelled but kept walking backwards. "Don't worry, there's a chemical toilet, state-of-the-art."

"You said that last year. If it's so state-of-the-art why do your tenants need the outhouse?" Inez said.

"It's a back-up. Nothing more," Astrid said.

"That thing needs a proper septic field this fall or I'm calling the islands trust."

Astrid waved and got into her van. The engine sputtered before kicking in, and she rumbled off. Rocks tumbled back into Wendy's stomach but she told herself the toilet worked. *Presto.*

Wendy walked up to meet her new neighbour on the lane. Inez looked to be in her sixties. Freckles spattered her pale cheeks. Playful, honey-lit brown curls bounced at her shoulders. She wore jeans, neon-pink sneakers, and a yellow sweatshirt liberally dribbled with food stains down the front. Wendy wondered if wearing one's leftovers was a prerequisite on Blackberry Drive. The dog barked again, startling Wendy. The woman hushed and petted the animal.

"That so-and-so," Inez said. "I could wring her cheap neck."

"Um. Hi. I'm Wendy. I'm renting her place."

"Oh my." She chuckled. "Inez. Welcome to Blackberry Drive."

They chatted over espresso and biscotti in Inez's bright expansive kitchen, very *much* renovated with oak cupboards, a marble kitchen island, and large windows overlooking the bay.

"So what are you up to on this wacky island?" Inez's wide, dark eyes bored into Wendy's. "Not another dope pusher, I hope, we've got enough of those layabouts already."

"No, no. I share a booth at the markets with this great lady who makes dog biscuits."

That perked Inez up. "Suzanne?"

Wendy nodded. "You know her?"

"Suzanne and I go way back. We were in high school together eons ago back in the city. Our school annual. Thick as thieves. I bought the best treats for Nigel from Suzanne at the market. They were shaped like baby deer. He gobbled them right up." Inez leaned down to the dog laying under the table. "You just love Suzanne's treats. Don't you?"

"Hello, Nigel," Wendy said. "I've never met a dog named Nigel."

"He's a Yorkshire Terrier." Inez scratched behind her dog's ears. "Nigel was the most English name I could think of."

"He has an amazing beard."

"Wait a minute." Inez gasped. "I remember seeing your adorable socks and sweaters. They're full of colour, aren't they? Like wearing rainbows. That's what I thought."

A ball of warmth glowed inside Wendy. "Thanks. That's really kind."

"I used to knit when my kids were little. I'd love to start again. Along with running a kayak shop. Wouldn't that be fun?" Inez giggled. "When I retire. Stop running back and forth to the city and find the time."

Wendy reached for her second biscotti.

"They're almond. From my dad's favourite place on the Drive. Have more. Go on. You're like a heron."

"A heron?"

"Elegant," Inez said. "But, well, you could handle another."

Wendy was five-foot-nine. Always slim, she had lost weight in the past month. She dipped her biscotti into her espresso and nibbled. "A kayak shop would be perfect on the island."

"That's what I tell my husband. I'm working on him."

Wendy considered how much of Inez's energy anyone could withstand. "I'm so glad I found the cabin."

"I'll tell you something." Inez looked at her conspiratorially. "Astrid's an odd duck. Different. She would love to quit her big fat doctor job, thanks to taxpayers like you and me, and spend all her days and nights there."

"Why doesn't she?"

"Her husband and daughter can't stand it. They won't set foot in that—well, you know."

Wendy suspected Inez wanted to say "dump" or "dive" but only just stopped herself. Wendy suddenly felt sorry for Astrid. She also realized she'd never been called a taxpayer before.

Wendy's cheque to Astrid went through, fortunately. She enjoyed hot, although not gushing, showers for a few days before the flow frittered away to a trickle. Less than two weeks in, though, something was not right with the "odourless" toilet. It smelled, and it was not a good smell—neither the fragrant scent of her black tea blends with lavender and anise hyssop nor of must and damp boots. She called Astrid three times and left messages. On the fourth try she reached her.

"Hello?" She sounded out of breath.

"It's Wendy. From the cabin."

"I'm just in the middle of something."

Wendy pictured Astrid sprinting up an alpine trail. "Did you get my messages?"

"All right, look," Astrid said, her tone clipped. "I'll send my plumber fix-it guy round to check the water pressure."

"What about the toilet manual?"

"I'll mail it. I have to go." She hung up.

The toilet manual did arrive in the mail the following Monday. With no sign of a handyman. She read through the entire manual. It appeared more complicated than Astrid had indicated. Apparently, it was important to add water to the top tank if the top flush reservoir lacked clean water. It also instructed: *Please use this toilet only from the sitting position. Standing means messy splashes.* Good to know with any male visitors.

Given the stench (maybe Astrid had friends who liked to spray standing up), she advanced directly to When to Empty and Clean. Following the diagram, she pulled out the "T" handle in the toilet's bottom waste reservoir tank under the seat and, yes indeed, the murky liquid was at the brim. That meant Full. Time to empty and clean it. She propped the door wide open, carted the entire toilet outside slowly so as not to trip, placed it next to the outhouse, and unscrewed the cap at the back of the small tank. Taking heed of the instruction to keep the cap facing up, she poured the waste into the abyss of the outhouse.

For the next step, washing, she moved the toilet over beside the garden hose and turned the outside faucet on. She waited a few seconds for action before remembering the hose was not an option at present, due to the less than torrential force of the cabin's water pressure.

Wendy didn't dare ask Inez if she could blast the crap out of the toilet, literally, on her side of the fence, but she took her bucket over. An older Asian man whom she assumed was Inez's husband busied himself emptying a wheelbarrow full of leaves into an already impressive pile while the dog chewed on a bone. She had noticed him before from a distance.

"Hey. I'm Wendy from next door."

"Oh, golly." He strolled over. He was not much taller than Inez. "I'm Jim," he said brightly.

"I'm sorry for interrupting your work."

"That's no trouble, nope, none at all. I was getting ready to burn as many leaves as possible in one go but as you probably know, there's an endless supply of Arbutus leaves and it's futile. Thankfully I'm retired. It keeps me out of trouble and endless games of Scrabble."

Wendy laughed. His voice was gentle, almost musical. "You look too young to be retired," she said, with his full head of black hair, his unwrinkled face.

"Oh, well," Jim said with a shy smile. "I've been around the block a bit."

"I have almost no water to clean my chemical toilet. Can I just borrow a bucket or two from your hose?"

"You certainly can. Take three or four or twelve if you like."

Jim found two more spare buckets in the garage. Together they filled the three pails and lined them up by the fence. Wendy walked around to the other side and Jim helped her to heft them over. He was in good shape. He told her she could come by for more if that didn't do the job and even offered to help clean the toilet.

"Oh no, that's okay. I can manage."

"Are you sure? Cleaning chemical toilets is known to be almost as hazardous as wrangling Arbutus leaves." He offered a coy smile.

She grinned. "I'm not going to inflict that on you. Toilets and leaves in one day. You won't have time for Scrabble. Thanks anyways."

Wendy used rubber gloves and an old dishrag as she poured water into the toilet, sloshing it round and rinsing three times to eradicate any noxious fumes once and for all. She discovered there was not actually "oodles" but only a quarter of a bottle of chemical toilet tank deodorant and sanitizer in the carry-all behind the cabin. Just a small dose of the blue sodium hydroxide solution was required, luckily. After she returned Jim's pails and packed the pristine toilet into the bathroom, she felt fuzzy-warm and satisfied. Fresh sea air filled the cabin. She made a cup of tea using water from her plastic jug which she refilled at the restaurant, finished a pair of men's socks for the fall fair, and smoked two cigarettes. She watched a loon down on the bay, floating, diving, reappearing. All before heading to town for her shift.

It was late September and a month into her cabin life. The island remained overrun with tourists on weekends, with plenty of day-trippers, but mid-week was slower now in town and her tips were down. Astrid's promised fix-it man never materialized; after two more messages Astrid texted her back saying: *Guy hurt back. Be there soon.* Wendy tried to focus on her knitting because she needed to finish at least five pairs of socks and another baby sweater to sell in her booth at the harvest festival this final weekend of September. Then there were the last four Saturday markets in October and that was pretty much it for tax-free tourist dollars. Concentration was proving elusive.

Three musician friends spent the weekend. They came over from the city to perform at a Friday night benefit at the hall, in the fight against the latest logging plans. Jumping from the rocks at high tide, they all frolicked in the bay, shrieking at the delicious cold, daring one another to swim out to the buoy, watching seal heads bob up and disappear. They waved at an imposing figure in a bright toque who rowed a dinghy from a moored sailboat to the rocky shore past Inez's property; the boater waved back. Later they made mojitos with fresh mint and sang Stan Rogers and the Beastie Boys to the ducks and seals. Inez and Jim's daughter

Jamie joined in the fun. Barely taller than her parents, Jamie was a rotund teddy bear with chipmunk cheeks, her mom's freckles, her dad's wry smile, and an endearing belly pudge under her baggy T-shirts. Jamie caught the ferry over from the city the odd weekend "to chill out from the city." They lit a bonfire and roasted oysters they gathered on the beach. There was a bottle of tequila passed round, hand to mouth, hand to mouth, and some powerful weed one of the musicians had acquired from his cousin's personal plot further north on one of the more remote islands. Not one but five of them used the chemical toilet. More than once. It was such a long way to the outhouse. Someone probably used the toilet from the standing position.

Now it was Monday and the festering fecal stench gnawed at her, assaulting her nostrils, infiltrating her mouth, tongue, and salivary glands, permeating her pores. Rotting shit particles, her shit, her friends' shit, floating into the main (and only) room next to the minute bathroom. She screamed and once more propped the door wide, donning plastic gloves to haul the useless thing outside. Odourless—not. It was wet and dripping as she toted it, opened the rickety plywood door with one hinge missing, and dumped it in the outhouse pit. Afterwards she hacked into the verdant salal bushes but nothing came up.

"Wendy!" Jamie's voice.

Wendy hunched over, hands on her thighs, shaky.

"Are you all right?"

She lifted her head. Jamie hovered at the fence, her ballcap cocked to the side, with a worried expression. "Was the weed bad? Oh jeez, I hope it wasn't the oysters."

Wendy righted herself. "That stupid toilet doesn't do anything except stew everything in its juices."

"That bites," Jamie said.

"It's like the most foul crock pot ever."

"I like crock pots. Nice autumn stew. Mmm. Get some organic potatoes happening, a bit of tender local chicken and onion and garlic. And a nice long firm bowel movement. Slice it up, throw it in."

Jamie mimed the chopping with a poker face. Wendy thought there might still be bile inside her. Nearby, Inez asked Jim where he put her bulbs, and Jim replied that he'd be right there.

"Thick brown gravy," Jamie said. "You don't even need gravy mix."

Wendy laughed. "That is truly disgusting. Hey. Don't you have a ferry to catch, like, yesterday and work to do as of right now?"

Jamie gestured for Wendy to come closer. She did. Jamie leaned over the fence, whispering, "I phoned in sick." She smelled of a fresh-smoked cigarette and strong coffee. It smelled good.

Wendy was coming back to life. She laughed again. "This is your lucky day because I'm pretty sure you helped make that gravy, although it was a team effort. The least you can do is fill up some buckets of water."

Inez's voice piped up. "Jamie! Who are you talking to?"

Jamie smiled. "Mom can't resist a good gossip session."

Inez ambled over in her jeans, sweatshirt, and gardening gloves. "Oh, it's Wendy. I'm planting my spring bulbs. A whole whack of them." She shouted behind her. "Jim, it's Wendy!"

Jim joined them. Jamie put an arm around her mother. "We were just talking about how diarrhea makes a really rich, savoury sauce in a chemical toilet crock pot," Jamie said.

"I'll pretend I didn't hear that," Jim said.

"That asinine thing's still not working?" Inez said.

Wendy's head jounced. "Not the running water either. The repair guy never showed up." She bit her lip, fighting the urge to snivel.

Inez planted her hands on her slim hips. "That ding-a-ling Astrid."

Jim tilted his head at his wife. "Now, Inez."

"Ding-a-ling, really, Mom? Language," Jamie said. "Wendy knits baby sweaters. She's a nice girl."

"I know she is, but Astrid is not even supposed to have running water without an approved septic field, that's what the guy told me at the islands trust or whichever one's in charge of all that." She pointed at the outhouse. "And look at that thing, she puts it right next to our place. The last tenant had parties every weekend and there were girls pooping not just in the outhouse but all around it. Remember that, Jamie? You went to one of those parties, didn't you?"

Jamie averted her eyes and surveyed the laneway behind her. "I might have stopped in for a few minutes max."

"Anyways," Inez said, "that crap flows right into my garden."

"I *am* getting more stomach aches in that cabin." Wendy contemplated spending the winter there, with mist, dark trees, and putrescent particles closing in, but what other choice did she have unless she moved back into the yurt or found another cabin? Most everyone had scooped up any affordable winter lodgings already. There were city people renting too, upping the going rate while building their luxury dream homes to retire in. She could leave the island altogether but to where? Back to the city and equally ludicrous rents for basement suites with postcard-sized windows? She started to cry for real this time before looking down to the bay, wiping her eyes, and pulling herself together.

"I would take you in myself," Inez said, "but Jim's sister is coming from Lethbridge."

"Then your cousin Rosa from Turin," Jim said.

"No way, you're not taking me in," said Wendy. "Maybe I should call someone else. Do you have a good repair fixer person that you use?"

"We have a guy who's good as gold," Inez said, "don't we, Jim?"

"One who's not smoking those marijuana cigarettes," Jim piped in.

"Like half the island," Inez added.

"While he's on the job, I might add," Jim said.

"You might indeed. I could tell you stories about the roofers we hired, couldn't I, Jim?"

"Yes, you certainly could, Inez."

"They were high up in more ways than one, let me tell you," Inez said. "One actually fell off the roof and landed in the shrubbery right under the window, I'm not kidding you. I was sitting on the couch with Nigel and bam, crash!"

Jamie made a mock-horror face. Jim smiled and winked.

Inez told Jim, "Go find our guy's name and phone number for Wendy."

"Right." Jim lingered.

"And then, Wendy, you just tell Astrid she's going to pay for it and that's the way it's going to be."

Jamie clenched her fist and raised her arm for battle. "Make her pay!" She reached over the fence to grasp Wendy's arm over and hefted it high. She did the same for her parents. Four arms, four fists.

"Okay," Jamie yelled, "make her pay!"

"Make her pay!" Inez and Wendy echoed.

Jim appeared mildly embarrassed although not surprised or angry. "I'd better dig up that phone number." He turned towards their house. Inez followed him.

Jamie patted Wendy's shoulder. "Hey. Don't take this the wrong way. But. Maybe you should use the outhouse for now. Just don't tell my mom."

It took Wendy a day and a half to muster up the gumption to call her landlord. When she finally did, she got Astrid's voice mail, again.

"I'm sorry to keep calling but your repair guy still hasn't showed up and I can't wait any longer. I'm feeling a bit sick with that smell and no water. I hope it's okay but I'm going to call someone else. I'll make sure they're not a rip-off or anything. I'll get the bill sent to you. Call me if that's not—." Beep. The voice mail ran out of room.

She reached Inez's "good-as-gold" repairman that evening. He said he didn't do the plumbing side but his brother did and was back on the island the next day.

Wendy showed up for her restaurant shift the following Wednesday, took her sweater off and changed into her work shoes in the cramped staff room as usual. Her boss Murray scurried past the doorway, then popped his bald head back in the door. "Oh, by the way. We move to winter hours next week."

"What do you mean?"

"Closed Monday through Wednesday. You'll be at two shifts a week."

"What? You're not serious?"

"I meant to tell you sooner. But you must have known we cut back in winter, we do it every year."

"It's only September."

"It's already slowing way down. Sorry. Welcome to the island." Murray vanished.

Wendy stood stunned. For a moment she misplaced herself until Murray called, "Table three. Wendy."

All through the piddly lunch crowd she craved a cigarette. She worked split shifts with two hours off in the afternoons. On her break, at last, she lit up steps away from the entrance even though her boss didn't like staff doing that. As she walked along the boardwalk, she checked her phone—she had missed the brother-plumber's call. "Damn it," Wendy cursed. She sat on a bench by the water and called right back. No answer. She closed her eyes and flopped her head into her palms.

"Wendy, is that you?" A familiar male voice with a mild quaver. Her ex. Jeremiah. Oh Christ, Wendy thought. Not now.

He sat down and put his arm round her. She tensed but sat up. "Hi, Jeremiah. Yes, it's me."

His familiar wheaten stubble refused to grow into a full manly beard. His scraggly hair was pulled back in a ponytail. His tunic hung slack, those faded blue hemp pants loose on his raw-boned frame and slender white ankles. She didn't think it was possible but he looked skinnier than ever on his vegan diet, endless fasting and cleansing, and manual farm labour. It was nasty, she knew, but she wondered if he had worms.

"Is everything all right?" He appeared genuinely concerned.

She didn't want to reveal weakness (read: wretched loneliness, missing him). She intended to say everything was fine, she was moving on tremendously since their last break-up, really for real the last because there was no way around only one of them wanting children, that being her, as for him it was no world to bring children into, what with climate change, airborne pollutants, consumer greed, and so on, and wasn't it grand them still being friends and all? But she didn't have the strength at that moment to lie and put on a brave face or remove his cloying arm.

"Everything's shit, literally." And she told him the short fast summary of the cabin compost toilet saga.

"That's frickin' not okay." He seemed energized by her predicament. "I'm with you, whatever it takes. I know the Landlord and Tenant Act inside out." It was true; he had been an activist in the city as rooming houses got demolished for condos, many of which turned out to leak. He had maintained it was karma.

He took out his harmonica and played a soulful tune, crooning, "I'll help you get that slum landlord, I'll help you toss her in the outhouse, I'm gonna get that darn landlord for you."

"I wouldn't go so far as slumlord," Wendy qualified. "She's a doctor, she's healing people." (Admittedly, that was hard to picture.) "Doctors are busy." Still, she wanted to kiss Jeremiah for the solidarity. She nearly did, which was mortifying.

"Wendy." He had that extra-spiritual tone for when he geared himself up to say something profound.

"What?" she snapped, then felt badly. "What?" Gentler.

"The yurt's still there if you need it. It's really warm and cozy now. It's got a woodstove and everything. And I'm there too."

Then he looked at her with beckoning blue eyes that she had loved not that long ago. She stood. A cold wind rustled through her bones. Her knees wobbled. That wind could knock her into his arms. She backed away.

"Thanks, that's good, yeah, I'll keep it in mind." Her words spewed out. "But I have to get back to work." She spun and sped away as quickly as she could without running.

She arranged for the plumber-brother, Ronny, to come on Monday morning at ten. Knitting, she waited. And waited. Four hours late, he arrived in his truck. He was younger than her, maybe in his late twenties, and chunky. His hair had a decent cowlick happening, it did not look combed or washed recently, but that was typical for the island and not a bad sign, especially as he shook Wendy's hand forcefully, saying, "Sorry for being late. Let's get your water sorted."

First Ronny investigated the chemical toilet.

"My landlord said it's state-of-the-art but I cleaned it out twice just like the manual said. It stinks no matter what."

Ronny guffawed, not an encouraging sign.

"What is it? Did I do it all wrong?"

"No, this is a really old one. I seen one of these useless relics kicking around at a friend's cabin. A bunch of us guys ended up trashing it with shovels one crazy night and hucking it in the dumpster behind the hall." He prodded the toilet with his boot as if considering a potential repeat of that fun. "Nope. Not worth fixing."

Next Ronny sized up the showerhead, checked beneath the sink, and headed outside. He peered under the cabin where there was a gap, then crawled underneath, re-emerging moments later. "I need to pick up some tools from another jobsite. It's just a few minutes away. And grab a bite to eat. I'll be back in an hour."

"How much will it cost?"

"Can't say for sure."

"Approximately?" she said.

Ronny scratched his head. "Could be one hour's work, could be four."

"I have to tell my landlord something."

"Hard to say." Ronny shrugged. "Two hundred. Three hundred."

"The landlord will be paying."

"I only take cash."

"I don't have any on me right now. I can call the landlord but she's in the city."

"Yeah. That's always the way round here." His easy grin told her he'd had this conversation before and wasn't going to budge. "It's up to you. Do you want water or don't you?"

She knew he was scamming Revenue Canada. So was she, for that matter. She made a mental calculation of how much she had in the bank. About four hundred dollars. Most of it had to go to next month's rent but she could dip into it. Astrid could deduct it from her rent.

"Fine. I have to go to the bank. And I need a receipt for my landlord."

Ronny took off. She phoned Astrid again. "It's me again. Wendy. I really need you to call me today because I have to get the plumbing fixed."

Ronny came back two hours later. He spent not a lot of time under the cabin.

"There's a leak and a damaged pipe. And some rotting wood. None of it's installed right in the first place. Par for the course round here. Plenty of cheap DIYs like this one."

"That doesn't sound promising."

"I just gotta run to the hardware store and pick up some more P traps."

"Okay." Pee traps? She had no clue what those were but suspected the cabin could really use them. "How much is this going to cost?"

"I'd say." Ronny scrunched his lips together, emitting an elongated grunt. "Gonna be at least three hundred, including the parts I replace."

"At least?"

"Maybe you should go get the cash ready. I'll be back tomorrow."

There was barely enough gas in the station wagon to get her to town. "You can do it, sugar," she told her car, stroking the dash, coasting in neutral down the hilly road to town. There also was less in the bank account than Wendy hoped. Just enough for the plumber. She rummaged, excavating loose change from the container beneath the radio (broken pre-island life, not worth fixing), and put eight dollars' worth of gas in the car. No buying cigarettes this week. She had half a dozen left in her pack to be rationed.

Ronny got the water running the following day. Wendy had to ask him twice but he wrote out a receipt for $315. The water pressure was somewhat better; she could fill the sink to wash her dishes and rinse the shampoo from her hair. The chemical toilet was not better. Reluctantly, she borrowed fifty dollars from Jeremiah for gas and food. She didn't say anything about cigarettes or wine but he knew her weaknesses. He kept telling her how glad he was to help her out. She felt guilty and wondered if she was using him. She didn't think she was, at least not very much.

Wendy left another message for Astrid explaining how much the repairs cost and asking for her address to mail the receipt. She had tossed out the envelope for the manual Astrid mailed without checking for a return address. Astrid didn't call back.

Later that week, clouds encroaching on the trees, Wendy sat on her deck wearing two sweaters, watching for loons and ducks on the bay, trying hard to think about ways to sneak more food from the restaurant, and trying very hard not to think about the rapturous pleasures of smoking and red wine.

"Wendy! Yoodle-hoo!" Inez called over the fence and waved.

Wendy waved back and walked over.

"I have a proposition for you." Inez smiled as if she had a naughty secret.

"That sounds mysterious."

Another one of Inez's giggles. There was a childlike spark to her. *She's got piss and vinegar.* Those words landed on Wendy suddenly. From where? She wasn't sure.

"I would like to know if you would give us the pleasure of your company on Sunday for Thanksgiving dinner. There's me and Jim and Jamie and our neighbours on the other side, Alice and Gertie. I don't know if you've met them but they're the salt of the earth. We've got a twenty-pound turkey from the farm up the hill and we need all the help we can get."

Wendy started to salivate. She flourished her arm to the side and took a bow. "I would be delighted to offer the pleasure of my company."

Inez clapped her hands together. "Yippee! Any time after five."

Wendy felt both taller and lighter. If nothing else, it was a free meal (and a chance to bum smokes from Jamie). It was more than that, though. Wendy welcomed the idea of being inside a warm house with other people. This past week the restaurant had been quieter, as had the previous Saturday market. Suzanne left early because she had family visiting and both grandchildren had come down with the flu. Then the wind whipped up and it poured with rain. Some of the market awnings toppled over. The park was one massive puddle. Fat slugs had a field day gliding through drenched grass. A ferry sailing was cancelled. Everyone seemed to be trying extra hard to have fun when it just... wasn't.

On the Thanksgiving Sunday, Wendy mashed the potatoes in Inez and Jim's kitchen while Jamie added butter and milk. She felt regal as she pulverized spuds on the kitchen island with her clear view of the bay. The neighbours, Gertie and Alice, arrived. Wendy had not officially met them, although she'd waved once or twice getting into her car as the pair drove along the lane in their red jeep. Jim hurried to greet them and hang up their coats. Gertie was an ample white woman with a pronounced limp. She took off her fuzzy turquoise toque at the door, revealing close-cropped snowy hair. Alice was several years younger, spry and vivacious, her afro trimmed short.

"That's Gertie's sailboat moored down the bay from us," Jamie said. "Gertie loves to fish."

At dinner Wendy had two helpings each of turkey dark meat, Jim's cornbread stuffing with sage and pancetta, gravy, mashed potatoes, Inez's cranberry sauce with orange zest and cinnamon, and Brussels sprouts. Red wine flowed freely. "This is delicious," she said. "Thank you so much for inviting me."

Inez puffed up with delight, telling her, "Eat some more."

Wendy thought of her mom's stuffing with apples and walnuts. "I can't remember the last time I had one of my mom's turkey dinners."

"You don't see her at Christmas?" Inez said.

"No." Everyone's eyes were on her.

"Did you lose your mom?" Inez said.

"No, it's just..." Ever since she moved across the country to the West Coast for university, she and her mother had not been ones to talk on the phone every week. She had chosen anthropology against her parents' arguments, being one, way too far away (which was the point in her mind, far from stodgy Ontario) and two, way too expensive, with student loans bound to be crushing (which proved bang-on, it taking her ten years to pay them off, but she'd never admit that to them) and three, totally impractical for finding any sort of decent job (also having some merit, but at the time she dismissed this as neither of her parents had gone past high school; she loved her courses and spending extra hours opening drawers of artifacts at the museum of anthropology). Her father visited once. It rained the entire time. Her mom had never been out west, not even for Wendy's wedding, which truthfully was not her mom's fault. It was a last-minute weekend ceremony in a friend's family lodge here on the island and her mother was terrified of flying. Her mom barely said a word on the phone when Wendy told her. The wedding weekend had been the genesis of her and Jeremiah's plan to move here.

"My family's really far away, that's all. Northern Ontario. It's not cheap to get there." It was years since she had been back. At that moment Wendy remembered. *Piss and vinegar.* Her mom's words. About Gran and her cigars and sailor mouth. And about Wendy too, when she was a girl, in a proud marvelling tone, like the time the school called after she kicked a boy in both shins when he pulled up her skirt to look at her panties.

"Our son lives way over on the east coast with his wife and the boys," Inez said. "They won't be coming this Christmas." She pursed her lips. "Never mind."

"Maybe in the spring, honey." Jim patted her arm.

The dinner table talk switched to docks. It took Wendy some time to figure things out, but it appeared that Inez and Alice were determined to go in together on building an elaborate new dock. And floats and walkways and ramps.

There were permit applications for moorage involved. And management plans to support the permit. It sounded complicated.

They would share the dock and the expense.

The dock would be situated on Alice and Gertie's side, the trail access on Inez and Jim's side.

It would add to their property values.

It would be safer for them. The rocks were slippery. Someone could slip and fall and hit their noggin, knock themselves out cold and get washed out with the tide.

"I practically have a heart attack every time Gertie goes down that steep path of ours," said Alice. Her timbre rose. "It's treacherous. Climbing over those giant slippery rocks covered in algae and razor-sharp barnacles and getting in and out of the dinghy. With her bum knee and all." Alice had her napkin balled tight in her hand.

"I'm careful," Gertie said. She stabbed at a morsel of turkey breast with her fork.

"If you fall, I can't pick you up." Alice fired Gertie a stern look.

"Are you telling me to go on a diet?" Gertie's fork hovered at her mouth.

"Don't change the subject. I told you it's an accident waiting to happen, Gertie, and none of us are getting any younger."

"That's for darn sure," Inez said. "I have to watch my step going downhill because I have no depth perception whatsoever."

"I'm not sure this dock's worth the cost," Gertie said.

"It would be a heck of a lot cheaper if we got more neighbours on board," Inez said. "Fat chance of Astrid coughing up for any improvements."

"That buoy off her property is falling apart," Alice said. "I swam by it all summer and it's barely floating." She wore a mauve linen shirt with short sleeves; Wendy admired her strong cinnamon-toned forearms.

"Last year she used our buoy for her sailboat even after we asked her not to," Inez said.

"I hate to tell you," Alice said, "but she used it again this summer. Gertie was out fishing when she saw her."

"Astrid told me she had your permission," Gertie said.

"That twerp," Inez said. "Speaking of buoys, I ran into the guy who does the maintenance, and he figures we're due because it's been over five years. He said to give him a call, he can come and check our buoys this month."

"Didn't a seal attack you when you were swimming this summer?" Jamie asked Alice.

"What? You're kidding, aren't you?" Wendy said. There were seals at their last raucous dip of the season. Jamie had a straight face.

Inez reached across the table to squeeze Alice's hand. "Tell Wendy about the seal."

Alice let out a great deep laugh. She had a dimple on her left side. "Oh, you guys."

"Didn't it try to mate with you or something?" Jamie said.

Gertie said, "Alice is known to be a very attractive seal."

"That's enough. It swam on top of me and sort of stayed there. Indefinitely."

"It was showing Alice how much it liked her," Gertie said. "It could hardly be faulted for that."

"It tried to hump you," Inez said gleefully.

"Mom, dogs hump. Seals mate," Jamie said.

"Seals can hump," Inez said.

"It's not the typical term one uses for seals." Jim nudged his Brussels sprouts to the side of his plate.

"I don't know if it was wanting to mate or hump or play or just tell me who was boss in its territory," Alice said. "All I know is it was on top of me and I was under it, submerged face-down, holding my breath for dear life."

"It's a good thing I wasn't watching or I might have gotten jealous about Alice starting a mer-seal family without me," Gertie said.

"Mer-seal! Oh, Gertie!" Inez laughed. It was a bit of a whoop.

"What happened next?" Wendy said.

"It felt like a thousand pounds pushing me down. I managed to roll onto my back and tried to push it off me." Alice demonstrated with both arms trying to toss a plump imaginary seal. "I could feel its fur, all coarse and oily, and a flipper with claws. I was kicking too."

"Omigod," Wendy said.

"I finally got out from under the darn thing and kicked a blue streak, came up for air and just flutter-kicked like the devil, did the back crawl like you wouldn't believe with my head up a little, watching if this killer seal was coming after me."

"Horny killer seal," Gertie added, deadpan.

Jamie and Inez exchanged a serious look before dissolving into laughter together.

"Cut it out, you guys," Alice said. "Scared the living daylights out of me. I don't think I've swum so fast since I was in college."

"I'm sorry, I'm going to pee my pants." Inez's eyes were teary.

"Inez," said Jim, gently chiding. "Maybe it's time for dessert."

Jim pulled out a rotary beater like the kind Wendy's Gran once had. As Inez made coffee, he laboured away on a bowl of whipping cream for what seemed an eternity. Jim never complained; in fact, he seemed to enjoy it.

"Jim, you could use an electric mixer, you know. I hear they have those nowadays," Gertie said.

"Ah, heck. And miss a trip down memory lane in small town Alberta? Mrs. Friesen down the road, first time I tasted whipped cream. That was weird," Jim said. "My first turkey too. I'll never forget…"

Inez cut in. "All right, Jim. Pie."

"Dad's famous for pie," Jamie told Wendy.

Jim's pecan pie was buttery-heaven, crunchy, and not too sweet, with a flaky crust. It went down perfectly with Inez's strong coffee.

"Wendy, give us the water-and-shit report," Inez commanded.

Jim cleared his throat. "People are still digesting their dessert and coffee."

"Ronny fixed the water," Wendy said.

"What about the chemical toilet?" Inez said.

Wendy swallowed. She glanced to Jamie, who looked worried, then back to Inez, who was narrowing her dark eyes. Birdlike, alert, they appeared to pierce directly into Wendy's brain and ferret out her secret outhouse use. "It's okay."

That evening Wendy stood outside with Jamie smoking on the front deck overlooking the bay. The stars were out and so was a three-quarter moon. Jamie gazed upwards. She was thirty-five, she'd said, not much younger than Wendy. Jamie wore an oversized plaid shirt over her jeans; in profile her small nose, turned up a little, accentuated her boyishness.

"You don't see stars like this in the city," Jamie said.

Wendy dipped her head in agreement as she exhaled. Jamie grabbed cushions from a bench underneath the kitchen window and arranged them on the deck, lay down with her head nestled on one, then patted the other. Wendy joined her.

"I'm thinking of moving here full-time," Jamie said.

"Cool. Your parents have a great place."

"Yeah. But no, do some house-sits, be a caretaker, save some moolah, eventually get my own place."

"On this island? What, did you win the lottery?"

Jamie didn't answer.

"Sorry, I can barely pay my rent," Wendy said. She was never one for saving a nickel, let alone enough for a down payment, but she sensed that this dream was real for Jamie. Who was Wendy to say it wouldn't work out if someone wanted it bad enough?

"Having your own place here, that would be amazing. Or I could help you build something," Wendy offered. "A tiny house."

"Really?" Jamie said eagerly. "I'm shit at building shit."

"Whoa, don't get too hyper. I'm not a carpenter or anything but I know how to wield a hammer, thanks to my dad. I've got a strong back and a weak mind, as he always said. Good for hauling lumber."

Jamie rolled over to face Wendy, propping herself on an elbow, and extended her free hand. "Give me your hand."

Wendy complied, expecting Jamie to hold her hand, which she thought would be okay and interesting and maybe nice. Instead, Jamie grasped and shook her hand, business-like.

"Deal," she said.

The oak and Arbutus trees shielded the view, but Wendy always checked to see if Inez and Jim were out in the garden before using the outhouse. Inez more than Jim—Wendy had a feeling that Jim would not report her—but best not to take chances. Their windows faced onto the bay and back to the lane, luckily, rather than towards Astrid's property. The reconnaissance was not a major inconvenience at night before bed. Wendy kept a honey bucket in case she couldn't hold it all in before morning.

When Wendy woke up on the holiday Monday morning after their Thanksgiving meal, however, she really needed to pee and had her period. Her cramps were intense, from her stomach all the way down her legs, and she was nauseous and didn't feel like budging. She was tempted to use the chemical toilet but knew it would be worse in the end as she'd be the one cleaning it out. She decided to drag herself to the outhouse and get her business all done in one place. The coast was clear. Usually, once inside, she guided the doorjamb closed with her fingers (it didn't have a latch or handle) because otherwise the door banged loudly, but she felt sluggish and forgot. The door clattered against the frame. She seated herself once again on the cool Styrofoam throne over the deep black pit. Then heard the call.

"Wendy, is that you?"

Shit. Inez.

Wendy stayed put. She tried to force the urine out quickly, hoping the sound of her yellow waterfall splashing in the depths wouldn't reach Inez's ears.

"Wendy, are you in the outhouse?"

"Leave her be, Inez." Jim.

"I swear I heard that rickety door slam."

"I didn't hear anything," he said. "We're going to be late."

"I'm just going to check."

"Please don't do that."

She heard footsteps crunch on her neighbours' gravel drive. Wendy hurriedly changed her tampon and wiped, tugged up her pajama pants, then squirted and spread sanitizer on her hands. Her heart pounded. She debated whether to stay put in the outhouse or make a run for it.

"Wendy? Is that you in there?"

Wendy froze. It was too late. Inez was right outside the outhouse on Wendy's side of the fence. She must have walked up to the lane and back down.

"Inez, dear, we need to go." Jim sounded a bit further away.

"The door's closed. There's someone in there."

"This isn't right, Inez."

Rap-rap. A knock on the outhouse door.

"It's private," said Jim.

Another knock, more forceful this time.

Wendy wanted to hold the door closed but there wasn't a decent place for her to grab and pull without her fingers showing around the doorjamb.

Inez, her voice softer, asked, "Wendy, are you all right?"

"Just a second." Wendy steeled herself and walked out to face Inez, dressed up in black slacks and a purple sweater sparkling from every thread. "It was only the once," Wendy said, "I didn't have time to clean the toilet yesterday."

Inez stared. "I don't know if I believe you."

"I believe Wendy." Jim was directly on the other side of the fence. "Inez. Come on."

"Oh, all right," Inez said. "That nincompoop Astrid."

"It won't happen again. I swear," said Wendy.

Inez muttered, "I don't have time for this bother. And now we're good and late for the brunch."

"That's what I told you," Jim said.

Inez huffed and walked away. Wendy's cheeks flushed with shame as she retreated to her cabin.

Around lunchtime there was a knock at her cabin door. Given the morning's episode, Wendy had no intention of answering, until a husky voice called out, "Don't worry, it's not the Outhouse Police. It's me."

She met Jamie at the door. "I heard what Mom did," Jamie said. "I'm so sorry. Jeez. She's like this queen bee buzzing around her house and her garden. I don't know what else to say."

"It's okay. I get it. It's pretty yucky. The outhouse is right next to her property."

"You're not just saying that?" She seemed to relax slightly.

"I love your mom. She's funny. And feisty." *She's got piss and vinegar.*

Jamie rolled her eyes and smiled. "Yeah. Sometimes. Hey. Do you want to take a spin before I catch the ferry back?"

"Sure."

"Your wheels? I'll spring for gas."

They took Wendy's station wagon with Jamie giving directions. Down the lane to the main road. Away from town, then left and down a narrow, meandering road, over the bridge across the estuary to a gravel pullout next to the ocean.

"Here," Jamie said. They got out.

On one side was a clearly new luxury home in dark-stained wood with massive, angled windows, dominating a cleared lot. On the other, a modest, well-kept older cabin with wood-shingle siding, artful port-hole windows, a hummingbird feeder, kayaks, a handmade stone firepit circled by driftwood benches.

"Something like this. It has a good feel to it." Jamie stood as close as she could without trespassing. "It's so DIY and perfect."

"It's gorgeous."

"You really think so?"

"Yeah. I really do," Wendy said.

Jamie nodded as if this was an important confirmation of what she knew to be true.

Island waterfront cost a fortune, but maybe Jamie could find a small plot of land in the hills on her own or go in with a friend. Build on someone else's property, even her parents' land. Just then Wendy accidentally grazed Jamie's arm with her hand, a gesture that could be construed as friendly and also casual. Jamie shuddered and edged away.

"Sorry, I didn't mean..."

Jamie took another step backwards, scratching her hair. "It's fine, yeah. Just a little jumpy, back to the city, work's kind of stressful, life, love, blah-dee-blah."

"It's okay." But Wendy wondered why her touch burned. She had no clue what Jamie's job was. Whether she had a lover. Anything at all.

The forecast for the following weekend was glorious—sun and temperatures up to sixteen degrees Celsius. This boded well for the market. Wendy threw her all into knitting. She could sell a pair of men's or women's socks for forty dollars. City people just loved buying homemade socks knitted on the islands for Christmas gifts.

With mint tea and her wool, she sat on the front porch on the sunny Friday afternoon clicking her needles on another set of rainbow socks, popular especially with the numerous gay and lesbian couples amongst the tourists. She craved a glass of wine but couldn't afford it. Maybe she'd splurge on one bottle after the market. Her father used to buy "wines under nine," bringing new finds home on weekends to sample with her mother. All under nine dollars. In the province nowadays that wouldn't buy more than cooking wine.

She looked up and saw Jim. He moseyed over to the fence. She joined him. "I'm working my way through my to-do list," he said. "It's pretty large."

"That doesn't sound very fun," she said.

"It's just the right kind of day for something at the top of my list. It's not supposed to rain. I'm going to seize the day, weatherstrip the stairs down to the water. The wood planks get something treacherous with the winter frost and mist. I wouldn't want Inez or Gertie or anyone to slip, right?"

Wendy wanted to hug him. "You're always so thoughtful."

"It's the least an old fart can do." He had the shy smile of a boy pleasing his favourite teacher. "I'd better get at it."

"Good luck."

Jim sauntered away, he never seemed to be in a rush. Inez came outside, emptying plant pots and washing them out with a hose, her neon-pink sneakers a glowing beacon to her movements. Wendy returned to her tea and knitting.

A few minutes later Wendy heard voices below. She couldn't make out the words. Then Inez called down, "Jim, who's there?"

Before long Jim appeared at the top of the stairs alongside a weedy figure. Astrid, a large packsack on her back, apparently on a monumental outing.

"What are you doing here?" Inez's tone was authoritative.

It was difficult to hear Astrid because of her tendency to mumble and rush her words. Something about "pop over, visit friends."

Wendy needed to get over there and talk to Astrid. About Things.

"I didn't quite catch that," Inez said.

"Astrid's here for the weekend," Jim said.

Sneaking, trying not to crunch the omnipresent Arbutus leaves, Wendy inched back towards the fence and saw red. Astrid's flaming hair was its own beast, as bedraggled as Wendy remembered from their first encounter; her long, pinched face was windburned and florid.

Inez approached, becoming louder. "What are you doing at our house?"

Astrid muttered something like "checked it out with Jim."

"Checked what out with Jim?" Inez had her hands on her hips again. She looked from Astrid to her husband, who had his arms out to her, palms up, his mouth open, as if ready to explain but trying to assess whether it was worth the risk. Inez glared back at Astrid.

"I explained it to Jim, it's all fine," Astrid said. "I tied my boat up at your buoy and rowed in and he said that was no problem."

Inez cast an evil eye at Jim.

More murmuring from Astrid. "Couldn't call. Clinic was completely batshit."

"Just for the night, Inez," Jim said. "I didn't think..."

"But she already used our buoy this summer. Gertie told us. Remember?" Inez shifted her steely gaze back to Astrid. "Even after we told you not to."

"You're blowing this out of proportion," Astrid said, adding something to the effect of "this isn't the time or place" and "none of your business." That last part was clear.

"It's darned well my business because look who's moored at my buoy out of the blue. Again. This is the last time. I mean it. What's the matter with your buoy anyways?" Inez asked.

From the turkey dinner and Alice's swimming report, Wendy knew full well that Inez knew full well about the sinking buoy.

"Nothing really," Astrid said, "just needs a bit of work."

"We're getting our buoys all serviced this month. Do you want the guy to check yours too?" Inez said.

Astrid made an indistinct humming noise. Presumably, she wished to avoid the matter and not spend any money if she wasn't forced to. Glancing towards her property as if seeking refuge or escape, Astrid saw Wendy at the fence. "Oh." She sounded deflated. "Hello."

"Hi." There seemed to Wendy to be an awfully long pause, perhaps it was only a second, but it spurred her to plunge in. "I didn't mean to be lurking, I mean, I was just outside on the deck knitting. It's the last market tomorrow. Socks, lots of socks. I just saw you here and thought, well, we haven't really connected much, text messages."

Another pause. Astrid leaned, tilted towards the laneway, ready to flee.

Wendy barrelled on. "You're probably busy. The plumbing receipt is right in the cabin, I know exactly where it is, I can go grab it now if you just hang on." She scanned Astrid's watery eyes for cues that she would indeed "hang on" but her face was pallid, emotionless.

Inez positioned her petite frame between Astrid and the laneway escape route. Astrid glowered at Inez; she clearly knew what was up.

Wendy's words tumbled faster. "Maybe you can just take it off next month's rent? I have more water now which is good, not exactly a monsoon from the taps but not a drought, enough to shower and wash the dishes. Sailing over by yourself, you're an adventurer, wow, I'd love to be brave like that. I'm glad you're here, a surprise, good surprise, not bad. It's so nice sorting things out in person."

She knew she was babbling. She willed herself to stop before she revealed the chemical toilet's ongoing malfunction in front of Inez.

Astrid still didn't reply. Her spine was rigid, her foot tapped the earth, her fingers twitched. Wendy's palms were moist.

"I gave Wendy the name of my plumber," Inez announced.

Wendy wished Inez hadn't said that.

Astrid puckered her mouth. It was plain that Inez was the last person on earth she wanted recommending tradespeople for her cabin.

"I hope that's okay," Wendy said. "I didn't know who to call."

"It's fine, all fine," she grumbled. "We'll sort it out later."

"Later this weekend?" Wendy wanted to settle the bill and discuss the toilet but not in front of Inez. "Because, it's just, the rent's due soon."

"I think we should sort it out right now," Inez said. "Wendy's been trying to reach you for eons."

Astrid frowned. Wendy sensed her icy judgement for confiding in Inez. "I can manage my own rental property and tenant relations, thank you very much."

"I don't know about that," Inez said.

Jim moved closer to Inez, touching her forearm. "Dear," he said quietly.

"And don't you think you should be checking on that chemical toilet of yours?" Inez said. "Not to mention your septic field."

"Everything's under control." A low buzzing emanated from Astrid's torso. She pulled out her cell phone and scrutinized it. "Gotta go. Friend's picking me up. Already waiting. Goodbye."

"What friend?" Inez said.

Astrid ignored her and maintained a wide berth around Inez and Jim, scooting past and up their driveway.

Inez tailed Astrid but once again she was no match on her short legs. Jim and Wendy joined Inez on the moss-edged lane. "Who the heck is this friend?" Inez said. The trio stood on the country road watching Astrid, arms swinging, continue her promenade towards the main road with no one else in sight.

Inez started in on Jim. "You let Astrid get away with using our buoy."

"I'm not sure what I was supposed to do, Inez," he said. "Astrid had already landed in her dinghy. She asked politely and promised it would only be for one night."

"That's not the point."

"It's not as if Astrid is taking up a buoy spot that we need. We don't have a sailboat ourselves, last time I checked."

"I do not want her at our buoy," Inez said. "Especially not without asking first. Too busy at the clinic, oh sure."

"Now, Inez, hang on." Jim's voice remained calm. "I wasn't about to row back out and let Astrid's sailboat go and bash into Gertie's boat or the other side of the bay."

"We can't let her wriggle out of this."

Jim scrunched his mouth at his wife. "Let it go, dear."

Wendy was not sure what all of "this" encompassed but it clearly was larger than her and expanding, with her becoming entangled. "Don't worry, Inez, I'll talk to her about the toilet. I'm sure she'll pay for the plumber."

"I wouldn't be so sure," Inez said.

Jim placed his hand on his wife's back. "Why don't we let Wendy follow up with Astrid while I tackle those stairs and you put your garden pots away?"

"All right. Fine," Inez snapped, but she returned to her pots.

Wendy wiped her clammy palms on her leggings. The autumn air was damp and thick and closing in.

Wendy didn't hear from her landlord the rest of that afternoon but tried not to dwell; there were socks to knit. Twice she picked up her phone and almost called but didn't.

Then at eight, knowing she'd be going full tilt all day at the Saturday market, and remembering Astrid was only mooring her boat for the night, Wendy called. No answer. She left a detailed message describing the amount of Ronny's plumbing bill, the receipt, and how she proposed to pay $375 in rent next month instead of the full $750.

Worried about being cut off, she ended the call, phoned back, and left a second message about the toilet. "That plumber, Ronny, he says the toilet's old and not worth fixing. I'm still having to use the outhouse. I don't have any choice and I'm worried about Inez finding out, kind of freaking, actually, so can you please buy a new chemical toilet? Or composting or whatever?"

Around one in the morning, she heard her phone make its resonant blup-blup indicating a text. As she fumbled for her phone, it reverberated again.

Astrid. The first one said: *Too much. Guy ripped you off.*

Then the second one: *My guy charges 100. Pay 650 rent.*

No mention of a toilet.

Wendy felt gut-punched. She wanted to text Astrid back but what would she say? That it wasn't fair? That she didn't have the money? And deserved a decent place to live? With Inez on the prowl, about to discover that Wendy's shit was spilling into her yard? It all sounded pitiful.

She couldn't get back to sleep. Her chest squeezed tight as an oyster shell. She reminded herself to breathe and inhaled deeply, guiding air from her toes up her legs, along her back, arms, and abdomen to her head's crown, then visualizing her happy place—floating belly-up on ocean waves. The salt water a dense velvet rocking her naked body, her arms cast wide, her breasts two contented fried eggs with sea below and sun beating down.

The meditation soothed her to sleep but she awoke at five-thirty. Under inky water, frantic for air, a murky shape holding her down. She felt its wiry whiskers worming their way into her ears, flippers flapping at her nipples. A hoarse barking—it was laughing at her! Spreading the stench of outhouse stew, mingled with the odiferous spring herring run, all of which she discerned even though she couldn't breathe. She had to flutter kick to the surface, strong like Alice, but her legs wouldn't work. She woke up coughing, panting, kicking her sweat-soaked sheets off before realizing she was on dry land with no crazed seal in sight. She waited until six before texting back to Astrid: *Your repair guy busy. Never heard from u. Can we pls talk? Im at market all day.*

When Wendy's alarm clock went off an hour later, an impenetrable dread cemented her to the bed. She could not summon her arm to silence the clamour. The alarm rang on, never-ending. A guttural scream erupted from her core, fuelling her ascent, eyes fiercely closed, onto all fours on her bed. She opened her eyes and reached and swatted the clock, sending it clacking across the wood floor. The alarm kept up its reveille. "Bugger clock." She moaned, hiding under her pillow. Defeated, she roused herself, retrieved the "bugger clock," and turned it off. A breeze skittered north over the bay towards the strait. A bald eagle soared, taunted by two seagulls. Squirrels chattered. A loon cried. She lay back down for just a moment. When she checked the time again, half an hour had drifted by.

She barely made it to the market in time, half-jogging from her car with her sock baskets. At least there was no rain, only cloud wisps and hints of blue; the air was fresh with the light wind but not cold. Suzanne, Wendy's market friend and stall-mate, in her windbreaker, her salt-and-pepper hair piled in a bun, already had her side of their table display set up in their usual spot. It was a prime location two stalls down from the soapmaker and across the central walkway from the fresh fish tacos. "I was getting worried," Suzanne said.

"I couldn't get out of bed."

"You had a rough night. Poor darling."

Wendy staved off tears.

"Hopefully, it involved a lot of really good screwing with barely legal young boys with stamina and hard pricks." Suzanne's face was inscrutable but she raised her eyebrows.

Wendy laughed. Suzanne was a naughty old woman, not really old—in her sixties like Inez, a retired librarian with a dignified air, three beloved Irish Setters, and a healthy sexual appetite.

"I wish," Wendy said.

"Well, do better next time. First things first. Sit down and let's get you your breakfast."

Suzanne served her a homemade rhubarb muffin and a cup of fair trade organic Nicaraguan coffee from the cart at the other end of the market. "Now. Why the rough night?"

"The stupid landlord." Suzanne knew about the predicament. Wendy updated her on Astrid's refusal to cover most of the plumbing repairs or even talk about it beyond murmuring and sprinting off.

"Someone needs to spear her in the ass with a pitchfork and toss her in front of a combine." Suzanne spent her childhood on the Prairies.

"And Inez, well, you know," Wendy said, "she's such a character and I love her. Every time I'm using that outhouse, I feel like I'm betraying her, spreading my, my detritus into her garden."

"It's not like you have a lot of alternatives. And one person doesn't spread *that* much 'detritus' around," Suzanne said, chuckling.

"I have to move out of there but I barely have money for rent. Have you heard of any house-sits or even just a room?"

Sadly, Suzanne hadn't. Wendy knew that staying with her was not a possibility. Suzanne and her husband had a two-bedroom bungalow; her daughter and grandchildren visited often from the city.

"Time to play our last game of the season," Suzanne piped up.

Early-bird tourists milled at the market's perimeter. "Do we have time?"

"You and I will make time."

Every now and then, Suzanne created a new shape of dog cookie and made Wendy guess what it was. They were generally bizarre, although they had to be at least tangentially related to dogs. Sometimes the treats were for sale, such as letter carriers, squirrels, deer, and other various island creatures which dogs love to chase and chow down on if given the opportunity. Sometimes they weren't, like the dog with an erect penis, right around the time Suzanne was breeding her youngest female.

The rule was: first Wendy had to guess without seeing the treat.

"A horny seal pushing my neighbour to the bottom of the bay while she fights for survival."

"I'm impressed," Suzanne said, "but no. Did that really happen?"

"True story." Wendy grinned.

"Also how is that related to dogs?"

"It's not. It's what popped up first."

Suzanne delved into a small brown paper bag and pulled out the latest mystery shape, beige-coloured and flecked with brown. It resembled a dog, sort of. Something strange protruded from its back.

"I have no clue." Wendy stole a glance at her sock baskets, still not on display. People with smart city jackets and expensive leather boots, not the rubber boots of islanders, strolled the walkway between the stalls.

"Trust your impulse."

"Okay. A sheepdog rescuing an injured lamb from foxes."

"Keep going," Suzanne said. Another rule was a minimum of three tries.

"A dog with a, oh jeez, a stuffed snake from the market for a toy."

"No." Suzanne's faint smile and the cock of her head rang of triumph.

Wendy wanted to play but she also needed to get her socks on the table to sell and make money for essentials like cigarettes. Liquor. And rent. "With a rabid squirrel attached as the dog flies through the trees trying to escape."

Her smile radiant, Suzanne raised her hands, flapping them in excitement like wings as soon as Wendy mentioned flying. "It's my Christmas special. A dog flying with angel wings."

Wendy looked anew at the light-brown speckled shape. Wings. Flying. When she was a girl, they had a special name for their Heinz 57 mutt when he lay on his tummy, his front paws splayed.

Wendy took the treat in her hand and sailed the winged dog through the air. Up and down and around she danced it. A young girl with her parents stopped to watch, mesmerized.

The girl looked about eight years old. She asked, "What are you doing?"

"It's Airplane Dog taking a spin through the clouds on his angel wings." Wendy continued the flight.

"Oh," the girl said.

The market wasn't nearly as crowded as in the summer. People moved more freely without bumping into each other, but her socks were getting snatched up. Wendy felt relief oozing into her shoulders with every purchase.

Near lunchtime she spied a slim man, his back to her, at the far end of the market. No blondish ponytail was visible, but the man sported an evergreen toque like the one she'd knitted Jeremiah for his birthday last spring. There was a woman with him. Wendy could make out more of her. Young, with a scarlet headband and wavy black hair cascading round her shoulders. Gazing at him. Saying something. Laughing. Was it... Lourdes from the organic farm? Wendy was certain it was. The touchy-feely one from Venezuela, barely into her twenties, always hugging everyone, drinking wine into the wee hours, dancing and wiggling her buttocks around the bonfire. The one he admitted to sleeping with during their second separation. The man pivoted to face the woman. It was definitely Jeremiah. They kissed. For several seconds. She felt her internal organs pierced by knitting needles.

A squeeze on her arm. Wendy started.

Suzanne said, "You've got a customer, darling."

Wendy faced a middle-aged man and woman. Suzanne spoke softly in her ear. "I saw them. Just breathe."

After Wendy sold two pairs of socks to the couple, barely listening as they prattled on about being from Seattle, there was a lull.

"Wendy. Wendy!" Suzanne said. "I want you to look at me."

Wendy obeyed. Her face contorted into a potential tear-fest which she summoned multiple muscles to staunch. Unsuccessfully.

"You were the one who ended it, remember?" Suzanne said.

"I know."

"And you know why you ended it. No babies. Not ever."

"I just wish..."

"I know."

"What if he... with her?"

Suzanne hugged her, then pulled away. "I don't say this lightly. Maybe it's time."

"Time for what?"

"For you to leave the island."

Wendy shook her head. No.

"There's a bigger sperm pool off-island. Who aren't all struggling artists and dope fiends."

At that moment Inez showed up at their stall. "Wendy, Suzanne, guess who I saw?" Inez's cheeks were rosy, her eyes keen. "I just had to run into the store for milk. There was Astrid. And a younger man, her so-called friend. Together. Past the fire hall. Crossing the street." Inez seized Wendy's arm. She was surprisingly strong. "Let's go!"

Wendy hesitated at this offensive move towards increased engagement in a larger war. On the other hand, Astrid could sail away within the hour. "Do you think this is a good idea?"

"I don't give a hoot," Inez said. "Let's hunt her down."

"What if she sees us tracking her?"

"You're well within your rights," Inez told Wendy. "Come on. We're losing precious minutes to nab her."

Suzanne laughed as if Inez's antics were par for the course. "Inez, you always were one to stir things up. Sounds like an adventure too good to miss. Go on. I'll be happy to sell socks if you tell me the gory details."

Wendy tilted her head down, discreetly wiped away a tear, and sniffled up drips of mucous before embarking with Inez.

They didn't travel overly quickly. Wendy slowed her pace to match Inez. Although she wasn't speedy, Inez was hyper-alert, her bright eyes all the while goggling this way and that hunting for Astrid and her "so-called friend" as she kept up a running commentary.

"A young man. Thirty at most. Maybe it's a fling. Except he has an earring. But most of the guys have them now so you can't tell, can you? Which way they're swinging."

"I'm hit-or-miss on that sort of thing." It had occurred to Wendy that Jamie might be queer or questioning, or perhaps love-weary like her.

"Maybe he's a disgruntled patient blackmailing her," Inez said. "Holy mackerel, this is juicy! Wait till Alice hears."

"Or—he's actually just a friend," Wendy said.

"Boring!" Inez retorted.

They reached the crosswalk leading away from the market and ocean towards the shops and made their way across the intersection. There was a fair bit of traffic.

Astrid was nowhere to be seen in the bookstore, the drugstore, or the bakery. Inez wanted to search at the marina but Wendy told her she needed to scoot back to the market.

Just then, as the women stood next to the stop sign, with Inez preoccupied scanning cars turning into the grocery store's lot, a smart red sports car pulled up. Astrid was in the passenger seat and she saw Wendy. They both froze. Astrid looked away. Wendy blurted, "Inez, it's her!"

Inez spun. "Where?"

Even though Astrid's window was up, Wendy whispered in Inez's ear. "Right here, stop sign."

Inez spotted her. "Jesus Murphy!" Without hesitation she stepped into the street beside their car, waved urgently at Astrid, and rapped her knuckles on the window.

Wendy could not believe it. She momentarily took leave of her body, hovering above the action like a flying dog. Snapping out of it, she yelled, "Inez, don't, you'll get hurt!" Astrid didn't react. Wendy grabbed at Inez's light jacket and tried to tug her back to the curb. The car eased away, veering left. Still on the road, Inez jammed her thumbs in her ears, fingers facing upwards and wiggling, and stuck out her tongue at the car.

"Omigod!" Wendy's heart raced. She burst out laughing and so did Inez. They made faces at each other with their wing-hands flying from their ears, cracking themselves up all over again.

Wendy sold all her latest socks save one pair that day, earning several hundred dollars. Suzanne gifted her the winged dog biscuit. Wendy bought cigarettes and a bottle of wine and filled up her gas tank. Still, the image of Jeremiah kissing that sensual young woman flashed for Wendy. Whispers peppered her. *Time to leave the island.* And no word from Astrid.

After six, the sun setting a brilliant orange, Wendy strolled over to Inez and Jim's and knocked on the door. Their terrier barked. Jim answered the door. The dog trotted over to lick Wendy's hand.

"Hey Nigel. Hi Jim. Sorry to bug you."

"You're no bother. You're the hero of the day. I owe you one for getting my wife to safety," Jim said. "And keeping her out of the slammer."

"Oh, you heard about that."

"It might be helpful for Inez to have a leash," he added in a perky tone. "Maybe just attached 'round her waist. We can add some padding so it won't chafe." His mouth opened into a sly half-smile.

"Jim. You're terrible." She laughed.

Jim looked pleased at his mischief.

"Have you seen Astrid?" Wendy said.

"No. But as far as I know, her sailboat's still there."

Wendy got back to her cabin and debated texting Astrid. Calling Jeremiah (and not about his fifty bucks). Taking a scenic drive in the vicinity of the organic farm. She thought about it a lot as she poured a glass of red wine. Took a generous gulp. Lit a cigarette. Inhaled. She regarded her wine. Her cigarettes. They cost her good money. They were delicious. They were being wasted, sullied, right now. Because of certain people.

"Fuck 'em," she grumbled. With vigour, again. Then, at the top of her lungs. "Fuck them with a seal flipper!" She took her wine and cigarettes out to the deck and made a mental note, an addendum, as she watched the stars, that most humans in her life were decent and thereby excluded from such curses.

Wendy picked her way down the switchback trail with Inez and Jim to their waterfront. It was already Sunday afternoon. Wendy was not optimistic; it was Inez's idea. Sure enough, the sailboat was gone.

"That sneaking stinker-bug," Inez said. "Wriggling away like that. I bet you she made her escape while we were walking Nigel."

"And I was sleeping in," Wendy said, omitting details of the red wine's throb on her temple. And her own surreptitious dawn visit to the outhouse.

She deposited her market earnings on the Monday morning and bought yarn supplies at the arts and craft store—enough to last her through two final markets' worth of socks, carefully digging through bargain baskets. Yarn was expensive. She would not do sweaters right now; they took more time and wool, and people were stingy about buying hand-knit sweaters for the price they deserved.

In the café Wendy updated her résumé on her ancient laptop and copied the file onto her thumb drive as she sipped her coffee. Over at the library, she printed out ten copies and then did the rounds around town, dropping off résumés at the other restaurant, the craft store, the medical office, the drugstore, the grocery store, anywhere she could think of. No one said they were hiring now. She wondered why she hadn't done this blitz sooner.

She also printed out and posted a notice at the café, the library, and the bakery. *Great Responsible Roommate Looking for Shared Accommodation or House/Pet Sit. Mature. Quiet. Responsible. References. Will do extra house and yard work. And knit socks! Wendy.* With her phone number at the bottom for people to tear off. She almost put "non-smoker, non-drinker" but her conscience stopped her.

There was nothing in the rental ads that she could afford.

She did cruise by the organic farm. She saw children out playing with a soccer ball.

She slowed. She didn't see Jeremiah or his whirling love-thing.

She didn't stop.

She drove all the way out to the provincial campground and walked along the grasses overlooking the tidal pools and rocky beach. It was gusty, bitter-cold, and spitting with rain coming at an angle off the ocean onto her face.

She took out her cell phone and hesitated before tapping in the contact. A woman answered.

"Mom? It's me. Wendy."

"Wendy. Holy kamoly."

"Yeah. I'm sorry I haven't called in a while." Wendy resisted the urge to say: *And you haven't called me either.*

"Gosh. What a surprise. How are you?" Her mother's voice sounded warm, soft as the fresh cinnamon buns Wendy remembered her making.

Where to start? She hadn't called her parents in months, definitely not since the last break-up with Jeremiah. The expensive apartment. Camping out here. Astrid and the outhouse. Her measly restaurant shifts. Scraping by.

"Wendy? Sweetheart?"

Wendy had planned to be brave, just check in and be a good daughter and tell her mom she was alive. This was what good daughters did once they got to a certain age, thirty at the latest, and stopped blaming their mothers for every little thing. Wendy also didn't want to give her mom ammunition to say, "I told you so." Yet at that word—*sweetheart*—Wendy melted and started to cry, which was somewhat humiliating.

"What's going on? Wen?"

"Just... I don't know." Wendy snuffled. Her words felt squished and flattened. "It's been so hard lately. All of it. I'm just really tired. And..." Wendy blubbered like a two-year-old who needed her nap. "Mom. I don't know what to do."

Her words expanded with air, sprang free. "Me and Jeremiah broke up. He has a new girlfriend who's barely out of high school. I'm not going back to his yurt. Ever. It's such a rip-off here. My hours got cut. Two shifts a week. It's pathetic. I'm just knitting and knitting so I can sell socks to rich tourists. This cabin. No water. No toilet. The landlord won't pay for anything. She won't even talk to me. She's like a cheap, mean robot turd. She just texts in the middle of the night. And the neighbour spies on me using the outhouse. I can't even go pee, Mom, I can't even go pee." She crumpled, her chest heaving.

"That's awful. I'm sorry, sweetheart."

Wendy's self-respect, the dregs of it, rose through her snivels. "But I'm not calling to ask for money, I'm not looking for handouts from you and Dad so don't go assuming that."

"I didn't assume anything. I'm just listening."

Mucous gushed from Wendy's nose. It was unfortunate that her cabin water wasn't as voluminous. She didn't have tissues and so wiped with her sleeve. "It's not all bad." She looked out on the wind-whipped sea dancing with frothy whitecaps. "It's beautiful here, Mom. And there's great people here like my neighbours. Even though Inez spies, she's totally hilarious, I love her, and her husband's the sweetest guy and their daughter's cool. And my friend Suzanne at the market, remember, I share a booth with her? She laughs no matter what crazy stuff happens. She makes insane dog treats like this one that totally reminded me of Airplane Dog. Remember Airplane Dog, Mom?"

"I sure do," her mother said. "He was the best dog ever. He was so gentle with you as a baby. I still have pictures of you two cuddled up together."

That did it. Wendy couldn't utter another word without bawling.

"Sweetheart? Are you still there?"

Her nose was clogged; she had to breathe through her mouth. "Mom. It's just, I'm not sure what to do next. Should I stay here and keep banging my head against the wall? Or pack up and leave like some loser."

"You're not a loser."

"I don't have a clue where to go, let alone how to pay for it. Not the city. And what will I do? Be a waitress all my life? Or go back to school and get back in debt after I finally paid off my last student loans?"

Her mother made a sympathetic moan. Wendy didn't recall her being such a good listener. "That's an awful lot weighing you down," her mom said. "What do you really want to do?"

"That's just it. I don't even know!" Wendy knew she was being whiny. "I don't want to be rushing through life so much I can't sit and look at the ocean. Not worrying every day. I don't want to be rich. Just more calm. Hopeful. I'm a hopeful person."

"You are," her mom said.

"Jeremiah doesn't want any kids because of climate change and radioactive fish. Can you believe that?" Wendy didn't mean to mention that. It sort of slipped out.

"So you're thinking you might like kids one day?"

She had told her mom that she wasn't sure. Wendy paused. "Maybe."

"Oh." Her mom's voice seemed to sing a little. "That would be wonderful."

"I'm sorry to just call and dump all this on you."

"It's okay. I'm glad you called."

"I haven't even asked how you and Dad are."

"We're all right. Your dad is off work for a bit. He might need hip surgery."

"Oh no," Wendy said.

"We miss you." Her mother's voice wavered. "I miss you."

"I miss you too."

"Maybe you can come home for Christmas."

Wendy knew the math. A plane ticket from Vancouver to Toronto and another flight—or a four-hour bus ride—to their small northern city. At peak holiday season. "Maybe, Mom."

"Or we can drive out there," said her mom. "I could see the ocean."

Wendy couldn't believe her ears. "Yeah, I think you'd love it."

After she told her mom to give her love to her dad, and they said goodbye, she stood where she had pitched her tent in August and worked her boot round in the grass. A ferry chugged along. It started to pour. She lifted her face into the wind and rain, letting sharp pelting drops mix with her tears and stream down her face for a long while. Like a virtual monsoon.

When Wendy returned from her restaurant shift later that week (with an extra container of contraband pasta and sauce), she found a handwritten note taped to her cabin door. *Guess what now?! Come over and hear all about the buoy!!! Inez (and Jim).*

Wendy walked over. Alice and Gertie were there too, sitting at the dining table with a coffee press, cups, and a plateful of biscotti.

"Wendy!" Inez said. "We bade farewell to Astrid's buoy!"

"What? You didn't really." Wendy's eyes widened. She sat down. Jim poured her a cup of coffee.

Alice chuckled. "We should be having champagne."

"Wait, I've got something better." Inez delved into her liquor cabinet and wielded a tall, narrow bottle with a flourish. "Frangelico will do the trick." She poured the caramel-hued liqueur generously into everyone's cup.

"I must say," said Gertie, "you're taking a disturbing amount of pleasure in this sabotage."

"It served Astrid right," Inez said.

"What happened?" Wendy said.

"The guy came to service our buoys all along the bay. We all sat on Alice and Gertie's little deck and watched. We got a brand-new buoy and a good, tough, strong chain and anchor."

"Life is pretty exciting on Blackberry Drive," Gertie said.

"It's nearly as good as a B.C. Lions football game and doesn't cost as much," Jim said. "Actually, scratch that. The new buoy did cost more."

"We had a picnic," Alice said. "I brought bread and cheese."

"And rum," Gertie added.

"Wow, some serious day-drinking happening here," Wendy said.

"Hot toddies," said Alice. "We had to stay warm."

"That's right." Inez giggled. "Astrid hadn't said a goldarned word to the guy about what to do with her buoy, which was barely even floating. Even though I told Astrid the guy was coming. And the guy said the chain is falling apart and the anchor isn't doing what it's supposed to and yadda, yadda, the whole contraption needs replacing. And the guy asked us, 'What do you want me to do with this rotting buoy next door to your property? I won't be coming back to this bay in a donkey's age.'"

Jim said, "I don't think the fellow said 'donkey's age,' Inez, he said it could be quite a while as he handles most of the buoys on the islands."

"Well, you know what I mean," said Inez. "And we all said, 'Just chuck it.'"

"I don't think I said that," Jim said.

"Me neither," said Gertie.

"*I* said he should just chuck it up on the shore," Inez said, "and he said, 'Are you sure?' and I said, 'Yes, you bet I'm sure,' and I looked at you, Alice."

Alice nodded. "And I said, 'You heard the lady, chuck it.'"

"I used to think men were the ones hard-wired for destruction but I'm having second thoughts," Gertie said.

"Chucking is not technically the same degree of destruction as trashing," Jim said.

"Wow," Wendy said. "What's Astrid going to do?"

"I don't know and I don't care," Inez said. "I hope she's good and mad."

"When she finds out," said Alice.

"The next time she comes sailing in," Inez said.

"You guys are really nuts. I hope I'm as tough as you at your age." Wendy meant it. They all seemed so *alive*. Playful. "I guess I better be careful not to cross you." She was joking but as she chewed her moist biscotti, dipped in coffee and sweet liqueur, washed down with more of the same, a sense of unease slithered down her throat, plopping into her stomach, as if free-falling and landing in the gooey depths of an outhouse pit.

Wendy did another go-round the following week of the places where she'd dropped off résumés. No one had news of openings. The housing situation had not improved either. Two people contacted her with offers far above her price range. One man phoned to say she could live and work on his farm for room and board. He told her where he lived, on the other side of the island with the "Honey for Sale" sign; she knew the spot right away.

She drove out to meet him and parked in the rutted dirt driveway. It was drizzling. The Victorian-style house was compact, most of its grey paint peeled off, with a porch for sitting. The structure sagged at the far end. An elderly white man in coveralls puttered near the lopsided house, poking piles with a pitchfork. She stepped out of her car.

Slow as a slug he walked over, hunched and frail, using the pitchfork as an oversized cane. He was shorter than Wendy, sallow-

PATTI FLATHER

skinned and terribly thin, reminding Wendy of a scarecrow with its head flopping down. "You the one who called?"

"Yes. Wendy. I always drive by this place," she said. "I just love these older houses. So much character."

He grunted. "Family's been here long before you lot."

"A lot of history," she said.

"Eyes are going. Back's going. Too much to keep it up."

Two border collies yapped at their heels. Several goats wandered the yard, bleating. There were shovels, crates, pails, and several beehive frames piled amok next to the house, the small barn, and a shed. The straw-strewn ground was muddy. As he showed her round, everything smelled dank, and then suddenly, putrid. She couldn't help but notice a small carcass—a kid?—rotting in the muck behind the barn. The animal appeared to have been there for some time. He probably could not see it with his failing eyesight, poor guy. His sense of smell likely was gone too. She wondered if she should tell him. She didn't.

Inside the house was more clutter—cardboard boxes and musty-smelling piles of newspapers and magazines. The free room was tiny. She felt guilty when she told him what her mother called a little white lie. "That's my phone vibrating," she said, digging it from her purse and examining it. "Shoot. I just got a message telling me I've got this other place."

"You don't want the room?"

"No. I'm sorry."

The man jerked his head and shuffled away.

Later that day she mailed her November rent cheque to Astrid's city address, minus the full amount she'd paid Ronny the plumber for the repairs and with a note that Astrid never called her back. Wendy had yet to have any real conversation with her landlord to sort out the rent and repairs. She was determined to give Astrid her month's notice but she needed an alternative with a working toilet.

The last weekend of October approached. The last Saturday market of the year. And Hallowe'en. Inez informed Wendy that the island didn't really do Hallowe'en, at least not the door-to-door part, because homes were too spread out. Instead, the community organized special activities for kids, plus a Saturday night dance at the hall that Wendy, Jamie, and her musician friends were going to attend.

It was the Friday morning before. Wendy hadn't dumped her honey bucket in four days. While it was not full (that would take multiple days for just one person), and while it had a lid, the stench grew exponentially with each use. Wendy thought of Jamie every time she looked at the pail on the floor next to her bed, knowing that it constituted its own energy-efficient crock pot.

She kept peeking out, searching for a safe window of opportunity to empty the bucket in the outhouse, checking whether Inez and Jim were outside, if their car was still parked there. However, it appeared to be another major yard work day for Jim. There he was, every single time, continuing his endless battle with Arbutus leaves. The third time, he saw her and waved. She strolled over to the fence.

"These Arbutus leaves are the darnedest things," he said. "They're slippery when they're wet. And they don't just decide to fall in the autumn like the Garry oaks. They like to do it any old time of year, the buggers."

Wendy smiled. "I think you might be fighting a losing battle."

"Well, I succeeded in getting most of this side done."

Just then Inez came out with their terrier. "I'm taking Nigel down to the creek. Do you guys want to come?"

"I'm going to focus on my leaves, thank you," Jim said.

"I'll come," Wendy said.

Unhurried, the women walked down the lane. The dog scrambled up and down the steep upper bank through the broom, holly, blackberry, and honeysuckle.

"He's looking for deer," Inez said. "I have to keep an eye out or he'll take off after them."

They didn't talk much. The dog relieved itself at the side of the road—a fragrant number two—and Inez bent down to examine the small, steaming mound, exclaiming, "Good job, Nigel!" Lavish log homes alternated with older, more humble dwellings, some with fallow vegetable gardens and leafless fruit trees, others shrouded in cedars and oaks. Dogs barked and visited with Nigel.

Wendy always smelled the fresh creek water first, then heard its rushing surge. A wooden bench, with a plaque in a woman's memory, overlooked the creek and imposing cedars. They sat down, the air tinged with rotting earth, clean flowing water.

"There's a raccoon momma who raised her little ones here every year. Like little bandits. They eat the acorns. And everything else." Inez pointed across the creek. "She would set up her den under that old fallen log. One summer she had five babies. Another summer there was just the one. She was a good momma. Teaching them how to get into our garbage."

"Oh-oh."

"But they weren't here this summer. I don't know why." Sadness washed over Inez's freckled face. "Nobody knows whether we'll be here today and gone tomorrow."

"I guess not," Wendy said.

"That's why we sprinkle in some zest every single day."

Zest. Wendy held that in her mouth, her heart.

Inez's dog had something in its mouth. "Oh, Nigel, what have you got? Is that doggie-do? Show me. Out."

The dog chewed, not wanting to relinquish its treasure, but Inez got her fingers involved and pried the dog's jaws open. "Come on. Out. Good boy. Eugh. Oh no." Inez dangled something long and dark green with brown spots. "Slimy slugs are not good for you."

Wendy grimaced as Inez tossed the slug into the ditch and wiped her hands on a tissue.

On the way back, Wendy said she was looking for work. "Have you heard of anything?"

"There's always the grocery store. Those checkout girls are the best," Inez said. "Or what about the school?"

"I'm not a teacher."

"Our vet said one of his grown-up kids is helping out subbing or with special-needs kids or something or other. It's worth a try."

"Thanks. I'll check that out," Wendy said. "What about you? What do you do for work?"

"Oh cripes. It's a long story. I studied history at university. My dad was a police officer and I ended up in police dispatch of all things." Inez leaned over to give Nigel a treat. "I stopped working for years when the kids were young. There was no daycare in those days. I loved being a mom but I could feel my brain shrivelling up. I got a part-time job in a law office. Before I knew it, I was a paralegal, just loved it. I finally went back to school for my law degree."

"That's amazing."

Inez chuckled. "Jim didn't know what hit him. No more homemade meals for him every night and his wife top of her class. He was not a happy camper."

"I can't picture Jim like that."

"Oh, he knows how to pout. We ate a lot of takeout and the kids watched TV till the cows came home. Then Jim learned to cook ten times better than me and he played with the kids more and, well, he always was the best guy alive but, you know, his father was interned in the Kootenays while his mom and the kids were stuck freezing in some shack on a sugar beet farm, they were separated for years."

"That's, I, that's awful."

"Canada, eh?"

"Anyways, the rest is history. Jim does my nonna's gnocchi, and my grandma's roast beef and Yorkshire pudding, better than I ever could. Plus any kind of sushi you could dream up."

"How old were you when you went back to school?"

"It must have been in my late thirties," Inez said.

"That's inspiring," Wendy said.

They approached Inez's house. At the top of the driveway, Wendy heard voices. The dog barked and scampered down to Jim. And another person, tall and gangly, a pack on their back, gesturing energetically with their arms.

Inez squinted. "Who is Jim talking to?"

"I think it's Astrid. She seems upset," Wendy said.

Jim edged back from those agitated limbs.

"What the heck has Astrid got to be upset about?" Inez said.

They headed down the driveway together, Inez swinging her arms.

Wendy lagged, unsure if Astrid was angry about the smaller rent cheque.

"What's going on?" Inez demanded.

Jim faced Inez with pleading eyes. He would clearly rather be somewhere, anywhere else.

"You!" Astrid said, striding to Inez, pointing at her accusingly. "You destroyed my property."

Inez stood her ground. "What on earth are you talking about?"

"You had my buoy destroyed so I am damn well going to use yours."

"Oh, for crying out loud, your buoy was rotten," said Inez, "your non-functioning buoy sinking into the bay, you couldn't even use it and you were too cheap to get it fixed."

"You listen. You had no right." Astrid jabbed the air with her index finger. "I saw it lying on the beach. That is my buoy. I'm going to need to use yours."

"You listen. You're trespassing." Inez stepped forward. She and Astrid were within spitting distance and spitting seemed likely. "You've got twenty-four hours to get that sailboat off our buoy or I'm calling the police."

"Go ahead and try. I'll sue you," Astrid hissed. "Just wait." She said to Wendy, "By the way, your rent cheque was short."

"But you never called me back," Wendy said. "I had to get things fixed."

"I'm not paying rip-off artists."

"You're the ripper-offer!" Inez roared.

"Maybe we should cool things down a little," Jim said quietly.

"Excuse me, but that's not fair," Wendy said. "I kept waiting to hear from you."

"Wasn't that long. I have a clinic to run, oodles of patients."

"I had no water. What was I supposed to do?"

"I didn't approve prior. Nothing to discuss. Mail me the rest pronto," Astrid said tartly. She spun round and hurried away up the drive.

"There she goes waltzing away," Inez said, "like nobody else matters."

A tsunami surged through Wendy. She bolted to the top of the drive, only to see Astrid speed-walking along the lane. "You have legal obligations under the Landlord and Tenant Act to keep the place in working order and you're not following them," she yelled. "I have friends who know the Act inside out."

Astrid marched towards the main road.

Her hands cupped at her mouth, Wendy thundered, "I'm the one who's not paying rip-off artists!" Trembling, she walked back down the drive.

"Whoo-hoo!" Inez shook her clenched fists.

Wendy's storm wave receded. She felt washed ashore. Beached. "What am I going to do?"

"You're not going to pay her a single cent more," Inez said.

"Not like that's even an option."

"Well. We'd better get ourselves into town for the bank and the groceries before Jamie comes," Inez told Jim.

Wendy returned to her cabin. To knit. Watch. And wait with her honey bucket.

A couple of hours passed before she heard a car. However, it wasn't her neighbours leaving, it was Jamie arriving for the weekend. She pondered going over to say hi but decided to wait. A week ago Jamie texted asking her to please pick up a ticket for the Hallowe'en dance and she'd pay it back. They cost twenty dollars and she'd bought one for herself too, opting to cut back on wine and cigarettes for a week.

At last, Wendy saw Jim and Inez outside on their front porch. Inez had her purse. Jim got in the car. Wendy went inside the cabin. She heard their car pull away.

With boiling water from the kettle at the ready, she put her rubber gloves on and lugged the honey bucket pail outside. She opened the outhouse door, went in, and emptied the pail. The door banged shut behind her. With the bucket out on the ground, she poured in the rainwater that she'd collected in her other plastic pail and went back into the outhouse with that rinse. She didn't worry about the rickety door.

Once more she came out with the bucket, poured the steaming water and vinegar in, and sloshed it round. She bent over and scrubbed it out thoroughly with an old rag she'd snitched from the restaurant just for this purpose.

"Wendy. What are you doing?" Inez was at the fence peering at the bucket.

Wendy squealed. "You scared me. I, I thought you went into town."

"Jim went but I changed my mind, I'll visit with Jamie and go in tomorrow," she said. "I heard the outhouse door clinging and clanging. Not just once. Why is that?"

Wendy's heart pulsed on fast-forward. "I just, put a bit of water in it. Washing water."

Inez frowned. "Why wouldn't you just put washing water in your sink?"

Wendy wanted to curl up like a small furry animal. She rooted around for a lie. "I don't know, it's a bit greasy."

Jamie appeared outside the house in sweats and running shoes. It looked like she was going for a run.

"Wendy," Inez said in a firm mother's voice.

Wendy's palms were moist. She stiffened.

Jamie came over. "Hi. Do you have your costume all ready? Because I have this idea for both of us." Her voice had a bounce to it. "Let me just say it's a doozy. Do you have flippers?"

Flippers were too much for Wendy to take in just now.

"It's okay if you don't, we can probably find some in town. But the flippers are pretty crucial."

Wendy wasn't sure if she was hearing properly.

"We're in the middle of something," Inez said tersely.

"In the middle of what, Mom?"

"You never mind. Wendy, tell me the truth."

"I am," Wendy said without confidence.

"You've been using the outhouse all along," Inez said.

"No," Wendy said, her voice tinny.

"Mom, Jesus," Jamie said.

Inez ignored her daughter, fixing her eyes on Wendy. "Haven't you?"

Wendy couldn't bring herself to speak.

"Because that idiotic chemical toilet isn't working. Isn't that right? Wendy?"

"Yes," she squeaked.

"I can't hear you," Inez said.

"Yes. That's right," she said. "Ronny the plumber guy said it's a really old one and not worth fixing and Astrid won't do anything about it." Her words were glued inside her throat; she had to extract them one by one.

"You lied to me."

"I know." She felt like a base creature, a brown-spotted slug sliming along the earth.

"Mom, don't do this," Jamie said, "this is not crisis material. Nobody has died here, no small children or animals have been harmed, this is totally minor, just chill out."

"Jamie, shut up," said Inez, her dark eyes anchored on Wendy. "Do you know what that feels like to be lied to?"

Then it spilled out of Wendy. "I'm so sorry. You've been wonderful to me and I don't know what to do. It's disgusting. I feel terrible. I'm trying to find another place, I put up notices everywhere, I'm looking for more work but it's just not happening."

"That's all well and good," Inez said. "It's a shitty situation all round."

Jamie smirked.

"It's *not* funny, Jamie," Inez said. "You know what?" She folded her arms across her chest. "I feel taken for a ride. I don't know what to say or feel."

Wendy withered. "You have every right to be angry and never talk to me again."

They stood in a stalemate. No one spoke for several seconds.

Jamie scowled at her mother. "This is shaping up to be a stellar weekend, thanks Mom."

"Oh, grow up," Inez said. "Everything on the island is not about you and your weekend shenanigans. It's not a holiday getaway fantasy for everyone, some people actually live here."

"Maybe I should just turn around and catch the next ferry," Jamie said.

Wendy felt at this moment that she—the slinking slug—was the cause of great ruin for these people, screwing up their weekend, wrecking their family.

Then it seemed as if all eyes were drawn simultaneously towards the versatile plastic bucket which once held laundry detergent and moments ago held Wendy's bodily fluids. She felt naked as they stared, although it was pristine now, a vinegar tang in the air. A loon called, haunting, and the trio gazed down to the bay with a chop on its water, a small sailboat swaying gently at Inez's buoy.

"Let's get her," Inez said.

"Not sure what you've got up your sleeve, Mom," said Jamie.

"Everything. The buoy. The septic field. Wendy. Let's really get her." Inez stomped her feet and cackled, her fury transforming into glee. "Where's that useless toilet? Bring it out."

The guilt that had quashed Wendy into the ground began to lift as Inez's judgement shifted from her to Astrid. "Ronny the plumber and his buddies trashed a toilet just like this one," Wendy said helpfully.

"Isn't that interesting?" Inez said.

"Mumsy," Jamie said, "are you thinking what I'm thinking?"

"You bet I am. Only worse. Go get that asinine thing."

Wendy and Jamie went in the cabin. Jamie carried the chemical toilet outside.

"Now we need to fill it up," Inez said.

Wendy gaped. "No, we're not really going to…"

"Tonight. We don't have much time. Get to work. Everybody has to pitch in. I'm going to grab a plastic bag and pick up Nigel's last business right now and whatever else I can find and give Alice a call."

"Prunes anyone?" Jamie said. They hooted with laughter.

Nevertheless, there was the question of what Astrid might do. Wicked things. "You guys, I can't. This is crazy and hilarious but what if she comes after me?"

"She won't," Inez said. "She's a big scrawny chicken."

"She's going to evict me for sure. I have nowhere else to live."

"You can stay with us," Inez said.

"No, you shouldn't have to put me up. Plus, you have family coming."

"Jim's sister broke her ankle. She's not coming until December. You can stay for the month," Inez said. "While you find something else."

"Thank you." Wendy embraced Inez, catching the faint scent of rose petals. She would knit the best rainbow socks ever for Inez and Jim.

Jamie joined in. "Can't miss out on a group hug."

They lifted the chemical toilet over the fence and put it on the driveway near the front door.

Wendy could not believe she actually did it, but she cruised with Inez along the laneway, wielding garden trowels and gathering dog poop in bags. There were a lot of dogs on Blackberry Drive.

Jim pulled up, got out of the car, and saw the toilet. "I'm afraid to ask what's going on here."

"We need a team effort," his wife said. "We're making a special present for Astrid and we're not going to waste a thing."

Consternation filled Jim's face. "Inez, no, not on your life, I'm not having any part of this."

Inez wheedled. "Come on, don't be a stick in the mud. It's going to be so much fun."

Jim shook his head. "This is not a good idea."

"It is a good idea," Inez said. "It's a great idea."

As it happened, Inez and Wendy and Jamie did "pitch in" and Jim didn't, although he helped Inez up off the toilet after she was done. The dog turds boosted the content. Alice and Gertie also chose not to personally contribute but Alice emptied her kitchen compost pail in. The toilet wasn't full but it wasn't empty either.

Jamie tied a thick red ribbon with a big bow round it and signed a gift card: *To Astrid, from all of us on Blackberry Drive* and taped it to the toilet.

Gertie volunteered the use of her dinghy. They transported the chemical toilet to the other border of their property, over the fence to Gertie and Alice's side. The whole lot of them, even Jim (to make sure no one got hurt), descended Alice and Gertie's trail to the water, with Jamie carrying the chemical toilet and Wendy spotting.

At the shore Jamie proposed they open the toilet lid just once. "Then we'll stand around it holding hands, take a deep breath together, and really smell the shit."

Inez giggled like a girl.

"Let's not and say we did," Alice said.

"Work with me here." Jamie pulled up the lid. She took Wendy's and her mother's hands, beckoning the others to join.

"You're not serious," Wendy said.

"This is about all of us. We need a ceremony," Jamie said passionately. "This is for Wendy and for my mom too. We need closure."

"Thank you," Inez said, leaning into her daughter.

"Well, if you put it that way," Jim said, taking Inez's hand.

"Closing the lid would be closure, wouldn't it?" said Gertie.

"Hurry up," said Inez, "the smell is revolting."

"Like stepping into a pile of fresh steaming dog's business with both of your bare feet," Jamie said, "and squishing your toes around to release all of the fragrance."

Wendy groaned. "That's certainly one way to describe it," Jim said.

"I did not need to hear that," Alice said. "Close that awful thing and get it out of here."

Jamie complied. She and Gertie loaded the toilet into the dinghy, while Jim reminded them to be careful not to slip on the seaweed. Gertie and Jamie got in. Gertie rowed over to Astrid's sailboat. Jamie clambered in. Gertie handed the toilet over. Jamie placed it in the sailboat and gave a thumbs up. Inez, Alice, and Wendy (but not Jim) cheered.

"Hang on, we need a picture," Wendy said. She pulled out her phone. "Ready. Go." Click.

Jamie got back into the dinghy and Gertie rowed them back to shore.

"Mission accomplished." Jamie stepped onto the rocks. "All we need is a live webcam."

Wendy regarded these people. Gertie tying up the boat. Alice extending her hand for support, Gertie swatting it off. Jim with arms around Inez and Jamie, Inez glowing, Jamie standing proud. She felt a wave of emotion. "You guys, you, you're just full of piss and vinegar."

"We're full of something, all right," Jim said.

Jamie said, "Is now a good time to talk coordinated costumes?"

Wendy grinned. "Sure."

"Can you take a leap of faith and trust me on this?"

"Oh boy. Okay."

"We need seaweed." Jamie poked around the translucent greenish-brown ribbons with hard bulbous anchors which had washed ashore. "Fresh and slimy preferably. And maybe a few mussel shells."

Wendy helped to gather. Inez asked, "What on earth does my sweet child have in mind?"

"You have to hold your horses, Mom, and wait until Hallowe'en."

That evening Wendy gathered her belongings into her old backpack and suitcase, stuffed her few remaining groceries into her reusable shopping bag, and put everything on the porch along with her knitting baskets. She could leave the cabin dirty for Astrid but that didn't sit right. She lit a candle, selected Joni Mitchell on her laptop playlist, put on the rubber gloves, boiled the last of her rainwater on the propane stove, then emptied in the last of the vinegar. She scrubbed the bathroom, counters, fridge, sink, bookshelf, windows, even the floor, feeling the ache in her arms and shoulders, her knee bones crunching on hardwood. The smiling father and child on the sailboat watched. Joni the poet songbird sang about aching life beauty. With each pass of the sponge, Wendy felt dirt sloughing off her. Astrid could never truthfully say she had been a bad tenant.

Wendy closed the cabin door for the last time and locked it. Unsure if she should put the key under the mat, she dropped it in her purse, deciding that she'd sort it out later. She waved at the cabin and blew it a kiss, then hoisted her bags over the fence onto Inez and Jim's side. Jamie carried them in. She settled into what Jamie called "the guest room," which included a small bedroom, a bathroom with a tub, and a glass door overlooking the bay. It was exquisite.

She and Jamie sat on the deck later in their sweaters, smoking and drinking wine.

"Are you going to tell me about these costumes?" she said.

"All right. Can't keep the cat in the bag forever. Or the seal away from the mer-seal."

"Are you seriously—?"

"One sec." She jumped up and disappeared inside. Moments later the deck light came on. Jamie reappeared with what looked like a blanket.

"I got it at this huge old sewing store in the city. Best costume place ever. Feel it."

Wendy ran her hands over faux fur.

"Okay, it's not exactly sealskin but it's grey. Add some flippers and whiskers..." Jamie unwrapped the fabric. "I'm not the greatest at sewing but I managed to make a little onesie here with arm holes. See, my head's going here."

"You're the seal? So I'm Alice the mer-seal?"

"You can wear your bathing suit, maybe with leggings underneath to stay warm. Goggles."

"No way." Wendy laughed in disbelief.

"Is that okay?" Jamie asked.

"Omigod. Yes, it's perfect," she said.

Jamie grinned. "I thought so. But I'm flexible here."

"Good to know."

"Here's the pièce de résistance, as they say." Jamie held the seal suit up and worked her arms and head through.

Wendy shrieked. There was a dildo attached.

"Horny seal," Jamie said.

Wendy could not stop laughing. "You're not really... going to dance... with that strap-on."

"Hell, yes. I'm bopping the night away." She started doing the swim, plugging her nose with one hand, holding her other arm above her head, wiggling her hips, and getting down low. She hopped up, yelled "pelvic thrust," and pumped her pelvis forward and back. The dildo quivered and dangled and shook.

Wendy had tears in her eyes. She snorted. "Who's wearing the seaweed?"

"I was thinking both of us."

Wendy tilted her head back and stared at the night sky. "Unbelievable." She took a gulp of wine and looked over at Jamie.

"Is this too weird?" Jamie said. "If it is, just say it."

"Can I ask you something?"

"Shoot," Jamie said.

"I might be reading too much into this. It's just, given that you've unveiled this horny seal dildo costume, and believe me, it's totally brilliant and hilarious and I'm all for it. I really like hanging out with you. I just want to be clear. I'm getting over a relationship and I'm not really sure where you're at and I don't want us getting our wires crossed."

Jamie was silent. Wendy feared she'd crossed an invisible line.

Jamie lit another cigarette and blew smoke up to the stars. "I'm seeing someone. But it's complicated. Long distance. She's in Peru. I met her when I was travelling. We Skype. She can't get a tourist visa. Blah-dee-blah. Sorry, don't mean to bore you."

"You can marry her."

"I can marry her." Jamie sighed. "So. That's where I'm at."

"It's okay. I get it."

"Yeah?"

"Yeah. Our costumes are going to kick ass tomorrow night."

Jamie nodded with a satisfied smile. "That they are."

The next morning Wendy carried her basket of socks for the final Saturday market out to her station wagon, still parked on Astrid's side. At the top of Inez and Jim's drive, ready to head down to Astrid's parking area, she stopped dead. Astrid strode towards her along the lane. Astrid saw her. Paused. Continued. Wendy had the impulse to whip round and make a run for it. Instead, she put her basket down and walked towards her.

"Hello," Wendy said, her tone even.

"Hello," she replied in the same manner. Neither friendly nor rude.

"I'm actually kind of glad to see you."

"Oh?" Astrid's voice was cool but mildly interested. "Yesterday you accused me of being a rip-off artist."

"I like telling people things in person," she said. "Not texting and leaving notes and endless messages."

She harrumphed. "Yes, well, not always practical in this day and age, is it?"

"I don't think you treated me fairly." She looked Astrid in the eyes. "Do you think you did?"

Astrid tried to keep her gaze but it was a battle, her eyes flitting away to the cabin, up the slope, landing back on Wendy ever so briefly, a heartbeat. Unsettled.

Astrid fixated on the cabin. "I gave you a place to live, very reasonable for this island. Those are hard to come by indeed." She cast her arm towards the bay. "You can't beat this view, people will pay oodles for this."

Their first meeting. The family photograph on the sailboat. Astrid's mention of the cabin no longer being practical, her husband and child too busy to return. It had been obvious all along that Astrid was unhappy. Wendy felt sorry for her landlord. "You miss this place, don't you?"

With a brittle laugh, she tossed her head towards Inez and Jim's. "I don't miss that woman. People like her are destroying this island. It'll be one big rich suburbia. You realize that, don't you?"

"Maybe that's true in some ways. But does that mean people like you can take advantage of people like me?"

"It isn't like that," she said, "I charged below market rent."

"I'm moving out. I'm not giving you any more money," Wendy said matter-of-factly. "What do you want me to do with the key?"

"Give it to me now."

Wendy handed it to Astrid, then picked up her sock basket and floated to her car, her feet springy, as if bouncing off cushions of moss. She put the basket in the front seat and looked back. Astrid was gone.

She gave her leg an enthusiastic double-shake behind her. Then the other one—Wendy's first-ever attempt at flutter kicking on dry land. Front crawl strokes with her arms, followed by a grinding oscillation of her hips, a wiggle and leap. She needed practice if she was to be an undulating mer-seal.

Stumbling Home

"ANOTHER FREEZING DEATH," my editor says. "Get me a couple of graphs from the cops."

Teenaged girl. Amanda Williams. Only eighteen. Froze to death. Wolf Rapids. Found morning after hockey tournament in unheated, abandoned house. Second freezing death since New Year's.

Jeez, how many are there in the Yukon?

Girl's cousin—"She was the first in our family to graduate." Cousin crying on phone. "She made a mistake. She thought the empty house was her own, one house over."

I underline the "18" in my notes. She wasn't much younger than me. I look out my second-floor window at the *Whitehorse News*; it's still dark at nine-thirty in the morning and the ice fog hasn't burned off. That girl was so close to home.

My editor, Verne with the freakish moustache, assigns me to cover the inquest next month. Yay. Me, my notebook, and the newspaper's Honda Civic with the passenger door falling off driving three hundred miles from Whitehorse to Wolf Rapids in the dark depths of winter. There will be almost no traffic on the final gravel stretch, no warm human to haul me out of the ditch after I spin out and throw Hudson's Bay blankets over me.

Did I mention this is my first winter here? Victoria doesn't GET winter, it gets an extended package on fall.

Later I'm lying cramped next to Rick in his single bed in his hot-plate bachelor dungeon. His long, skinny frame, fed on beer and canned stew, accentuates his carved cheekbones, full lips. He seems to outclass the narrow bed, his cubicle of a home.

"Amanda who?" he asks.

"Williams. Amanda Williams."

"Christ. That might be Ronald Williams's sister."

"You know her?"

He shakes his head. "I went to high school with Ronald. He lived in the dorms. Met her once, she must have been grade eight. Jeez."

I wonder which corner of that lonely house Amanda curled up in.

"I'm going to die on this road trip."

He holds a strand of my mousy hair across his dark forearm, touches my face gently, and smirks. "You won't die."

"Yeah. I will. In that shit-bucket *News* beast." He thinks I'm joking but I'm not.

"That's the difference between you and me. You see the worst in things and I see the best."

"Is this a cultural thing or a girl-guy thing?"

Rick's from around here. He works for the Council of Yukon Indians. He quit grade ten after they said he had to take French for his language credit—he wanted to study Native languages but they didn't offer it. "Don't know," he says.

"It's not that I don't want to go to Wolf Rapids."

"Then what is it?"

Just before I moved to Whitehorse, I took the ferry to say goodbye to my boyfriend on the Sunshine Coast. Fun fun. This woman, maybe in her forties, watched me read a newspaper that my editor sent down. She told me she used to live in Whitehorse. "The dark, that's what killed me," the woman said. She had bags under her eyes. "I was getting depressed and it wasn't even November. Then I had a week's work in this hole called Wolf Rapids. That's what did me in. Took me six more months to get out of the Yukon." Her face loomed close like in some horror movie. "When that happens, don't wait six months like I did."

"Hello?" says Rick. "Anyone there?"

"I'd rather go in summer," I tell him. "Not forty below."

He makes chicken sounds. I try to beat him up but he pins me and rubs his chin whiskers on my neck.

At night I dream that an avalanche smothers me, not just me but my last lover, my grade one teacher, and the entire house I grew up in, even the front lawn and gigantic monkey tree. I'm trapped in white dark. Rick's laughing as I punch my arm up through the snow to breathe.

These were the rules I set for myself when I flew up last September for the newspaper job: No more one-night stands, Unemployment Insurance, or rooms shared by rodents. Not as much red wine. (That would be tough.) I knew I was setting my sights high, that these standards were rigorous, possibly unachievable, but I couldn't travel much further to start over and still be in the same country.

I moved in with two old university friends, job-seeking refugees from the right-wing Socred government in British Columbia. It was autumn briefly, until wind shook the trees naked in a night.

Rick was shy but helpful when I met him at a news conference. He patiently explained the mapping of his First Nation's traditional territory. Six weeks later, snow on the ground and my belly full of beer, I covered his mouth in wet kisses outside the Taku Hotel on Main Street and hauled him into my shared condo. (I never said anything about beer.) We rolled around in the living room before tiptoeing up the stairs together, collapsing on my mattress on the floor. His intricately beaded mitts, trimmed with beaver fur, stayed downstairs by the winter boots, a clue for my housemates the next morning. They both admitted later that they assumed I'd brought home Rick's cousin, the one with a reputation as a ladykiller. Like proud parents they were thrilled when Rick walked downstairs to breakfast.

I spent an orphans' Christmas with my roommates and Rick. He gave me a Royal Family pop-up book because he remembered how I hate the monarchy. On Boxing Day when we watched *Deliverance*, his arm reached behind and grabbed my shoulder during the rape scene. I screamed. We made love in the afternoon. I hoped my roommates didn't hear. It was the best Christmas ever.

"Rick, I'm going to live! The coroner postponed the inquest because the temperature isn't going above minus thirty-five!"

He squeezes my hand. We're having lunch at the No Pop, which is not wise since I'm short for rent. I'm not sure where it disappeared to—restaurants, cabs, not that much wine. I can't believe how easily Rick lends me five twenties.

"Do you have enough for yourself?"

"It's only money. Can't take it with you."

"No," I say. "Let's do cheesecake," and we do.

He kisses me goodbye outside the restaurant. I start crying for no reason. Rick's going, "What? Michelle, what is it?" My face is on his shoulder. I don't answer.

When I get home there's a letter in the mail from my ex. Double yay. After all those years with Theo, Sean was a brief, intense rebound, a friend of a friend, sweet and haunted. I stuff the letter under my mattress for two days before retrieving it. "Why can't we be together?" Because you don't want to be in the frozen north on a bearskin rug and I DON'T WANT TO BE DOWN THERE, as I said a MILLION times before. Maybe there was more to it, our drinking binges, Sean's pot-smoking and sad eyes. Or it was time for me to leave home. What home.

What if I'd returned to clean-living Theo in our basement suite after my trip to Europe? Settled for a community rag in some logging or pulp mill town. Hustled my way up to a big-city paper. Or quit journalism altogether—but for what? I push the letter back under the mattress.

Rick phones me at work the next morning with a hot tip that all the First Nations have pulled out of land claim negotiations. After I tell Verne, leave messages with the feds, and get a curt denial from the one chief I track down in Dawson City, Rick calls back. "Did you get the story?" he asks, then bursts out laughing.

I yell into the phone, "Asshole jerk scumbag!" Verne peers out of his office, pulling up his sweatpants. How many pairs does he have? One probably... nauseating. "It's my boyfriend. It's okay." I want to be mad, I'm holding my face together, but then I'm laughing too.

There's a territorial meeting for me to cover at the library that evening—the left-wing NDP government consulting Yukoners on the environment. Four real people show up, not counting bureaucrats. On the walk home into the wind, I watch mist rising from the Yukon River, not quite frozen over.

Rick's boss calls me at ten the next morning in the middle of our news meeting. Rick, who doesn't have a phone, hasn't shown up. "No," I say. "I didn't see him last night."

After deadline I walk over to his building near the clay cliffs, tramp through snow to his postage-stamp window at the back, and peer in. Rick's dressed and asleep, face up and jacket zipper down with no covers on. I bang on the window. He doesn't budge. I'm kind of scared but it looks like his chest is rising and falling. I bang harder. Still nothing. Is this what I look like passed out after a bottle of wine? I climb the stairs and knock for the landlord. No answer. On the way back to work I try to convince myself he's warm, not to worry. That evening Rick calls from a payphone. He cabs it over and sinks down on the couch.

"Must have been some night," I say.

"I can't sit home in that dark hole. Walked downtown for something to eat." He grins sheepishly. "Ran into my uncle at the Taku. Guess we got a little crazy." He kisses my forehead. "I love you."

How could I be angry?

He's not angry either when Sean flies up two weeks later, rents a car, and drives me out of town for the weekend.

"I'll be at the Taku," Rick tells me before the plane lands, "so don't go there. Please."

Two hours later I'm lying naked on a motel room bed. Gold pans painted with mountains and fireweed hang from the stained-wood walls. I feel like shit.

In March the river ice breaks up a little more each day. A guy climbs the stairs to our smoky newsroom and announces that his wife is missing. I interview him.

Clean-cut. Suit and tie. Says he found her car abandoned on the bank above the river. "She was depressed all winter. It was like she was somewhere else."

The husband calls me back the next day. He's so loud I hold the phone away from my ear. "Goddamned cops tell me I'm a suspect!"

Teenaged boys find the body at the river's edge below the hospital a week later. Verne hears it on the police scanner and sends me over. "Don't forget the camera," he says. I throw it into my pack along with the car keys and head out to the newspaper's dented-up car.

Parking at the roadside, I walk down the bank through the willows. Police have covered her body, except for the feet. My eyes are drawn to her feet. Why did they lead her here? I take a photograph without thinking. Verne runs it on the front page that afternoon.

Rick meets me at my office after work. On our walk in the slush back to my condo, we stop on the bridge. I point out where her husband said her car had been parked, and where her body lay.

"I shouldn't have taken her picture."

He throws a rock onto the river ice. "Can't take it back now."

"She was lost. She drove away from her house in bare feet and her nightie. The cops said she never went in the river. She must have wandered around and then fell or something." An icy wind attacks us. "I'm not used to this. People freezing in the dark."

He wraps his arms around me. "I'll keep you warm. Move in with me."

"What?"

"I love you," he says. "Move in with me."

"Wow. I don't know."

He lands a rock on open water and starts walking. I hurry to catch up.

Two days before summer solstice, packed and ready for Wolf Rapids, I meet Rick for lunch at the No Pop. He gives me a single red rose. "You look like you need it lately," he says.

"What do you mean?"

"To cheer you up."

I sniff the rose. "You sure you're not mad at me?"

"For what?"

"Getting my own apartment." I move in July first.

He picks at poppy seeds on his plate. "You need your own space."

"I've never had a place of my own before."

He looks out the window.

"You'll still be over lots," I tell him.

"Yeah." He smiles at me. "In the bedroom."

Outside the restaurant he pecks my lips and walks away. I'm thinking he'll turn and wave but he doesn't. I wrap the base of the rose in wet toilet paper from the No Pop bathroom and lay it on the newspaper beast's dash. Three petals have unfolded. The colour is rich velvet. My parents bickered over everything, even the colour of roses in our garden. Orange, my dad said. No, pink, said my mom. Why did they stay together? I'm in shorts and a tank top and hot already in this shit-bucket. The rose is going to fry on the drive up. I buy a coffee at Tags, drive up Two Mile Hill onto the Alaska Highway, and head north. Bad coffee is a prerequisite for road trips.

The Wolf River flows past the north end of town. On its far bank the mountains rise sharply. The main street slices the town into Native and white, more or less, with the First Nations people closer to the river. It's just as Rick described it.

MOTE, reads a sign on my left with a faded spot for the missing letter. I pull into the gravel parking lot. The Wolf Rapids Motel is a squat, L-shaped log structure that has seen better days but its bright white doors and red roof are hopeful. After I check in, a woman in her fifties heats up ham and scalloped potatoes in the small restaurant. It's past eight and the kitchen is closed. With my ripped army shorts, unshaved legs, and sandals, I know I look more like a hippie chick than a reporter. The new CBC Radio reporter, Tara, marches in. She just moved to Whitehorse from Toronto. She has linen shorts that barely look wrinkled after the drive.

"That road is hideous—it has more potholes than pavement," she announces, then scans the restaurant and frowns.

"This food is great," I say, more to the woman than Tara.

The woman's face lights up. "I made it myself."

Tara walks out.

After dinner I wander past the band store and gas station to the new log houses on the Native side. There are a lot of dogs. Kids are playing. They watch me. I can't get over this light. It's past nine o'clock but the sun washes warm over me, old cars and wildflowers alike. It feels peaceful.

A short elderly man stops. It's hard to understand him.

"Seven kids."

"You have seven kids? Wow."

"They all gone," he says. "No more."

"Did they move away?"

"No. All die."

I think I see tears in his eyes. "I'm sorry."

I walk back to the motel. In the dimly lit bar, the one bar in town, hangs the largest—and only—collection of baseball hats I've ever seen. Wesley the night bartender tells me why his slo-pitch team is the best in Wolf Rapids. "'Cause we work together, play hockey and ball together, and drink together. There's a bond, like this." Wesley locks his hands together and gives them a tough little shake. I like him.

Wesley's friend Lawrence asks me, "So you got a boyfriend in Whitehorse?" Lawrence, who's on the fire crew, has the hint of a smile. He's in his twenties like me, with a broad handsome face, shoulder-length brown hair, and the hint of a belly under his white T-shirt and jeans.

"Yeah, I have a boyfriend."

"Good guy?"

"Yeah."

"Bet he's not Indian."

"What's that got to do with anything?"

Lawrence's smile widens but his voice pierces. "I knew it. He's a white guy."

"He's Indian."

"That so." He raises his eyebrows. I take a swig of beer. Lawrence has Coke.

"Do you have a girlfriend?"

He shakes his head. "We broke up. Got two boys. They're down South."

He's my age and has two kids. I can't imagine taking care of some little creature, tucking it in at night, reading Winnie-the-Pooh.

Tara from CBC is already at the community hall, pen poised and hair perfect, when I arrive and take a seat on one of the folding chairs. I pull my pen and notebook out for the first witness.

Faded jeans and muscle shirt. Bartender at hockey tournament. Not Wesley. Huge white guy. Ex-biker, he tells coroner. Remembers serving Amanda several rye and Cokes, finally cuts her off. Inquest lawyer: "When did you decide not to serve Amanda?" Bartender: "After I saw her trip and fall."

Tara files her story through the lone payphone in the motel lobby while I wait. There's a list tacked up next to the check-in desk with the names of people who aren't allowed to buy off-sale booze anymore. I remember hearing that there's no liquor store in Wolf Rapids. Next to the list is a paper with "Do We Want a Dry Community?" in big letters. I connect my laptop computer to the payphone and file before calling Rick at work, collect. The operator says I can't bill it to my home number. "He's at lunch," a woman says and hangs up.

Cold night last January. Forty-four below. Lawyer: "Were there special measures for people under the influence to get home safely?" Tournament organizer: "No."

It's after five when the day's last witness steps down. As I get up to leave, I see Lawrence in the back row of chairs. He's staring straight ahead. I hover nearby, thinking I'll say hi, but he's not looking my way. Someone bumps me and I move on, out of the hall and into blazing sun. I walk back to the motel. It's too bad that Rick has no phone. He has slo-pitch tonight anyways. He probably rode his bike there.

After dropping my notebook off, I walk north along the main street towards the ball diamond near the river and the bridge leading to the next stretch of gravel highway. A few spectators sit on faded wood benches. I join them. A thin freckled woman, very pretty, is at bat. The young woman next to me yells, "Yay, Shelly! Hit one for the teachers!" Wesley is pitching and Lawrence is playing short. Wesley throws a strike. The catcher bobbles it. Lawrence gives me a wave.

It's still sunny and warm. Three kids play with a bat and ball. The river is a rush of glints between the birch trees. This light could feed me forever.

"You won't believe what we're getting!" Lawrence, grinning ear-to-ear, sits between Wesley and me. The beers and his Coke are on the table.

"What? Caviar?" I say with a touch of sarcasm.

"We don't need to pay big bucks for fish eggs," says Lawrence. "Got plenty around here."

"Okay. What then?"

"Lobster. Steak and lobster." Lawrence looks well pleased with himself. "The truck gets in Friday."

"Two more days," Wesley says. "Can't wait."

"You should come to our barbecue," Lawrence says, touching my arm. My skin tingles. "Stay for the weekend."

I can't keep his gaze. I stand up suddenly. "I have to go. Have to work early."

"And call your boyfriend," Lawrence adds softly.

"No." Why am I lying? Because he's attractive and I'm tempted? My face burns.

On my way out I notice the clock behind the bar counter, underneath the baseball caps. It's midnight. June twenty-first. The longest day of the year. Outside it's barely even dusk. I head past the row of motel rooms and into the lobby. Rick's team always goes to the Taku after a game. I plug several quarters into the payphone and ask the operator to call the bar. "Rick wasn't in tonight," a bartender yells over the din. I hang up and re-read the list of people who can't buy booze to take home or to the riverbank. Outside my room I stop for a second, then return to the bar.

"You sure like Coke," I tell Lawrence.

"It beats the point-five they sell here. Low-down Wesley won't order the good fake beer."

"It's out of my hands, man," says Wesley. "I'm just the bartender."

"You don't drink at all." I realize I'm on my fourth beer.

"Not anymore," Lawrence says.

"But you're in a bar."

"She's observant, eh Wesley? Must have learned that at reporter school."

I ask Lawrence, "Why don't you drink?"

"Why do you drink?" He's smiling but there's something hard beneath it. I want to push my beer away.

"I never met a guy who didn't drink. I'm curious."

"She's curious too, Wesley."

Wesley fixes mock wide eyes at me. "Yup, I can see that."

"A real reporter from White-arse." Lawrence leans back in his chair. "How long did you say you're staying here with us? In beautiful Wolf Rapids?"

"Um…"

"Not long enough," Lawrence says.

I try to lighten things up. "Your sober-up story takes that long?"

"Yeah." Lawrence watches me with a bemused look. I catch a flash of what he sees. A young white woman from the city, who's never been to his town before, takes notes all day about a drunk teenager freezing to death, then hits the bar at night to give the small-town boys a thrill. Wait a minute. Who's giving who the thrill?

"I gotta go," I tell Lawrence, avoiding his eyes. "Save that story for tomorrow."

"Might be too late."

"I'll take the chance." I walk out, wondering if he's watching or laughing or couldn't care less.

My head flops down towards my chest. I jerk it back up, opening my eyes and hoping nobody noticed. What a way to spend my first summer solstice north of sixty. A cop is testifying. I pinch myself to stay awake. Tara taps her pen on a small notebook. The band chief takes the stand. He holds himself together until the end, then starts to cry. I join him, wiping my nose with my hand.

Final witness. Lady. Last one to see Amanda alive. "I saw her standing by the doors. I remember thinking, 'Where did her jacket get to? It's so cold.' When I looked back, Amanda was gone. I found a purple coat on the bleachers. I think it was hers."

At four o'clock the jury starts deliberating. The inquest lawyer promises to call us at the motel restaurant with the decision.

I walk back and call Rick collect at work. A guy answers. "He never showed up today."

In the restaurant I have no appetite for my spaghetti.

"They call this a salad," says Tara, turning over wilted lettuce. "I hope they hurry up. I can't wait to leave."

"I like it here," I tell her.

"Busy girl. Enjoying the local nightlife, are we?"

"You bet." I get up and refill my coffee at the side table. Lawrence and Wesley walk in. Lawrence smiles at me. I spill my coffee.

"And the wildlife," Tara adds.

"How much do you reporters get paid," Wesley asks, "to sit around drinking beer and coffee?"

"Doesn't look like you've been fighting fires," I say. "I hear you sit and watch them burn."

Wesley seats himself next to Tara.

She shifts in her vinyl chair. "We're waiting for the jury," she says coolly.

"I know," Lawrence says.

I sit back down and Lawrence joins us. Tara assesses his long hair and cocky face. She turns to dark-skinned Wesley in his Toronto Blue Jays ball cap. His eyes are on her already. "I think I'll check on the jury," Tara says. She picks up her tray and leaves.

Wesley laughs. "We scared her off. Big bad Indians."

Lawrence asks me, "Aren't you scared of us, too?"
I laugh and blush. "Yeah right."
He pokes my arm. "I know what you're scared of. That I don't drink."
I nod. "You're right." Then add in a rush, "But I think it's good. I mean, I couldn't do it. I was going to cut back when I moved up here and then..."
"In a place like this," Lawrence says, "there's no in between. You either do or you don't, and you don't do it halfway."
I can't think of anything to say. The woman who runs the restaurant comes over to let me know the jury is back.

Death from hypothermia. Alcohol a contributing factor. Don't serve booze to minors. Board up abandoned houses.
I'm suddenly furious. Three days of public gut-wrenching, Amanda is dead, and this is the best you can do?
Outside the hall in the hot dry early evening, Tara and I interview the chief. He seems to choose each word carefully. "It's not enough," he says, his voice quiet. "I wish the jury went further." A middle-aged woman touches the chief's arm, squeezes it, then walks past.
"Thank you for speaking with us about this. I know it's really hard," I say.
"Can I get your phone number in case I have more questions later?" Tara asks.
He hesitates, then says, "Excuse me," and turns away.
"It's not like covering stories in the city, you know," I say to Tara.
She faces me. "A girl died and you want to coddle these people. Or party with them."
"Or treat them like real people."
In my motel room I type up my story. I see Amanda beaming in her graduation photo, the one in the newspaper obituary. Dark bangs. Roses in her arms. A beautiful young woman. Who drank too much, she certainly wasn't the first, without a friend guiding her home.

That woman on the ferry, she's haunting me now. Her dark-circled eyes. Her voice. "This hole called Wolf Rapids. That's what did me in." Go away, weird lady. It's not a hole. I can't file that to Verne. I hear Tara playing the chief's comments over and over on her tape deck on the other side of the thin walls.

Lawrence leans towards me in the bar. He smells of aftershave. "I'm going back to school. I'm going to be a teacher." His face is wide open. This is his dream. He's telling it to me. I touch his arm. Remembering Rick, I slide my fingers away.

I take a swig of beer. "Whoa. A father and a teacher. I am way too irresponsible to have kids."

"You'd get responsible pretty quick."

"How old are they?"

"One and three." He digs in his wallet and pulls out a picture of two chubby boys.

"Aw. You must be on the phone every night with them."

He doesn't answer.

"You call them sometimes, though."

"It's not that fucking simple." He sounds mad.

"Okay."

"You make it sound like I abandoned them."

"Sorry. I didn't mean to."

"After fire season I'm gonna go down and see them."

"I believe you." I can't tell if I mean it. It's too quiet as he drinks his pop and I peel my beer label.

A few minutes later he stands up. "I want to show you something." We leave the bar and climb into his truck. "My uncle's," he says.

"Where are we going?"

"Don't worry."

He drives to the end of town and beyond, at the north end across the river. The truck turns onto a narrow dirt road and rocks its way through deep ruts. I hold the dash for balance. Before long a clearing emerges. He stops. Dogs bark as we get out of the truck. On one side is a picturesque log home framed by spruce trees.

Lawrence walks towards the shoreline of a small lake. My sandals slip in the sand as I follow so I take them off. The water is glassy. There's a corral with three horses further down next to the beach. The lake reflects pale pink and orange from the setting sun.

"It's beautiful," I tell him.

"It's my mom and dad's place."

"You're so lucky."

He pokes the sand with his runner. "I know people like you think we're a bunch of drunks."

"I don't think that."

"I didn't mean you. But lots of people. They don't bother to understand."

"I'll try to understand."

"Amanda was my cousin."

"Oh God." I realize Lawrence hasn't mentioned the inquest before.

"She... she was the only girl playing hockey. When our grandma broke her leg, she was over every day helping. She loved jujubes, except not the red ones." His large hands cover his face. He sighs and looks up. "Imagine waking up and seeing this every day."

Neither of us says anything. He will see his kids. How could he not?

Suddenly he grabs my hand and pulls me towards the water. "Let's go swimming. This'll be something to remember from Wolf Rapids."

"Agh! Let go!" I dig my bare heels into the sand and pull backwards. "Didn't you douse enough fires today?"

He lets go, unbuttons his shirt, and takes it off, followed by his shoes and socks.

"I'm not going in."

"Yes, you are. You can tell your friends back in Whitehorse about this lake. How you went swimming with a crazy Indian."

I don't move. Lawrence is just in his jeans. He smiles confidently. He's sure he's going to lure me in. I'm sure he won't and I don't exactly know why, although he is sweeter than most guys I've woken up with. He runs into the lake and dives. After surfacing, he stands tall with his hair slicked down his neck and back, his wet jeans glued to his legs.

"It's warm."

"I don't believe you."

"Maybe I'd better throw you in!"

"No." Something in the way I say this makes his smile go poof. After a few seconds he says, "All right," and I feel bad.

"I shouldn't," I say. "I can't." The sun is just setting, which is impossible because it's after midnight but I'm not down south anymore. I'm so far from there. I stare down. My big toes are grotesque. I never saw my toes so clearly after midnight.

"It's not about you."

He walks out of the lake. I pick up my sandals. We get in the truck without saying anything. When he drops me at the motel, I say, "Goodbye." And then, "Sorry."

"'Bye, Michelle," he says.

Later I cry into my pillow but not too loud. I can't give Tara next door the pleasure of my misery.

Early the next day, I walk and walk in the sun. At the river I cross the wooden footbridge and follow the river trail. The ground is covered in lupines and wild strawberries. They're miniature and still green.

When I pull the beast out from the motel, Lawrence and Wesley wave me down on the main street. I stop the car.

"Make sure you have enough gas," Lawrence says. "It's a long way back to Whitehorse."

I can't believe he still gives a damn. "I just wanted to say about—"

"Forget it."

I take a different route back. The drive is spectacular. Too bad I'm not enjoying it. Stunning, narrow canyons force blue-green water between cliffs. Jacob's Ladder and delphinium dot the mountainsides in blue alongside a dirt road with almost no traffic. I can barely breathe with the heat, the dust, and no air conditioning.

In Whitehorse I go straight to Rick's work. It's after five but he's still there. I can't read his face.

"Hi," he says. His voice is flat. What the hell's going on? We don't talk in the dusty shit-box on the way to his dungeon pad. We sit on his bed with the faded plaid comforter.

He stares at smiling elders in a Native language poster on the wall. Finally, he says, "I, uh, met somebody at the solstice dance."

"What's that supposed to mean? You went home with her?"

"You could say that."

"Was it the booze?" I'm wishing it was the booze.

"I was drunk. But it wasn't just the booze. I wanted to."

"You gave me a rose for chrissake."

"You're always so depressed," he says, still not looking at me. "I obviously can't make you happy."

I laugh out loud.

"What?" Rick asks but I keep laughing. Those payphone calls to Rick who was never there. He says yes and I say no. I did it. I proved I could. What was Rick trying to prove? If I had said yes too and spent the solstice screwing Lawrence, would things be different right now on this sagging bed?

Then I start to cry and Rick joins in. This is pathetic. We lie squished on the bed for what seems like hours.

I ask him, "Do you still love me?"

"I don't know."

We don't make love. We have sex and it's not like those first wet, drunken kisses outside the Taku, or rolling around on my living room floor. More like motel walls and painted gold pans. When it's over it's like being home.

Sarah Is Under the Table

LEAH LIKES THE IDEA OF LEARNING to make real bannock with her
mother-in-law. It might help. You know, things, such as having
this docile stranger with the long black braid living in the spare
bedroom, the south-facing room with Leah's sewing machine,
designs, and half-finished quilts that she stuffed in the closet last
spring. Four, no, almost five months ago, since Margaret's husband
died suddenly, tragically, and it was clear that she couldn't go back
to Jensen Landing, not alone, not how she is.

"What do we need, Mugs? Flour?" Leah wears the beaded
slippers Mugs gave her for Christmas, although they're tight on her
size nine feet.

"Aaha'," Mugs says.

Zach, still in his sleeper, clangs two pots together on the kitchen
floor. Mugs shudders.

"What else?"

Hesitation. "Lard. Sugar." She pauses again, searching for words
in the August sky and spruce trees outside the apartment window.
"Salt. Oil. Baking powder."

Leah places ingredients on the green enamel table, twenty-five
dollars at a garage sale. "How much flour?" she asks.

"Aah. Four cups." Mugs tucks her rosebud-pink cardigan into
the stretchy waistband of her navy polyester slacks, then tugs the
pants higher, snug in the crotch.

Leah tries not to laugh. "Oh, Mugs." Even her nickname makes
Leah smile. It's from Mugs' younger sister, who couldn't wrap her

tongue around "Margaret" when they were kids. Leah can't imagine Martin, tall, lean and wiry, coming out of this squat woman on a biting winter day.

The bright April evening when Martin's parents arrived at the Whitehorse apartment with two small suitcases, Leah whispered to Martin in bed, "I forgot how short your mom is." They had met only once before, just after Zach was born. This time the plan was a brief stay while his father had hernia surgery at Whitehorse General. None of Martin's siblings lived nearby.

"Lots of us up north aren't tall," Martin told her matter-of-factly. "Less body area to keep warm."

She stroked his forehead. "Not you. Guess it's your Viking blood." He grinned before rolling over. Martin's grandfather on his dad's side had been a Norwegian trader and sometime prospector who had a way with Native languages. He married a First Nations woman at Jensen Landing. "Half-breed, they called Dad back then," Martin had said; Leah didn't like the term. Leah's roots were firmly in the British Isles. Farmers. Shopkeepers. Stonemasons.

"Tell me again about the blizzard you were born in," she said.

"It was a total white-out. Dad took her to the nursing station by dog team. They found the way together. By memory."

Steadying the measuring cup, Leah pours flour. Zach sits on the floor, his sparse walnut-brown wisps filling in closer to Martin's straight black hair than Leah's blonde strands. The baby picks up a pot and slams it down. Clang. "Sssh!" his grandmother says. Zach eyes her, mouth open, then resumes the percussion.

Cupping her left hand, Mugs spoons in granules from the sugar bowl, then opens her hand into the bigger bowl. "Small handful of sugar," Mugs says. "Small handful of baking powder. Sprinkle of salt."

"How much lard?"

"A big handful. Like this." Mugs slices a piece of lard and puts it in the bowl. "Now mix it up."

Leah cuts and works the dough with a pastry blender. Gripping the smallest pot, Zach hammers on the stockpot. Mugs shuts her eyes tight, balls her shoulders forwards, and turns to the one-year-old. "Anaa! Don't do that!" Mugs points towards their cramped living room with its sagging Ikea couch, eighteen-inch television borrowed from Martin's cousin, and a pile of newspapers. "Look! Puppy!"

Zach looks for the puppy, pointing just like his grandmother. *Don't trick my baby.* "I don't think there's any puppy here," Leah says. "Let's get this bannock going. Now what, Mugs?"

"Water. Or milk. And a little oil." Mugs pours with ease, then puts her hands in the bowl.

"We can have the bannock with the blueberry jam I made. Martin and I picked the berries up at Log Cabin last year." Martin didn't want to leave. You could not get him out of a berry patch. Leah's chest crumples in tight. Her teacher friend Gwen was up the Skagway Road last week, said the berries were good. *How the hell are we getting up there this Labour Day with your mother in tow? Is she gonna open the car door on the highway again, like when we were doing a hundred and forty fucking clicks on the way to Jensen Landing? Huh?*

Leah watches Mugs' hands come alive working the sticky mass. She has gravitated to the kitchen since her move to their place, washing dishes on what Leah deems the wrong side of the sink, drying cups, rearranging forks and knives. Maybe Mugs dreams of cooking again for her own children, or workers at the old mine. Always Leah wants her out. Hating herself for it. *Go sit on the couch and rip Kleenexes.* That's what Mugs does, like an automaton. Maybe she dreams of something else.

"One time when I was a girl we pick blueberries," Mugs says. "Up on the hill." Leah tries to imagine a mountain slope in north-central Yukon where Mugs grew up. The willow and bearberry leaves already turning colour.

"Black bear come bothering us. Skinny one. Sick."

"What happened?"

"He come near my sister."

"Was she okay?"

Her hands move continuously. "My mother shoot him."

"Holy cow."

"Go get the tray now."

Leah pulls two cookie sheets out of a cupboard and greases them with buttered wax paper. How little she knows of this woman's life, her experiences out on the land.

Mugs forms the dough into round biscuit shapes and places them on the sheets. "When I was a young woman, my brothers go fishing. Their boat tip over. They drown."

Martin never told her. Heat rises on Leah's face, equalling shame. Nothing like that has happened to her. "That's so sad. I'm sorry."

"I need a fork."

Leah hands her one. Mugs pokes the tines into each patty three or four times. The oven is set at four hundred degrees.

Leah slides each sheet in. "How do you say bannock, Mugs?"

"Łuh ch'uh."

Leah can't get the first letter right. It's like wind through the poplars when her mother-in-law does it. It has something soft to do with the tongue, a sound Leah has never learned.

The afternoon stretches, unending elastic, longer than that last day of school before summer holidays, the final hours of labour before Zach's head emerged, covered in dark wet hair.

Wiping, wiping—Mugs dries the mixing bowl with a tea towel. She walks into the living room and bends over near the coffee table, speaking in her language. Gwich'in.

"Mugs?"

Mugs straightens but keeps her eyes on the carpet. "Stop bothering me!"

"Is it Sarah again?"

Refocusing on Leah, Mugs says, "Aaha'. Sarah. Always making mischief."

The first time Sarah appeared in the apartment was after Martin's father died. The morning of his scheduled surgery, Solomon complained of a "sonofabitch" headache. His left eyelid drooped. When he collapsed, Leah called 9-1-1 and the ambulance arrived within minutes. He was pronounced dead at the hospital. A brain aneurysm.

It was somewhat of a blur but about a week later, after the funeral, Leah noticed Mugs staring at the coffee table, no—under the table—with narrowed eyes.

"What are you doing here?" Mugs demanded.

"What is it, Mugs?"

"Quit hiding. I see you." Her tone was firm.

Leah came closer. "What do you see?"

Mugs shook her head slightly, piqued, her gaze fixed. "That Sarah. I see her under the table." She advanced towards the table, brandishing her arm. "Shoo!"

That evening Leah asked Martin about her. "She's an old friend of Mom's. Their family was always at fish camp with us," Martin said. He smiled. Maybe something about fish camp.

"Where is Sarah now?"

"The old folks' home in Dawson City. Pretty sad."

After that Leah took her mother-in-law, with Zach in tow, to her own family doctor. Leah told him, "I didn't really know Mugs before. But things don't seem right since she lost her husband. Just getting in and out of our car, she stiffens up and grabs your hand like she's terrified. Walking down the stairs, anything, she seems confused."

Mugs sat still, clutching her purse. Zach tugged for a breast under Leah's shirt. Leah gently took his hand away. Zach whined.

"And you see your old friend Sarah all the time hiding under the coffee table, don't you, Mugs?"

"Yeah," Mugs said, nodding.

"How are you doing, Mugs?" Dr. Khan asked.

"Good."

"It seems like Mugs has some form of dementia," he said. "We'll try an anti-hallucinatory drug."

"Is that really necessary?" Leah asked.

"It's standard with dementia presenting with hallucinations," Dr. Khan said.

They were out of the doctor's office with the prescription in ten minutes. That evening, when Leah told Martin about it, he didn't say a word.

This time Leah walks over to Mugs, gingerly patting her shoulder. "That Sarah sure is a pest, huh." Mugs nods and Leah pats. When she was growing up in her high-ceilinged house, almost no one came to visit. Their grandparents and other relatives lived far away. Her family was not touchy-feely, either. The physical pleasures of breastfeeding Zach, sleeping in a family bed at Martin's suggestion—both were complete surprises to Leah. Comforting this seventy-year-old woman feels strange. Leah keeps patting, thinking about taking her hand away. She feels Mugs' body relax. Suddenly, she giggles like a young girl. Leah wonders what Sarah has done— tickled her friend? Leah can't help but laugh too.

Zach's chubby legs dangle from the front of the grocery cart. He's wearing the exquisite slippers Mugs sewed for him just after he was born: tanned moosehide, beaded red flowers, babiche ties. Leah's at the end of the vegetables. Mugs' shuffle-steps keep her stuck in the strawberries, staring down, gripping her handbag with both hands. Leah fetches her and guides her by the elbow. Mugs seems scared and unsure where she is. At the till, *finally*, Leah unloads with one hand, keeping Zach back from the candy bars with the other. The cashier re-weighs the broccoli. Leah notices Mugs leaning on the scale and the cashier giving them a cold glare.

"Mugs, let's move your hand away from there." Leah takes her hand and places it on the counter, then turns back to Zach, who has grabbed a chocolate bar and crammed it in his mouth, wrapper and all. Leah snatches it away and puts it back, anywhere in the display, not caring where. The cashier purses her mouth. Glancing back, Leah sees her mother-in-law's hand back on the scale. *Great.* Zach starts his I-want-it cry. An older man in line behind Leah sighs, marching off to another till. In her mind Leah hops on her bike and rides away without a helmet down the Long Lake trail. She dives in the lake naked, drinks a bottle of red in the shallows, and slides unconscious into brown-grey muck that passes for a beach, letting horse-flies nest on her eyelids. She's been a good girl. Her last drink was at the funeral.

She and Martin, they've been trying to make things work. It's been a stormy ride. They broke up twice, had other flings, tried to pick up the pieces. He took off to Mexico for a week with some environmental lawyer. She went on wild weekend road trips without him, to the hot springs, to Alaska. They argued drunkenly under the midnight sun at the music festival in Dawson City. At some point that summer she decided they were worth fighting for. And he did too. On the Labour Day weekend almost two years ago, they moved into the apartment together and went picking wild blueberries. She got pregnant later that fall. His pure joy at the news amazed her.

As dinner time approaches, Leah listens to CBC Radio's Yukon afternoon show. It's her lifeline to adults, community, a world outside. After the five-thirty local news she hovers near their apartment door. It's nearly six o'clock when Martin steps through. She practically jumps him, grabbing his shoulders and kissing him before he hucks his backpack down.

"Hey." He kisses her back. Zach toddles over and hugs his leg. Scooping him up, Martin brushes his chin whiskers against his son's cheek. Zach giggles.

"Come and sit down." He still holds Zach as Leah drags him to the table. Mugs, her back stiff, perches at the edge of a kitchen chair as if ready to leap, worrying a dish cloth in her fingers.

"Łuh ch'uh," Leah says proudly. Trying to make wind through the poplars on the letter "Ł," her tongue's tip on the roof of her mouth, as she places the bannock in front of him.

"Wow. You made this?" He strokes Zach's head.

"Me and your mom."

"Thanks, Mom." Martin pecks his mother's cheek, then eats three in a row with butter and jam, giving Zach little bites, grinning at his sticky, blue-smattered cheeks.

Tugging Martin's earlobe, Leah says, "Now I can teach you."

He grins. "Yeah."

In bed that night, Zach nursed to sleep between them, Leah says again, "Łuh ch'uh. Do you know that word?"

"Sure. Mom always made bannock. Łuh is flour. Or ashes. Ch'uh is water."

"See, you do know Gwich'in."

"Just a few words."

"I think you know more."

"I know English." Martin rolls away from her. "And how to swear in Norwegian."

Leah suspects she should shut up. "I can't believe your parents didn't speak Gwich'in to you."

"I can't believe your parents didn't speak Gaelic or whatever the hell to you."

This isn't turning out right. "It's just sad, I mean, because they were fluent."

"Only Mom was fluent. Dad could understand it."

"Sorry, I just mean it's sad that it's being lost and Zach might not ever learn it. I wanted your mom to speak only in Gwich'in to Zach, but she won't so I try to pull words out of her here and there."

Martin yanks on the covers. "It wasn't something they were taught to be proud of." His voice is irritated. "Okay?"

"Okay."

He closes his eyes. She sits up. *Oh no, the breakers.* She gets up, checking that they're turned off. They're not. *Trust Martin not to do it.* Last month they woke up to smoke and burning rubber, Mugs' attempt to boil water with the electric kettle on a stove burner. Now they have to cut the power to the kitchen at night and when they're out.

No electricity and no liquor, not a drop in the apartment since the wake for Solomon. Not because of Mugs, who stopped drinking years ago. Martin and Leah were doing good, six months sober. It wasn't like they drank all the time and not when she was pregnant. When they did, though—it wasn't *really* Leah with a problem, she was a happy drunk, at least until she cried. Martin got the blackouts. But all those relatives converging from north and south, gathering in the apartment, strong women telling Leah to "cut celery like this" for potato salad. Demanding, "Where's your salt?" Ordering, "Go get a coffee urn at Super A." Mugs ripping Kleenexes and crying. Anglican women praying with her in a circle in the living room. Children and grandchildren bringing her plates of moose nose, fried rabbit, nilii gaii, and uutsik which she barely picked at. And no grandpa to teach Zach how to hunt caribou. Ever.

Back inside the bedroom, Leah stands watching Martin doze off in bed. Just like that. A hard day's work, bannock, and off to sleep. *Must be nice.* In this moment she despises him for that.

"Martin."

He groans. "What?"

"When are you going to switch to part-time?" He is never home before six and often later. From his *interesting* research job in the territorial cabinet offices.

"Huh?"

"So you can help with your mom and I can look for work again. Zach's old enough."

He rubs his eyes, covers his face with his hands.

"Well?" There's a cutting tone in her question.

"Quit nagging."

What did her father say to her mother? *You sound like a fishwife.* Here she is now, a fishwife at twenty-seven.

"I don't want to work part-time," Martin says.

I bet you don't. "She's *your* mom. I barely know her. And I want to work at least a couple of days a week. You know, talk to grownups once in a while."

He gives her a half-smile, his throwing-hands-to-the-gods kind of face. "What can we do?"

"I don't know. Maybe put her on the wait list for Stewart Lodge."

His smile vanishes. "I seen the people in those places. Nobody visits them."

"That doesn't mean you wouldn't." With a guilty twinge, Leah imagines having to force her own mother, a feisty hotel manager, into an antiseptic cage. Leah wishes she could afford a ticket south to see her this fall. Even phoning is so expensive. She knows there's no easy answer for Martin.

He sits up on the edge of the bed, his face falling back into his hands. "I'm not sending Mom to an old folks' home."

"Then what are we going to do?"

He covers his face again.

"Talk to me!"

He gets up and puts on a pair of jeans and a T-shirt.

"Stewart Lodge is just down the street from us."

"NO!" he yells. "Just no." Turning away, he wipes his eyes. "I can't."

She walks closer and touches his shoulder. "Then I'll go to work."

Pushing her away, he rushes out of the room.

"Martin, wait."

Zach wakes up and cries to breastfeed. Leah hears the apartment door slam. Pounding her thigh in frustration, she lets Zach sob. His howls are unbearable. She lays down before long to feed her baby.

The next morning Leah finds Mugs in the bathroom in an agitated state. She's wearing Zach's—*Zach's*—red pullover, the one Leah's mother knitted for her grandchild's first birthday. More like Mugs is strangling in it. How in hell did she get it on? She's panting, short breaths, a pair of sharp sewing scissors gripped awkwardly in her hand, attempting to slice downwards from the neckline and free herself. It's too late for the pullover; the first cuts have been made. Leah takes the scissors, snipping, dissecting the wool from the bottom edge to the neckline without a word. One hand underneath, preventing a nick to Mugs' skin, pulling each sleeve slowly off her plump arms. Putting the scissors down, Leah picks up the sweater and buries her face in the soft crimson wool. Mugs has vanished.

Martin walks into the bathroom and puts his arm around Leah. "What is it?" he asks.

She holds up the remains of the sweater.

His eyes widen. "Oh no." He kisses tears off her cheek, then turns. "Mom?"

He heads into the hall. Leah follows. Mugs sits motionless on her single bed in the spare room in her bra and underpants. Martin takes the sweater, walks over, and sits beside her.

"Mom. What happened?"

She strokes the wool. "Oh. Too tight."

"Mom, this is Zach's sweater."

"Was," Leah bursts out.

Mugs looks at her son. "Oh."

"Fuck!" Leah storms off and flops onto their family bed, crying. This wakes Zach who wails and searches for his mother's breast.

Martin stands in the doorway. "She feels bad about it."

So what.

"Well." Martin stands motionless, watching the carpet. "I guess I better go."

"Must be nice." Spitting it out. "To go out. To work. While someone else babysits your mother."

Now he says, "Fuck." His face is blank. He has gone far inside, deeper than when they drank. He disappears. Leah hears the front door slam. After Zach nurses back to sleep, she looks out the bedroom window. There is snow on the ground and in the spruce. In August. Vancouver never stole a summer away. She presses her face against the cold glass.

The same morning, this is what Mugs teaches Leah:

Tok. Breast milk.

Thiinjii. Go to sleep.

Nit'ii nihthan. I love you.

For lunch Leah heats up baked beans from a can. She spoons some into the plastic plate on Zach's high chair tray, then brings a bowlful to Mugs with bread on the side. Mugs takes a bite of beans and grimaces. While Zach smears sauce on his face, Leah watches Mugs tear off pieces of bread. The beans remain in the bowl.

Afterwards Leah unpins Zach's cloth diapers, T-shirts, and sleepers from the mini-clothesline strung along the balcony. The snow has melted with the sun but there is an autumn chill in the wind. She inhales the fresh air smell in her baby's clothes. Mugs joins her.

"We make beans all the time," Mugs says.

"You made them for Martin and your other kids?"

"No. That school. Chooutla." Mugs reaches her hand to the balcony, searching as if blind.

"Chooutla? Oh." Now she remembers Martin telling her. The Indian agent came and took his mother and her siblings hundreds of miles south to Carcross. "Residential school."

"Aaha'." Her small hands rest on the brown wood rail.

"How old were you?"

"Aah. Little. Five, six."

Zach hurdles onto the balcony in a rush of small steps and collides with Leah's leg, wrapping small arms round it. He's starting to "cruise," as her mom calls it, but is not full-out walking yet.

"That's so young," Leah says. If Zach had been born then, they would have sent him too. The only escape was if your father was legally white, which was how Martin's dad deked out of it. That Norwegian blood.

"All morning we work there. Then school after lunch."

"That's not much time for school." When Leah was a girl, she never heard of such things. Once, in Girl Guides, she visited a kind elder—a skilled weaver—at her house to earn a badge, which was better than building a terrarium or doing knots. On the way to seaside parks or ski hills, Leah's family drove past reserves countless times, places where the houses and yards looked different for just a few blocks. She was aware that a handful of students in her school were "Native Indian." It wasn't until university that she learned what reserves and residential schools really were, what they were for. And was shocked.

"My brother got sick. They put him in a little room."

"A hospital room?"

"Akwaa. I never see him after that."

Leah searches her mother-in-law's impassive face.

"I never eat beans since that time," Mugs says.

Mugs' dark eyes bore into spruce trees.

They are not picking blueberries for Labour Day. They are driving north to Jensen Landing again. *I'm locking the car doors this time.* Wet snow turns to slush on the highway, hanging heavy before melting in the poplar ridges. Many of the leaves have fallen. Bright rusty-red splatches of bearberry peek through the sodden blanket, but the granite-grey sky, oppressive, mocking, promises half a year of winter. No more giddy endless light for soccer and slo-pitch and fishing. Laughing around the campfire as the temperature drops and the mosquitoes come out and it's dusk at midnight. Endless possibility. Summer's gone.

Five hours after leaving Whitehorse, they reach the village. At a compact brown rancher, they park in the rutted driveway behind a mud-spattered truck with Northwest Territories plates and a dented-up car. Martin's burly Uncle Larry is outside having a smoke. His embrace is powerful. He helps them coax Mugs from the passenger seat.

Martin's relatives are in a flurry of activity inside, sorting through his parents' things. A life. Leah lays her coat down in a corner of the living room. Her back against the wall, she breastfeeds Zach on the floor until he falls asleep.

In the kitchen the women grab pots and plates, cramming them into boxes. Mugs moves forks and knives on the counter. All of a sudden, she's crying. Leah hesitates before putting an arm around her. Does it get any easier? "It's hard moving," Leah says.

"I see my husband. In the tree there." Mugs points out the kitchen window.

"You miss him, don't you?" Leah feels the woman's body quake.

Martin sits on his parents' bed with a shoebox full of loose photographs. Leah joins him, placing Zach on her lap. Children in winter, their faces surrounded by fox-fur parka hoods. Inside, sitting around a simple kitchen. Solomon and Mugs, her smile filling her face, wearing a fitted calf-length dress, outside in summer. "This was their wedding day. Their honeymoon was setting up a wall tent way upriver. The river was low and they got stuck just out of town so they just set up camp there." Martin tries to laugh it off but it doesn't work. His eyes well up.

"After my parents' wedding Dad took Mom to Whistler," Leah says. "She said they hiked up a mountain in the rain and had nothing but soggy tuna sandwiches. While she nursed her blisters in their motel room, my dad got drunk with his old tree-planting buddies." Martin wipes his eyes. Leah stops there, while it's funny. No need to mention her mother's fear that she had made a mistake. Did Mugs ever wonder with Solomon? Martin said one time she tossed her cup of tea in her husband's face and all Solomon said was, "Needs sugar." And what about Martin and Zach and herself? The new trio. A quartet thanks to Mugs. *What about us?*

Zach is on the move and the place isn't baby proof. When she picks him up, he squirms and fusses. She roams the small house, wanting to hand the baby over to Martin. She's annoyed to find him standing on the duplex back steps in the evening sun with Larry, their coats on, drinking beer. Maybe it's his grin that says: This isn't my first. Maybe it's that he's not drinking with her.

Leah and Zach curl up that night on a mattress in the hallway; Martin's aunt and uncle have the bedroom. The volume rises as Martin, his uncle, and cousins drink and tell stories in the living room. Martin's belly laugh reverberates. The sleeping baby beside Leah is suddenly one more *thing* reining her in. Just after two a.m. Leah leaps up, yelling, "Why don't you go to sleep!" She storms out and down the back steps without a coat into the frosty dark night, onto dusty roads and along the river trail that Solomon walked every morning of his retirement. Martin said his father knew every bend in the river. She wonders if Solomon ever saw himself heading out to check fish nets again and waved at that image of his younger self—a handsome single man, floating by. Free.

It's Uncle Larry, not Martin, who finds her as she hurries back, afraid that someone will trip and fall over Zach.

Larry looks worried. "We didn't know where you went."
"Me neither."

A few hours of freedom, and more within reach. The owner of the quilt store says she's looking for help by the end of October, a theatre company's looking for a costume designer, the groceries are in the car, and Zach's on a wait list for a family day home two days a week.

Leah twirls Zach in the public pool's shallows, holds him close, and bounces him. "We're kangaroos!" Her baby likes that. "Swimming bunnies! Splash, splash, splash!" He startles when the sloshing water gets his face, he's not ready for that. Leah lays Zach on his back in the water, one hand supporting him underneath. Her baby kicks and cries at the sensation, struggling to bring his head up. "Okay. No back floats."

Leah refuses to take Mugs out grocery shopping anymore. She turns off the breakers instead, leaving her mother-in-law behind to rearrange the kitchen. It's been okay, mostly. One day Mugs forgot to hang up the phone. It turned out that it was Leah's mom back in Vancouver; she called back later, asking in an anxious tone, "Is everything okay?" Leah insisted that she was fine, she wasn't sure why, something about not wanting to admit to her mother that she was far from it. Another time Zach found a sharp kitchen knife on the living room floor. Now Leah checks when she gets home. Mugs probably would enjoy sewing again but Leah's sure she would leave pins and needles everywhere, so that's just too bad.

Keeping Zach in his car seat, Leah carries groceries in. The apartment door is wide open. "Mugs?" Silence. She lets the bags down and walks through. "Mugs. Mugs!" The place is empty.

Martin's not in a meeting, fortunately. After he meets her at home, they split up, Zach in Leah's back carrier. An hour later Martin finds his mother baby-stepping, clutching her black purse, near the Yukon River bridge. It's only minus five Celsius but the wind is fierce. She's wearing her boots but no jacket, just a cardigan.

Leah can't leave her alone.

The home care lady is late. *Damnit.* Zach has his snowsuit and boots on. There is fresh snow outside, hardly surprising in November. Everything is packed and ready for their two hours of freedom—swimsuits and towels, bananas, an extra cloth diaper in a plastic bag. If the worker doesn't show up soon, public swimming will be over.

From the couch Mugs converses angrily with Sarah, alternating between Gwich'in and English. "I told you! Get going now!"

Here we go again. So much for the anti-hallucinatory drugs. "I don't think Sarah is there, Mugs. She's living in Dawson City, remember?"

Mugs doesn't respond. There's a small pile of shredded Kleenexes in her lap. "Anaa!" Don't. Leah knows that word. Mugs waves her tissue under the coffee table.

"I think it's bath day, Mugs," Leah says in a false syrup voice. *Let me outta here.*

On Tuesdays the home care lady, Kate, drives Mugs to the mall. They walk back and forth along the small strip of stores, buy new underwear, and have tea and fries in the coffee shop. On Thursdays Kate stays home with Mugs, bathing her in their tub. In her fifties, also First Nations, Kate unbraids Mugs' long hair. She lathers shampoo in and soothes her charge when the water frightens her. She helps her clean her privates and towels her dry firmly, as if Mugs were her own mother, or daughter. Kate brushes her grey-streaked black hair lovingly before braiding it for another week, securing the sides with bobby-pins. She even brings moose meat.

Leah knows bits of this, imagines the remainder, all of which she should do. If she was a good daughter-in-law. But Martin doesn't do it either.

From phone calls and appointments, Leah learned that if Mugs was not a real legal status Indian, the Yukon territorial government would give her three home care visits a week. Because she has "status," she is entitled to only two visits courtesy of the federal Department of Indian Affairs in Ottawa.

"It's so racist," she said to Martin.

Martin scoffed. "No shit."

Mugs has status because she reclaimed it the year before; the government had taken it away when she married Solomon. He was non-status because his mother married non-status, that Norwegian trader. Zach will have status, his children won't—disenfranchisement postponed a couple of generations. Not ended. Leah once tried to explain the maze of discriminatory laws in the Indian Act to her own mom without success.

Leah and Mugs haven't made bannock in months.

When Leah asks Mugs for a word in Gwich'in, she struggles to find it. And can't.

Zach seems scared of his grandmother.

Kate is twenty minutes late now. *Damnit damn.* Zach fusses, trapped and hot in his snowsuit. "It's okay, honey." Leah strokes Zach's cheek, resisting the urge to yell at something, anything. "Just a couple more minutes and we're going in the car and we're going swimming, okay?"

Leah searches by the phone for Kate's number. Zach starts to cry. A knock at the door. Kate opens it and strides in. "Sorry I'm late."

Leah picks Zach up, grabs their bag and edges out, averting her eyes. "Goodbye," she says, knowing she's being rude. Making a beeline down the stairs.

It's late morning at the Catholic-run emergency shelter. Leah spots her mother-in-law on the far side of the room, slumped in a chair, a blanket around her. Leah glances at Martin. His arms wrap around Zach; he cannot seem to move. Leah rushes over and hugs Mugs so hard she says, "Oh!"

Martin joins them. He touches his mother's hair near her forehead. "Mom."

A young woman, one of the members of the religious order that operates the shelter, comes to fill them in.

"On the Alaska Highway?" Martin says.

"That's right," the woman says. "Past the Kopper King." A good hour's walk for a healthy young person.

"Jeez." Martin stares at the linoleum.

"How did you walk that far, Mugs?" Leah asks. No answer.

"It was a trucker," says the woman. "Three in the morning. Said he saw her in his headlights. She was off the road a little ways on the other side of the ditch. No coat. Just that light sweater."

"Jeez," Martin says again.

"She's a lucky lady. It went down to minus twenty last night."

Martin and Leah catch each other's eyes. There's nothing to say.

"I'm sure glad you phoned around. She had no ID so the driver wasn't sure what to do."

"But her purse," Leah says. "She never leaves without it."

The woman smiles sympathetically. Martin takes his mother's arm and guides her up, supporting her back as if it might snap. "Come on, Mom. Let's go home."

Mugs' purse is not at home. In the afternoon Leah cruises the highway near the trailer court with Mugs and Zach, pulling over at a black object in the snow. Putting her hazard lights on, she gets out and picks up the purse. Inside she finds bobby-pins, Mugs' wallet, photographs of her husband and children, and Kleenexes.

That night Martin wraps a bungee cord around Mugs' bedroom door, stretching and securing it across the hall on the bathroom doorknob. Leah watches, then tests it. He looks at her, his eyes questioning. As if she has the answer.

They make love for the first time in weeks.

Leah wakes up and looks at the alarm clock. Just after four a.m. She hears a noise. Break-in? No. The next-door bedroom. "Martin." She pushes him. Nothing.

"Sarah!" The voice is angry. "Anaa! Sarah, stop that!" The door opening a little, closing. Opening, closing. Over and over. Then. Tiny cries.

Shut up, shut up. Hands over her ears, Leah hides under the pillow. After a few minutes, she tosses the pillow off. The room is quiet except for Martin's long breaths and Zach's short puffs. Fumbling in the closet, she retrieves a brown bag and pulls the bottle out. She walks out quietly, ducking under the bungee cord at Mugs' door—it's open a crack—to fetch a glass from the kitchen.

As she sits in bed drinking the glass of wine, Zach turns, half-asleep, searching for a nipple. Leah leans on her side to nurse, propped up by one arm, the other holding the wine precariously.

Open, close, open, close. The door again. "Sarah!"

Her right nipple, Zach's favourite, slips away from his lips.

"Tok, Mommy, tok."

Back and forth, sharp jerks. Zach mewls.

"Martin." Reaching, she puts the glass on the bedside table and nudges him. "Wake up."

He moans.

"Your mom. Listen."

Pounding now. "Sarah! Let me out," she demands.

"Oh jeez," he says.

Mugs whimpers. Leah can barely breathe. Zach cries out for the breast.

Martin gets up and stands outside the door. "Mom, it's nighttime. You're okay."

More joggling of the doorknob.

"Please, Mom. Go back to sleep." He pauses. "I love you."

Her tiny cries turn to sobs. Martin's face is in his hands. Leah goes to him and puts her arm on his back. He turns away.

"I can't take this," he says.

"I know. It's not right," she says, "we can't, not like this."

Zach wails full-out now, drowning out his grandmother.

"Okay, fine," Martin says abruptly.

"Okay, what?"

"We'll..." His voice wavers. "Put her somewhere. Safe."

Now he's crying too. Leah holds him.

Zach, snuffling, has worn himself out. He doesn't understand why his mother's not coming to him.

Leah lets go of Martin. "Mommy's sorry, baby. I'm here now." She leans over and catches her baby's sweet breath. She pushes the half-finished glass away and lies back down on the bed to feed her son.

Sinkhole

I TELL THEM OVER AND OVER we need more guys. These young men we take care of, you have to watch them with both eyes. They're like kids. They don't know better. Innocent.

All last year they stretched us tight. Not enough workers. Not replacing guys on medical. Short every week and extra shifts and "Edgar, can you work another four hours with Charley even though you worked ten and no break." No please, no thank you. Stuff like that all the time. I got my own little guys. They're nine and twelve. I'm a single dad. Their mom helps out but she's away a lot with work. They're saying hang on 'til April, we're getting new money, and we're hanging, we're pulled thin through the winter. Like that maple syrup the French people pour into the snow at Rendezvous, wrap it frozen 'round a popsicle stick. My boys love that stuff. It gets really hard. Sometimes it breaks.

Then it's April but it's still winter because winter lasts six months here, which is crazy, but it's okay because us guys, we got a good basketball league, we got the indoor running track, lots of stuff. And I have my plaid hat with earflaps, my Sorel boots, like every other winter guy. I come in for our staff meeting. My boss Rose has Critical Incident Review. She always has that. Not my case. This time she's dragging Jonah across gravel shit, for what? Because his guy stole a pack of gum and the guy who owns the bookstore complained about no-brain criminals running loose on Main Street and scaring away customers. Jonah's not saying anything. He's barely moving, except his fingers tap-tapping his legs under the table.

Rose has pretty petals on the outside. Blonde hair she gets cut and blow-dried every other week. Fancy-looking pantsuits. My boss is one of those people, she says one nice thing like a flower opening up. But the flower smells like cat piss.

She says, "We're a team. We're not laying blame. We're making things better for you and our clients." And then she says, "You cannot take your eyes off your client for a single second." Her eyes. Rose is one of those people, she's a toad, she's on top of one rock along the shore and she's ready to jump to the next rock because it's bigger, it's got a juicier bug to eat on it, and the rock after that with a fatter bug still. Her eyes bulge. Everybody knows she's doing her master's so she can get a bigshot government job.

"You stretch and stretch tighter," I say. "You stretch a rubber band, one day it's gonna snap and hit you in the face."

Jonah's not saying anything, just touching that gold crucifix on the chain round his neck. Chris, the only First Nations guy on our team, says "Yup" under his breath. He's our union rep. Nobody else wanted it. He's young, he's got a ponytail. All winter he looked more tired than an old donkey.

Rose straightens up and fixes her fancy collar. "I'm not sure that I'm liking your tone here, Edgar."

My tone. "We're people. We're working damn hard."

"The union's worried 'bout workload. And safety," says Chris. That guy never raises his voice.

"We're working on the issues together," Rose says.

"You guys better hurry or we're gonna break," I say. "You're going to break us."

"Then maybe you're in the wrong line of work," Rose says.

"I... You..." My voice is a stone dropping to the bottom of the sinkhole. "Are you saying—?"

"Am I saying what, Edgar?" Rose's voice can split stone.

"Take it easy, everyone," Chris says. "Been a long winter."

Jonah lets out his breath.

I grab my voice, lift it to the surface. "Are you threatening us?"

I can barely see her. Like she's hiding in mist coming up off the water.

"You're awfully defensive today," she says.

"It's fine," Jonah says. "We know. We watch our guys better."

"That's right." Rose points her finger at us like a machine gun. "You're all on the front line. Your job is to watch your clients like a hawk."

We had a swimming hole when we were kids. It was a sinkhole, round and wide and really deep. My mama said it was from where the earth caved in a long time ago, sucking a family in their hut down with it. Mama said the earth got hungry, opened its mouth, and swallowed them up. Then pooed them out the other side.

The sinkhole had frogs and ferns, and turtles peeking their heads out of the water. The everywhere green cooled you down and lifted you up and made you clean. And the little fish darted and flashed yellow-gold. They had their quick moves.

I took my younger sister there. She didn't swim yet. She was only learning to be a shining fish. I watched her close. Do you know how hard it is to never take your eyes away? Even for the most precious? Try it. You'll see. I was the hawk circling. I was her brother.

My main guy Charley is a good guy pretty much. He's a bit younger than me on the outside and way younger inside his head. He lives in a group home. He can do some things. Brush his teeth. Take a piss and shake it out. He swings and sprays it like it's a hose. It's pretty funny even though I'm the one wiping it up, but he tries, you know? He can go for a walk up and down the stairs by the clay cliffs, slow and steady. Looking at his short legs and chubby doughnut you would be surprised, but Charley has super cardio. And bowling, he's pretty good at that, he did that in Special Olympics and won a medal. Other things, not so much. Taking a bath. Shaving, I help him with that. Cooking is kind of risky. He forgets about a pot of Kraft Dinner or the kettle for his bedtime hot chocolate.

Oh, he can really eat. The fridge, you gotta watch that. He pretty much will gobble whatever he can without chewing and then throw up and start over. Like a dog. Those retrievers, we had one of those when my boys were little. That thing would goddamn well eat itself to death if you let it. They lock Charley's fridge at night. Same for beer, guy can't stop, when he can get it. He finds ways. And he can make babies. He made two of them. He's a guy. Yeah.

It starts with Tim Hortons. I didn't know it then. It's about a week after Rose who's not a rose gives her "we're a team" bullshit, which really means "your asses are always on the line."

We go to Tim Hortons near Main Street, the old one, because that's Charley's favourite. It has big windows. "Like to watch people going by," he says. There's more of that near Main Street. Sometimes we have a double date. I joke about that.

"Hey Charley, you and me and Jonah and Frederick gonna have a double-double double date today?" Double-milk double-sugar. People here love Tim Hortons coffee and doughnuts. Coffee's pretty weak and doughnuts are nothing like my mama's but it's warm especially when it's dark and forty below so your balls shrink in tight and small. For protection, like a possum playing dead. I am never getting used to blue-ball cold in this country.

We're having our double-double double date. With a window seat. Jonah's from Syria, he's pretty fresh here, he got out when that Arab Spring started. Always dancing, throwing his long hair around, or tapping the table to his own beat. His guy Frederick is a little guy with those pimples, you know, acne, all over his face. Frederick lives for heavy metal. Today his T-shirt is Megadeth.

Everything's melting outside because it's April, warming up in the days now and we got record snow this winter. Flooding up the drains and cars are going by splashing and spraying people on the sidewalk. Every time someone gets soaked, Charley and Frederick hoot and stand up and give the high-five across the table. Charley keeps saying, "Another one bites the dust," and Frederick keeps saying, "Burned," and Charley's fat cheeks shake. Another thing, those two can really laugh and get you going too so it's not feeling like work. They remind me of my youngest son when he was little, his mama holding him, and I would hide anywhere and pop out.

Under the table. Behind the door. "Where's Papa? There he is!" Squealing with laughter. Over and over. Big baby cheeks. He never got tired of it. Neither did me and my wife. Back then.

Charley sees his Special O coach walking by. It's a young lady volunteer who's really patient with the guys. Charley waves and his coach waves back with a giant smile.

"There goes your girlfriend," Frederick says.

"Shut up," Charley says.

Frederick holds up his half-eaten doughnut and sticks his finger in and out of it. Charley tries to grab the doughnut but Frederick pulls it away and jumps up, giggling.

"Whoa there, Frederick," says Jonah. "Remember, what kind of a place are we in?"

Frederick frowns.

"Frederick," Jonah says.

"Public place." He lets out a gigantic sigh.

"Yes," says Jonah. "Do the gentlemen do the crude things with doughnuts here? With the ladies all around?"

Frederick rolls his eyes. He sits down and pushes his doughnut away.

"You're burned, Frederick," says Charley.

"The ladies don't dance with the crude guys," Jonah says.

Charley stands up and says, "I gotta go to the bathroom."

"I'll come with you," I say.

Frederick laughs. "Need Edgar to wipe your bum, Charley?"

"Shut up," Charley says. He punches Frederick in the arm.

"Ow, fuck," Frederick yells. Other people look at our table.

"Hey, hey, no punching," I say. "He was teasing. Right, Frederick?"

Frederick glares at Charley. "Bum-bum," Frederick says.

Charley gives Frederick the finger.

I know what Rose says. Like a hawk. But these guys know when you treat them like babies. A few seconds is not going to hurt. "Go ahead, Charley," I say.

Charley walks to the can. I figure I'll go check on him in a minute if he's not back. Me and Jonah talk about our men's league game last Friday. We play in a school gym. Jonah's on my team. The ref let the game get out of hand.

"He should have handed David a foul right away for that cheap shot," I say. "Hip checks Larry right out of bounds when he's going up for a basket."

"That's fucking cheap," Frederick says.

"Yeah," Jonah says, nodding. He's a really easy guy all the time. An Arab Buddha.

"Ref's gotta keep it down, under control. Then we're not going for revenge. Larry's the one who fouls out in the third. Our best guy," I say. "Shoulda been David."

Charley's not back. I go into the men's can and get blasted right away with shit smell. One of the doors is closed. I lean down and see black boots. And water.

"Charley? Hey Charley?" He's not answering. I try the door but it's locked. "Charley, buddy, open up in there."

"Can't."

"What you doing in there?"

No answer.

"It's not smelling so sweet. Are you sick to your stomach?"

"Yeah."

"You can't sit there all day. Your ass is gonna stick to that thing. You know that, eh? We're gonna bring in that Jaws of Life to rescue you. Pull your ass off that seat before it gets sucked into the water. You don't want that, do you?"

"No."

Charley has big lips. I can pretty well imagine his pouty bottom lip sticking out. "Come on. Open the door for Edgar."

He opens the door. It's not good. His fly is open. He shit his pants. Shit everywhere. Runny shit. On the seat. On the back of his pants. His hands. His boots. Brown water bits on the floor. The toilet's full with paper. He really tried to wipe.

I'm looking, I'm seeing this in two seconds flat. I'm shitting, I'm swimming, I'm sinking down, gasping for air. I blink. I'm coming up. Tim Hortons. Charley.

"The toilet overflowed, eh?"

Poor guy. Charley starts to cry. I pat him on his shoulder. "It's okay. It's an accident, right? You had upset stomach."

"It's gross," Charley says.

"We're gonna get you cleaned up and smelling fresh like spring. Like the pussy willows, they're coming out now. They smell sweet. We can rub your bum with those willows, huh?"

Charley giggles. "Perverted, Edgar."

"I know. Just kidding." I grab lots of that brown paper towel by the sink and wet it good. "Hold still, buddy." I wipe off his boots and the back of his pants best I can.

"I'm all wet," Charley says.

"Gonna get you home soon. Come on out here and wash your hands." I lead him over to the sink. "Extra soap today, okay?"

"Yeah, tons of soap."

I take more wet brown paper and wipe the toilet seat and the floor around it before I wash my hands, extra soap too.

"Everyone's gonna say Charley pooed his pants," he says.

"No way, man. This is what we're gonna do," I say. "Take your hoodie off. We're gonna wrap it round your butt like you're so hot 'cause its springtime. We're gonna walk back like that all cool and no one's gonna know."

"Really, Edgar?" Charley looks at me with his brown eyes so trusting.

I help him tie his hoodie arms around his waist. Before we go, I tell one of the young Filipino guys at the counter, "Sorry man, but the guys' bathroom needs a makeover."

I never tell Rose this time. We're not having Critical Incident Review for this. What's she gonna say? "You left him, Edgar." While I gave him a few seconds of freedom. Not like I can stop a guy taking a messy crap but she'll twist it to make me look bad.

I go home at the end of the day and cook dinner for my boys. Ravioli. The younger one washes the dishes, the older one dries. Michael and Joseph. They're good boys. Next year Joseph starts high school. They're begging me to make doughnuts like I used to but I say, "Sorry guys, maybe on the weekend." I help them with their homework. Make lunches. Watch some sports. I go to bed. Hoping I don't dream.

Our swimming hole back home was deep green. They have plants in the woods up here that are really thick, soft carpets. You push it down, it bounces back, like a ball that needs air. Moss. It was green like that.

My sister, she was my responsibility. My mama was working. My papa was working. I had my sister under my wing. Sometimes I didn't like her tucked down there. She slowed me down with my friends. But I didn't have a choice.

And my sister, she was tiny when she was born. Two months early. She was smaller than the other kids. She needed her big brother.

We had contests. Who could hold their breath longest. We dove down deep. Greener, darker, blacker, to the centre of the earth. Maybe I'd find the mine full of gold where Papa worked, never seeing the sun.

You go past your limit. Your body's sucked up all your air. You're starting to die.

Enough.

Push the water down like the turtle, make your hands wide, fingers together, flipper circles out and down.

The last few metres are the longest. You have to fight the urge to open your mouth and breathe in the water. Too soon.

You're burning.

You're dying.

You burst through the surface, hungry, gasping, sucking in air, you would drink all the air in the world if you could, swallow so much you pass out and explode and sink down to Papa's mine.

You win. You're alive.

It's okay to dream that.

I didn't want Lucy to try that. Not yet.

"Papa." Michael stands over me in his pajamas. "Papa, are you okay?" He's looking worried.

"My son," I say.

"Sounded like you were choking."

"I'm okay."

He's not moving. "Bad dream again?"

"Good dream." I reach up and mess up his hair. "Go back to bed, little guy."

He does.

Then there's Main Street. Things are starting to go sideways. Bit by bit. Now I see it.

It's a week later. Snow's gone except a few spots on the trails. Garbage everywhere. Brown, dusty roads full of the winter's gravel, wind making sand tornadoes. No green on the trees yet but the swans are back on the river. Two of them. Charley likes the swans and so do I. Swans stay together for life. We like their loyalty. Their long necks. Their honking. We sit by the river, plug our noses, and honk at them together. "Honk-honk." It's pretty fun and my job is good.

We're walking back along Main Street towards Charley's group home. Lots of people out. It's always windy and cools off in a flash when the clouds hide the sun but some people wear T-shirts and shorts. Teenagers trying to look tough and sexy. Smoking and swearing. Hacky Sack and skateboards. The street guys and girls who don't have a home like Charley and are out celebrating the spring.

Then we hear, "Charley," beside us. An old woman's voice. A hungry voice.

Charley's body tightens. I know that flip. From swans to survival.

"Charley, help your old mother out. Fifty bucks. For breakfast." She laughs and her buddies join in. "Bacon and eggs and toast and hash browns. Come on, my boy."

His mama's just skin and bones. She was supposed to be back in Fisher Lake. Instead she's coming at Charley with her hand out, no teeth, only gums in her smile.

We talk about triggers where we work. Triggers aren't guns.

This hand. This voice. This smile. This is Charley's trigger. It lights him up and sets him on fire. Gas and lighter, poof. His mama runs on vodka like my old car runs on gasoline.

Cooking wine. Mouthwash. Poor people's poison. That's what she filled her babies with, running through her blood into theirs so they stay babies forever. But not innocent. Charley stayed with her six years before the social workers took him. He knows things he doesn't want to know. He remembers. You always do.

He can't move. I can see he's trying to speak and nothing comes out, even his air is stuck. I'm thinking she's his mama and she had a hard life like a lot of us, they sent her to one of those schools and bad things happened to her. But he's my guy and we need to keep walking.

I say, "Charley, let's go, we gotta get you home before bowling practice." I don't touch him. Not now.

She's grinning and I'm wondering what happened to all her teeth.

"Twenty bucks." His mama grabs his arm and snap, his body screams, arm kicking back like it's starting a chain saw, hitting her in the face.

Now Charley runs. Off down the sidewalk, back the way we came, and I'm running after him. He's not quick up here but he's got quick moves, fast feet, even if he runs like a crooked zombie waving his arms up and down.

The light is red but he's running out into traffic with the road full of gravel. A car honks and brakes slam and he slips and falls hard in that intersection and he's not hit, I'm pretty sure he's not hit, thank God, but he's howling, he's crying. Poor guy. I think he banged his elbow. I'm hoping nothing's busted.

I lead him off to the sidewalk. His legs give out. I hold him up and get him to a bench. He's sitting and wailing like a calf for its mama's milk, holding his elbow tight to his chest. People are crowding round. If it was me or my boys, maybe we go home first, put some ice on it, see how it is. Us guys are always falling down. But I have to be extra safe, because this is work. Protocols.

My phone, it's not in my pocket, I must have left it in my car at the group home. All these people are standing over us. An older guy asks if he can help. I say, "Yeah, man, can you call 9-1-1?" He does and he waits with me, he's a good guy.

They let me go in the ambulance with Charley. Once we check in to Emergency, I use their phone to call my boss like I'm supposed to. "I was right with him. His mother grabbed him, and he took off," I say.

"I expect a full report," says Stinky Rose Petal. "I am not happy about this."

Like I'm happy. Stuck at the hospital with Charley waiting for x-rays. At least he's not wailing any more, just little moans. His body caved in, a turtle pulled back into its hard shell. Only Charley's shell is soft.

Three hours later. It turns out he's only got scrapes and bruises from hitting the pavement. Rose has to pick us up at the hospital and drive us back to the group home. It's after six. She's not saying much. Except, "Get your paperwork in immediately." She drives away in the work minivan.

I grab my phone in my car to call the boys. There's a message from my son Joseph. "We finished volleyball practice, Papa, where are you?" A text. *Papa r u coming?* Another three calls from him.

I'm a good dad. I'm there for them. My papa couldn't be there. He was working in the mine six, seven days a week. He was angry, he was tired, and I didn't see it then. But once I became a young man, you know, the mine bosses, security guards, the police and the military, a few guys running the whole country, getting fat, I could see how that sucked Papa down. Not me. I gotta be there for my sons, they're my best guys.

But Joseph and his buddy are waiting for me. And I'm not there, I forgot, he has no one else to call and his little brother's home alone. Their mother's a nurse, she's working up in Wolf Rapids for a few months filling in for someone. Good money. I told her sure, take it, me and the boys will be fine. Me and my wife split up a couple years ago but we're good, you know, friends, the boys go back and forth between us.

I phone Joseph.

"Papa. Where are you?" He sounds scared but trying not to be. "I'm so sorry, buddy," I say. "My guy got hurt and I had to take him to hospital."

"Charley?" my son asks. "Is he okay?" I tell the boys stories about me and Charley. They met him a few times. Cheered him on at bowling. Charley loved that.

"He's fine. He's gonna have a nice bruise on his elbow, that's all. Are you guys still at school?"

My boy says, "Dustin's mom took us home."

"Is Michael okay? Did you make a snack for you and your brother?" Usually the boys take the school bus home together and make some macaroni. Now Joseph has more after-school stuff and the little guy's on his own for a bit so I try to leave snacks out for him. This morning I ran out of time.

"I got it covered, Papa," Joseph says. "We zapped a bunch of pizzas and grated more mozza on top. Then we piled on the salsa and put olives on. We made mountains basically."

Basically. Joseph's word of the month. I laugh out loud in the car as we pull up to the group home. Goddamn, I love those boys. "I'll be there soon," I say.

I'm still smiling when I get out of my car by the office a few blocks away, even though I know I got shit-piles of paperwork to fill out by the end of tomorrow. I see Chris leaving. He's here late too. His fists are tight, he's looking straight ahead. He's got this, you know, bandage, on one arm and scratches on his face. His hair is loose down his back and His Idle No More T-shirt is ripped in front—Chris is really strong into Indigenous rights and I respect the guy for that. He lights up a cigarette, sucks in the smoke, and looks up at the sky.

"Hey, Chris," I say.

He jumps back and says, "Fuck, you scared me."

"Bad day?"

He says, "Yeah."

"Me too," I say. "Charley banged up his elbow pretty good."

"Junior frickin' had a tantrum and took a fork to me." He holds out his arm.

Chris's guy Junior has a head injury from his ATV crash. He gets depressed and moody and throws a punch now and then. Junior's the youngest of our guys, maybe twenty. "Shit," I say, "did you need stitches?"

Chris shakes his head. "He went for my face. Thank Christ he missed my eyes."

"Jesus."

Chris is tall and fit, a good-looking guy with a girlfriend and baby on the way. "All my kid needs is a blind dad."

"Oh no, don't say that."

"Said he was gonna kill me." He's messing with his hair, his eyes are bullets shooting back and forth like some druggie guy.

"Are you sure you're okay?"

"I gotta get outta here," he says and rushes past me.

The swimming hole was so deep, you could swim down past Papa's mine, past the dark black centre of the earth and come out the other side. Where that family from the hut was living like nothing ever happened. The ones who got sucked down. Where it was only cool green swimming holes. The water was clean. Papas never went down into the mines. People ate warm doughnuts sprinkled with sugar all the time. Mamas didn't cry. And we were gonna go there one day. That's what I told Lucy. She believed me. She believed everything I told her.

Maybe I shouldn't have told her that. She was only learning to swim.

Like I said, things are going sideways. Little things, not so little. The pool.

It's May and the leaves are finally coming out, making everyone almost drunk with sunshine 'til eleven o'clock and the everywhere green. This is why everybody lives here, right? We get kind of crazy to pack it all in outside. It catches and spreads to anyone, even if you grew up somewhere nothing like here. This kind of place where people live to play, and it's okay.

Jonah and Chris are biking to work now. They're on a team for the bike relay to Haines, you know, in Alaska. It's pretty much United Nations with Jonah from Syria, this other guy from Iraq, plus David from basketball and Chris, they got the First Nations covered. Our basketball league is over but there's ultimate Frisbee. I tried it last year at Rotary Park, it was pretty fun, I'm thinking I might do that again.

Things are supposed to be better at work because we have our new budget, new money. The scratches on Chris's arm are healing up good from where Junior took a fork to him. Then just before May long weekend we hear Chris is off on medical. No one's saying much about why but me and Jonah are figuring stress. I ask Rose, "Are we hiring someone else to cover?"

All she says is, "We'll see."

I ask her, "How are we dealing with Junior?"

"Exactly like you're trained to. Stick to routines to a T. Watch them like a hawk. That's your job. Do it."

Rose calls someone in for a few days. Auxiliary. An older guy, how dumb is that with Junior? This guy puts his back out right away helping Junior get groceries. So now he's gone. Rose says there's no one else to call in. Me and Jonah don't believe her. We're carrying Chris's load, we got an extra client to watch like a hawk. Basically.

We take the guys from their group home to the pool twice a week, Tuesdays and Fridays, at the Canada Games Centre. They built it up on the hill. That really blew my mind. Ice rinks, indoor fields, the gym and running track, pool and water slide and hot tub and giant windows you can see the mountains from. Subway sandwiches. Art everywhere. Never could I imagine a government would build something like this for people. When the Canada Games were here, me and the boys watched everything. Judo, wheelchair basketball, speed skating, lots of stuff. It was really good. Yeah, it's a kind of paradise really.

I used to think that.

We're having a slow start this Tuesday morning. Jonah's half an hour late for work. That guy's never late, just like he's never mad.

Good thing Rose was off at some meeting. Jonah rushes in. He didn't shave and his hair, it's pretty curly and it's kinda crazy.

"Hey man," I say. "Where were you?"

"Sorry I'm late." He's not looking me in the eye.

"What happened? You sleep in? Your hair looks like it had a war with your pillow."

Jonah shakes his head. He's mumbling, something like, phone call, three a.m., family back home.

"Is everything all right?"

He looks at me and he doesn't speak. It's like he's trying and he can't and I know exactly what that is. Then he says, "There's a fucking war on in Syria. What do you think?"

I want to pat him on the back but I know better. "I'm sorry, man. I think our world is poisoned by some really sick people."

He doesn't say anything.

"But they can't kill love. We gotta put love wherever we can, every minute, every day."

Jonah's looking at me a long time. "I never asked you about where you come from."

"I…" Now my voice is sinking.

"Right, hey, it's okay," Jonah says. "We better go pick up the guys."

We grab our work minivan. When me and Jonah walk up to their group home, Charley's standing at the door holding his swim bag with two hands like he's ready to jump off the diving board. Charley says, "Let's go already, Edgar. I been waiting like a century."

"You got all your swim stuff?"

He groans. "Yeah." And pulls everything out of his plastic bag. "Goggles, check. Shorts, check. Towel, check."

I high-five him. He grins.

Junior is in the easy chair in the living room with his feet up on the table and a big bulb of a head. He likes it shaved. You can see a long pink scar above his ear on one side, curving like a skinny moon, but maybe he doesn't care. It's from his crash.

"Hi, Junior," I say. "You got your swim stuff?"

He nods over at a backpack. I give him a thumbs up.

"Frederick," Jonah calls. "Time to go swimming."

"Where's Frederick?" I ask Charley.

"Frederick's pissed," Charley says.

Jonah asks, "How come?"

"'Cause his girlfriend is two-timing, that's how come," says Charley. "Caught her sucking face with Boris after soccer practice last night."

"Oh boy," says Jonah. "Not again."

"A-gain, oh yeah," says Charley. "Frederick never learns. Women."

"Bitches," Junior says.

"Hey, don't talk like that," I say. "Women are our mothers and sisters. They bring us into this world."

"Bitches," Junior says again. Me and Jonah look at each other like, oh shit, this guy's not like our guys.

Charley's girlfriend moved to Ontario with her family last fall but they still Skype a lot. Frederick's girlfriend June-Bell is in Special O with them and Boris. June-Bell's about five feet tall and loves to dance and flirt. So this two-timing is pretty much a regular thing.

"Splash, come on, buddy." Jonah goes up the stairs. "We're gonna do cannonballs, right?"

We hear Frederick telling him, "Not coming."

"Frederick," Charley shouts up the stairs. "Come on. Swimming. Girls in bikinis."

Charley starts chanting, "Girlsinbikinisgirlsinbikinisgirlsinbikinis."

Frederick shows up at the top of the stairs in his underwear. He's got a really big gut and man boobs and skinny bowlegs. "Okay," he says.

Me and Jonah and Charley start laughing. Even Junior joins in. I'm thinking, it's gonna be all right.

It's quiet at the pool in the mornings. Charley loves the pool so he gets into his shorts no problem and sits on a bench in the change room and waits. Frederick is still pretty cranky. He puts his shorts on backwards. When Jonah tells him, Frederick gets all worked up, flapping his arms like a duck taking off on the water. "It's okay,"

Jonah says nice and gentle. "Just sit here and take them off and put them on the other way. Not so bad, huh?"

Junior's got his shorts on too. He's muscular and into working out. Chris took him to the gym a lot. Junior starts to head out. He likes to be independent. "Hang on Junior," I say. "Let's go out together."

"I'm not waiting for babies," Junior says.

"We're not babies. Come on, Charley," I say. "Let's head out with Junior."

Jonah says, "Me and Frederick will be right there."

Out on the deck the sun shines in through the giant windows. The pool is clear.

We start in the shallow end. Charley really likes floating on his back in the lazy river. We do it about twenty times at least. He could do that forever. Junior does it a couple of times before he joins Jonah and Frederick in the deep end.

Charley's kind of scared about the water slide. What we do is we go up the stairs together. I get him all ready, sitting at the top of the slide with his hands at both sides. "Okay, here we go, we're at the Olympics, ladies and gentlemen," I say. "Charley Wilson from Yukon Territory, Canada, he's been training all year, he's the famous world champion, he's gonna do the luge, he's gonna race down on the ice faster than any human before. This is the moment everybody's been waiting for. Ready?"

Then Charley says, "Ready, coach," and I give him a little push and off he goes. The rule is, I have to come down right after. We do that about twelve times. It's good cardio going up those stairs.

Frederick and Jonah hang out in the deep end for monster cannonballs and splashing. Junior does lengths. He lost some coordination after he bashed his head but he gets going pretty fast. Charley's not big on swimming in the deep end. He likes me to pull him around on those big foam mats and we judge cannonballs.

Jonah does silly dance moves on the diving board, rolling his shoulders up and back, one after the other, tossing his head around like he's some hot player-guy, turning away and wiggling his bum.

Frederick laughs. Then Jonah races off and flies and makes his body into a tight water bomb.

"Eight and a half," I say.

Frederick is pretty funny. He sort of jogs in slow motion along the board and then stops at the end. When he jumps he can't really get his legs in tight and lands with them spread out.

"Eleven," I say.

"No way, that sucked. Another ball buster," Charley says. "How does that feel, Frederick?"

Junior takes a break from doing lengths to yell out nasty scores like "negative zero."

At the end we're all in the hot tub hanging out and it's good. But we got a slow start so we're coming up on lunch time. We always buy Subway and sit at the tables to eat but we're late and these guys, you know, little things like being hungry, it's not good. Routines. So I'm saying, "Okay guys, let's get changed and grab some lunch."

"This is lame. We just got in," Junior says.

"I'm not even hungry," says Frederick.

"You're gonna be hungry soon," says Jonah.

"I'm hungry now," says Charley.

"You're always hungry, you pig," says Junior, poking Charley in the arm. "That's why the fucking fridge is locked for all of us." Poke, poke.

"Ow, don't." Charley holds his arm and turns away.

"Charley needs his lunch and so do I," I say.

Junior tells Frederick and Charley, "You guys are grownups and you let them treat you like you're still in diapers."

"Do not," says Frederick.

"Maybe you should be in diapers, Charley," Junior says. "Heard about Tim Hortons, chocolate doughnut shit spread all over the can, huh?"

Charley's arm's getting ready for chainsaw action.

"Cut it out, Junior," I say.

Junior gets things going, stirring it up, like. Back home we call those people, you know, agitators. They put them in the mines.

Unions. Everywhere. Pay them with whiskey, pay them with cash. They're the first ones at a protest to throw rocks, Molotov cocktails, making it okay to start firing. I'm not saying somebody put Junior in that group home to cause trouble. It's just, he's that kind of guy.

"Charley," I say, to stop him from whacking Junior, "what kind of Subway you gonna get today?"

"Chicken bacon ranch melt thousand island sauce no onions no olives," says Charley. But he's still keeping his eyes on Junior.

It's not easy to get three grown guys out of the hot tub when two of them don't want to go. It comes down to, "Okay, no Subway lunch for anyone, it's gonna be baloney sandwiches back home if you don't get out right now."

Frederick and Charley and me and Jonah get out and stand there, and finally Junior. He takes his time getting out slow as he can. He's dragging behind us, acting mister macho in his muscle body and skin head, looking the lifeguard girl up and down.

I'm kind of on edge, out of the rhythm, you get a rhythm going in a good basketball game with your team, me and Jonah try to get a good rhythm with our guys, it's hard enough and now Junior's just putting us off our game. I'm feeling, like, stress, watching Junior, expecting him to do something.

We get in the showers and rinse off and grab our stuff out of the lockers. My hawk eyes are on Junior. A few little boys, maybe a school group, are laughing and yelling, getting their swim shorts on. My cell phone rings. It's Michael, my youngest. I'm keeping my eyes on Junior and I'm still checking Charley. He's on the next bench over. I answer.

"Papa, I puked in the hall," Michael says. "Can you come and get me?"

"Where are you?"

"In the office," my boy says.

"Okay, son. I'll come soon as I can. Might be a little while."

"Then can Mama come?"

"She's still away, remember? Just rest. I'll be there."

I'm on the phone for five seconds, maybe ten. Junior's got his pants on. The boys race out to the pool. I put my phone away and turn to see how Charley's doing and he's gone. Disappeared. "Where's Charley?" I say.

Junior ignores me. Jonah says, "Charley was just here." I check in the cans by the shower. Nobody.

"Charley. Hey, Charley." I'm calling out. I'm hunting for him right away. I run out on the pool deck and call. I ask the lifeguard. "Have you seen my guy, Charley?" She hasn't seen him.

I rush back through the guys' change room and into the hallway with all the shoes. I hear my guy talking like he's talking to a friend but I can't make out the words. Where the hell is he? I hear a tiny cry and a rock's jammed in my throat. "Charley," I yell and, "I'm coming in." I push through the doors to the Ladies. He's standing there with a little girl in a bikini. With his shorts down and, yeah, okay, he has a hard-on but no way, he didn't, they're standing apart, okay, close but not touching, she's not moving, and he didn't touch her down there, anywhere, his hands, I can see them, no, I don't think he would have. He's a kid, he wants to play. But he's also a man. Nothing happens. I know she's crying, she's scared, but she has her bikini on, she's okay.

"Charley," I say. "Pull your shorts up."

But before he does a lady comes in looking for this little girl. The lady starts screaming, "Get away, you freak!" and, "Police! Police!" Asking me, "How did he get in here?" Grabbing him. Charley hits her. The lady yells. Charley runs. The little girl never moves. And I'm sinking down past the green to the black of Papa's mine. Where people die. They don't get to come out the other side.

My little sister begged me and begged me. "Teach me to swim, Edgar."

"You're too little," I always told her.

"No, I'm not," she said.

One day Lucy jumped in anyways. But she couldn't swim, she was taking in water, going under, before I made my quick move and swam over to hold her up. I had to teach her. She was ready.

"Push the water down like the turtle, make your hands wide, fingers together, flipper circles out and down."

Oh, she was good. She learned like that. Slippery strong and fast. She had gold in her hair. Papa said that was the only good thing came out of that mine. When the sunlight came down into the sinkhole, little bits here and there, it caught the green of the ferns. The gold of her hair. She was our shining fish.

The cops come, a guy and a lady. They're both big like bouncers. She puts handcuffs on Charley. He cries like a sad dog.

"He's a boy in a man's body," I tell them. "He never hurt her."

"Edgar, come with me," Charley says.

"I'm sorry, Charley. I can't. You gotta be brave and good, okay?"

He's looking at me with his trusting eyes. The cops take him away.

I pick up my sick little guy at school, hug him close. Bury my face in Michael's messy blond hair, the colour of sunshine.

I have to go to the police station in the afternoon and give my statement. They let me wait 'til Joseph's done school so he can stay home with his brother. I sit in a little room with those same cops. The door is closed. They want my name and address. I can't swallow and I start thinking, like, what if I can't swallow ever again and my spit piles up in my mouth and, you know, blocks the air, and I never see my little guys again.

"Hey. Mister Lombard. Edgar. Sir. Are you all right?" The lady.

"Water. Could I please?"

The guy gets me a glass of water. I take a sip. It goes down my throat. Okay.

I tell them everything. I got nothing to hide.

"Can I see Charley?" I ask.

"Not now," the lady says.

The next morning Rose phones me when I'm rushing the boys out the door to catch their bus. "You're suspended with pay while we investigate." They're doing Critical Incident Review but Rose says it's not her this time, it's someone higher up. She says, "You need to come in Friday at one for a meeting."

I'm allowed to have someone from my union with me so I ask my local. This short bald guy shows up. He has one of those little pointy beards, you know, a goatee. Armand. He pumps my hand when we meet, I'm thinking he's got my back, I can do this. I sit next to Armand and tell Mister Higher Up in his suit across the table about everything, play by play, not enough guys all winter, building up. Rose sits quiet for once. They're recording. Higher Up's a calm guy with grey hair, nodding and taking notes. Armand pats my arm at the end. "Good job," he says. I'm thinking it's gonna be okay.

After the weekend it gets in the newspapers, on the radio, the police saying a little girl was attacked at the pool. Now they have to make somebody pay. They fire me. Kick me out. Just like that. Six years I'm doing this job, taking care of guys nobody else wants to see. I got two little boys. Single dad. I never left my guys. Discharge with cause. What cause?

My union. I tell Armand, "Look, man, we file a grievance. I took my eyes off him for five seconds. We're watching an extra guy, a hard case. I told you that."

"We'll see." He doesn't shake my hand this time.

Then no word, nothing from my union. Every week I'm phoning. Until three weeks later Armand says, "No go, Edgar."

"What the hell is 'no go'?"

He says, "Our hands are tied. We can't win this one."

I can't believe it. The union can't see the rights they have in this country sitting in front of them like a full plate of meat and fish. They don't want to take those rights and chew them and swallow. Who do they think struggled for these rights? People.

Where I come from, they kill union members. Miners. Students. Journalists. Lawyers. Politicians. Teachers. Anybody who speaks out. But they hurt them first, this army of monsters with hearts darker than the centre of the earth. We knew some of their names. Red Devil. The Knife. The Wolf.

I'm not just watching guys. I'm educated. I was a union leader. I know my rights. And this is not right. They're throwing me away for vultures to pick out my eyeballs. They don't care. I'm the lamb.

They cut my throat and let me bleed so they can save themselves and tell the newspapers and the parents everything is okay. It's not okay. I meet Jonah and Chris at Tim Hortons one night. It's July. My little guys are with their mom for the week. She came down from the nursing station for a visit.

Chris's girlfriend had a baby boy. "He weighs eighteen pounds already," Chris says. "Just smiling all the time, he's a jolly guy."

"Way to go," I say. I'm happy for him, trying to be positive.

"You do diapers?" Jonah asks.

"Yup. All part of the deal."

"I did lots of diapers with my boys," I say.

"My father, never," says Jonah.

"Is Charley doing okay?" I ask Jonah. I'm not even supposed to say hi to Charley. He's not in jail but everything will be in court. What if I see Charley walking by right now? I'm gonna wave at him. Fuck them.

"Charley asks about you. He misses you. But don't worry, Edgar," Jonah says. "The new worker's treating him nice."

"That's good."

"Guess what?" Jonah says. "I applied for a job at Northwestel. Accounting department."

"Cool," says Chris.

"You got a degree in that, right?" I say.

"Yeah, totally," says Jonah.

"I got news," says Chris. "I start up at the college this fall. For teaching."

Jonah's mouth opens up wide, then he grins. "Right on."

"Teacher," I say. The word sits like a smooth stone on my tongue.

"Edgar, don't sound so shocked. Don't think I can do it?"

"Oh no, sorry, man, you're gonna be great," I say. "I was a teacher back home. High school."

"No way," Jonah says.

"You never told us," says Chris.

A lady at another table is looking at me. Her son was in Michael's class. She whispers something to her friend. They're staring. They look away quick when they see me.

Sucked down. No air, no sun, only the dark centre of the earth.

"Edgar. Edgar, my friend. Here. Have some coffee."

Jonah's talking to me. Holding my cup out. He's not touching. He knows not to.

I want to throw up. I'm going to throw up.

"They don't put my name in the papers but people know. Parents at my boys' school know. Their kids tell my kids I let perverts run loose. Joseph got in a fight and ended up in the principal's office on his last day of school. They should take hot metal and burn it into my skin. I'm the guy who let the pervert attack a little girl. Nobody wants to hire me. I raise my boys here, I volunteer, I work hard. Now my name, my reputation, gone. Nothing. And what about my boys? They're innocent. How am I gonna be there for them?"

Next thing there's coffee spilled all over our table, dripping on to my shorts, the floor. A broken mug on the floor. More people are looking at me. I'm shaking, I'm not swallowing. I have to get out of here.

"Edgar, wait, don't go," Jonah says.

Stone-hard faces, judging.

"It's okay, I got it." Chris wipes up the mess with napkins.

"Sit down. Let it go," Jonah says. He holds his hand out to me. "My friend."

I sit back down.

"Sometimes you gotta walk away," Jonah says. "You and me both know that."

"Look how long it took us to get land claims here," says Chris, "and we're still fighting for respect. It never ends, brother."

I don't say anything. I'm thinking, maybe I don't walk away. I run. Maybe the boys stay with their mother. Maybe it's better like that.

Back home we were going to show everyone. What's not right. We were speaking out. We were protesting.

They had eyes always watching. They watched us get on a bus, get off a bus. They sat behind us on the bus. They watched us go to work, they watched us come home. They watched the people we love. Our lovers. Our mothers and our fathers and our sisters.

They watched. They hunted. They chased. And they had quick feet.

Sometimes they took us in. For a few days, weeks, months. Sometimes they let us out. Me, I was lucky. Only eighteen days in the dark with The Wolf. His breath stank of tobacco and cinnamon. Those smells still make me vomit. When I limped out I left behind nails, shit, and blood. I still had my fingers, my toes, my ears, eyes, and balls. My scars and my nightmares.

I didn't stop speaking out.

Lucy went missing on the way home from college one night. We walked the way she walked, to home and back, in her footsteps. We checked with her friends. Nothing. By then Papa was almost dead from the mine, his lungs drowning, sucking for air that never came.

The next morning me and Mama went to the police station. The officer was fat. His shirt buttons looked ready to pop. He said, "She probably ran off with her boyfriend." He laughed in a dirty way. I wanted to slap him but my mama held my arm.

Me and my uncles, my cousins, my friends, we searched the ditches and fields, the quarry, the dump, places where people turned up. We didn't tell Mama that. Every day we looked. Nothing. A week later a little boy came to our door with his papa. "The sinkhole," the man said.

She was floating face up. I swam out and carried her to the edge. We laid her on the soft and green. Our golden shining fish. Our baby. Seventeen years old. She had no nails left on her fingers, her toes. I knew. They used her as a message to me.

We carried her body to the police station. I tried not to let Mama see. But she said, "I was the first to see her and I will be the last." I can never forget how my mama howled.

The police told us Lucy drowned. But I taught her to swim.

I held Mama through the funeral the best I could.

And then I ran in the night. I walked through the mountains, I waded through rivers, I got to the border, I looked back once and said goodbye.

And my wife, my beautiful wife, she was born here in this country, she tried to understand. But she couldn't take the nightmares.

I never swim again.

Until Charley.

When I went for the job they told me the guys go swimming. I needed that job. I was looking for work for a long time. I swam for Charley because I had to. It made him happy.

And you can see the bottom of that pool.

It's the beginning of August. Summer is short here. Joseph is begging me, "Take us to Long Lake. Take us swimming. Please, Papa."

I told my guys all these years, their papa can't swim. Their mother is the one who takes them. "I don't want to go to the lake," I say. "It's not safe."

"That's not fair. Mom can't take us all summer 'cause she's not here," Joseph says.

She came down for that one week but she's staying away working 'til the end of August.

"You never do anything fun with us anymore," Joseph says. "And there's nothing to eat."

"We had popcorn yesterday," Michael says.

"It's all gone," says Joseph.

"I'm sorry, I forgot to get groceries, I'll get them today." Their mom sent money but I'm their dad, I didn't want to take it.

Michael pokes his big brother. "Joseph, stop. Papa's got more nightmares."

They're looking at me. Joseph is frowning. Michael has questions in his eyes, I can see he's worried about me. They're my boys and it's summer. I'm their papa. What am I doing to them?

"All right. We're gonna get a whole bunch of snacks."

"Doughnuts. And chips," Joseph says.

"Yeah. And we're gonna go swimming. Let's go."

"Yes!" Joseph yells, raising his fist in victory.

But little Michael says, "Are you sure, Papa? It's okay if we don't."

I crouch down and look into his brown eyes. "My sweet boy." I mess up his thick hair. It gets even lighter in summer. There's a clump of knots. He hates combing his hair and I guess I haven't done it for a while. "I'm sure," I say.

We eat our box of Tim's doughnuts in the car on the way there. I park and we walk along the trail through the trees until the boys find their favourite little beach. Their mother's a good swimmer and they had lessons. But the water's cold here. This lake gets deep pretty fast. I tell them not to go out far. I watch them like a hawk. They splash around, throw mud at each other. It's slimy green-black with, you know, that algae. They take an air mattress and pump it up and float around. They're only a little ways out so I sit on a log and try to relax, take my shoes off and feel the sand. I never take my eyes off them.

But they're laughing and fooling around. Pushing each other off. Going further out. Next thing Joseph kicks away with the mattress and his little brother tries to keep up.

"Hey, you guys, that's too far." I jump up.

"Joseph, wait," Michael says.

Joseph's giggling and saying, "Gotta catch me."

I run to the water. "Joseph, stop. You guys come back." I can hear every word they say like they're right next to me but they don't hear me or they're ignoring me. They get further out. It's cloudy today, not so warm and only Tuesday, we have the lake to ourselves.

"Michael. Joseph. Come. Back. Right. Now." I scream loud as I can. They're still not hearing. Then I see the air mattress go flat.

I don't want to. I have to. I step into the lake. My feet sink in soft muck.

Joseph's dragging the leaking mattress, telling his brother to come on. Michael's not coming.

Slime locks round my ankles.

"Hurry up," Joseph says. "We gotta fix this."

Swallows my breath.

Joseph swims back to Michael. He's trying to help his brother and hold on to the mattress. It's not working. Joseph says, "Papa, Michael's got a cramp."

I never taught them to push the water down like the turtle.

Joseph tells Michael, "Let me carry you. Lie back," but Michael won't do it.

Ooze fills my lungs.

"Papa! Help us!" Joseph howls.

Sucking me down.

Even though he's fighting to keep his head up, Michael's saying, "No, Papa." He doesn't want me to get hurt. He's swallowing water, he's getting scared and making it worse. Then his head goes under.

Lift my foot. Set it free.

The muck is the colour of my boys' first baby poo after they were born, before their first mama's milk. Dark green-black.

I yank one foot free, then the other and dive under water, my arms gliding, shooting me out. I swim slippery-fast, pushing water with flipper hands. I pull Michael up and tell him, "It's okay." Lean his head against my chest and kick back to shallow water, stand up and carry him to the shore. Lay him on the sand. He's coughing and shivering. I rub him off really good with a towel, his head too, his golden hair. I wrap him up and hold him tight even though I'm still wet. We sit in the sand, he puts his head into my neck, and we stay there like that.

Joseph's standing over us guarding and crying. "I'm sorry we went out so far, Papa. Is Michael gonna be okay?"

Then Michael's face leaves my neck. "I'm okay, Joseph."

Snot pours out of Joseph's nose. He wipes it with his arm.

"Papa," Michael says. "You do know how to swim." He has this look in his eyes like I have superpowers.

"Yeah, Papa," Joseph says. "You're an awesome swimmer."

I make my hands wide, pulling Joseph into the hug. These are my guys. These are always my guys.

Because things are not right. Because it starts with our children. Because I want to be a teacher again. Because I'm good with kids. I'm telling you. That's why you should take me into your program.

I'm not getting sucked down to the centre of the earth. I'm gonna come out the other side. Where families eat warm dough-nuts sprinkled with sugar. That's another thing. I know how to make doughnuts.

Such a Lovely Afternoon

IT WAS SUNNY AND WARM and that Pacific Ocean breeze fluttered on my skin. I lay in my bikini on a lawn chair, free, my toddler and my man half a country away.

Shadow blocked my sun. Andy towered over me in her shorts and a sports bra, cider in hand, her strawberry-blonde hair pulled high with a scrunchie.

"Funny way to spend Mother's Day," Andy said, "lounging in your bathing suit in your dead mother's backyard."

"Mom would say, 'Get off your duffs, girls.'"

"Yeah, totally." Andy laid the cold bottle against my belly. I yelped and she jumped away laughing. "Payback. I'm bigger than you now."

She took a swig of cider. I stared. My youngest sister was nearly six feet tall and ripped. Even the scar above her left eyebrow looked rugged. It was from rugby in high school after I was long gone, she'd told me. She was four years younger than me. Her face now much older. Somehow Andy had become broken. Licking her wounds, moving into Mom's spare room last year.

A glint on Andy's ear. "Are those Mom's pearl earrings?"

"Yeah, I just felt like wearing them." Andy sank into her lawn chair. "Okay?"

I didn't know how I felt about that. Andy used to "borrow" my clothes, never to be seen again. Maybe I did the same to Kim, our eldest sister.

"Okay. Not okay then," Andy said lightly.

"Okay. Just, let's go through her things together. With Kim too."

Moments before, Andy and I had finished the edging. My sisters had trimmed the grass and hedges, weeded the flower beds, planted geraniums and marigolds, and put up hanging baskets before I flew in. Kim was managing the estate, including the sale of the house, and the debts. Our mother adored the best of everything and lived for the moment. Often generous—and often strapped, she borrowed money from each of her girls regularly, surreptitiously, a little here, a little there. There was no will to be found.

"Terri," Andy said to me, "I want to behave well, you know? Towards Dude."

I knew she meant the fiancé. Things had gone badly. A hyper-energetic Type A with a twitching eye, older than Mom, some kind of investor, it was never quite clear. Dwayne was from that generation of white men used to being in control. He was against my request to view Mom's body right away before she got puffy, not that I let him stop me. Then he had a conniption when our father showed up for the funeral. "Mom would want us to treat her fiancé well," I said. "Even if Dude's a douche-bag."

Andy leaned forward in her lawn chair. "Us girls need to stick together, you, me, and Kim. No matter what."

"You're right. No matter what." I ruffled her ponytail.

A yelp from Snookie startled me. Our aging family pet, a chunky Golden Retriever with a whitened muzzle, lay asleep dreaming in the shade. Andy had taken care of the dog when Mom travelled with her fiancé.

"What about you?" I asked. "Are you done. With him?"

Andy nursed her cider.

"God, Andy, no, the way that scumbag treated you."

Andy wielded her bottle like a weapon. "Spare me your fucking pity. And don't you dare judge me. Run back to your perfect little house on the prairie. Pancake flat, far, far away."

I wanted to say it wasn't easy for me either. Finding space to breathe, in between all of you. Leaving to build a life of my own. Severed from ocean, from blood. I said nothing.

The scarlet runner beans Mom had planted crept up the white lattice along the back stairs. Her sweet peas by the garage were in full bloom. A lavender sweet pea stood alone at the west side of the house, the single plant that had survived the winter, the one blooming when she died eight weeks before.

Her attic is twilight dust brown, holding me, shadow people, and her belongings. Here's a photograph, one of Mom's favourites, mauve wildflowers on the Oregon coast. Suddenly, I sense her alive behind me. I must be more discreet. Should I tell Mom what's going to happen to her? Hurry, decide, don't wake up yet...

My palms were damp, my forehead too. I didn't mean to fall asleep outside. Still groggy, I phoned Grandma from Mom's kitchen. She picked up after nine rings. She told me she'd been up making jam since five. She's eighty-eight. She's been on her own since Grandpa died. I never flew in for his funeral. I couldn't afford it, and Mom didn't offer to pay.

"Well," Grandma sighed. "I'd picked all the boysenberries, and the raspberries, and the loganberries until oh, about two this morning." She took a deep breath between each berry. "Another day and they'd be overripe. I couldn't let them go to waste."

Her jam jars, shelves upon shelves in the basement pantry, sat unappetizingly close to Grandpa's larger jars of pickled fetuses, baby animals, a biology teacher's bag of tricks. Her jars had labels like Ginger Peach and Pear Chutney in pinched handwriting, not much neater than her daughter's notorious scrawl. Each label was dated, as with every note she made. Photos. Recipes. Cards. Is jam from 1971 still safe to eat? Grandpa's jars didn't have labels.

"Grandma, you could have frozen the berries."

"Althea was my youngest. Tomorrow I've got to go to the courthouse, and Kim will pick me up shortly before eight-thirty, and the hearing begins shortly after nine, and that lady, that foreign lady called me."

"Lola-Maria from Victim Services? She's from the Philippines, Grandma. She's Canadian now."

"Yes. Well. Mr. and Mrs. Lancaster from our church have a son, John. Or is it George?"

Out the back-door window, I watched the sun glittering on the inlet between roofs and cedar trees.

"Their son George Lancaster met a young girl in Japan, a Japanese. Not Chinese. I don't know if she's a Christian or a Buddhist. And they're engaged to be married."

Grandma paused. Smiling to myself, I guessed that her tangentially related jaunt into the Lancaster family had another unstated point—trying to figure out how her blonde granddaughter, me, had met and fallen in love with a different-coloured boy. Without getting married in any church. "He's very dark," she had told me in a confiding tone just after she met Bal.

"Althea was a dear thing." Her voice on the phone seemed to shrink. "When I went out to sell magazines door to door, she put her little arms around my legs. She said 'Please Mommy, don't go.'"

I saw Mom as a toddler, white-blonde wisps, holding on for dear life. Millie, sobbing, would not let go of me yesterday at the airport. Bal had to pry her away. Walking through security wiping tears and snot with my sleeve, I felt like I was abandoning our little one.

"Grandma. I'll see you in the morning, okay?"

With my sisters' approval I was driving Mom's new car, gleaming red, an expensive luxury compact with hefty monthly payments, according to Kim. Andy and I ate Thai food in a delicate truce before arguing over who would pay the bill. Andy wanted me to cover it since she was between jobs and I hadn't been around to help. I pointed out that she had free rent and I had to pay for my flight. We split the bill.

At sunset we hung out at the cemetery with a view of the Fraser River flowing towards the sea. I sprawled on the grass next to the grave. She sat cross-legged and smoked—she'd started again last month. We brought sweet peas and said nothing for a while.

"She talks with anybody and everybody, Ter. About Mom."

"Who?"

"Grandma. I took her out for lunch. We had to wait in the lobby for a table. Grandma starts talking to the people sitting across from us, complete strangers with little kids. Tells them all about her daughter being murdered. She went on and on."

"No way."

The sun slid away.

"How are you doing?" I asked.

"*Now* you're asking?"

"Yes. I am."

She shrugged, then looked straight at me. "I literally can't remember most of the past two months. It's like being in a fog, you know?"

"Yeah. I feel like I'm swimming out of control. With this undertow. I can't see it. And it's sweeping me away."

"Oh yeah," she agreed.

"There's real time and then this other time. It doesn't fit into clocks. It blurs edges and makes you feel one beat off."

"I'm with you," Andy said. "I'm so there."

She touched my arm. Her fingers were rough. I felt safe.

"I want you to visit. Please."

Andy gave my arm a squeeze. "Maybe," she said.

Kim and Grandma were late. Andy smoked outside on the courthouse steps. I stood upwind scanning the street—the rec centre with the pool we all practically lived in as kids, thanks to Mom's old life as a swim instructor. The pedestrian arch I spat on cars from, the gas station across the busy thoroughfare. It used to be a big old-fashioned house and garden belonging to my mother's aunt. The night before the demolition Mom and I had sneaked in and dug up the filbert nut tree to plant behind our picnic table.

Kim appeared from around the corner, one hand resting gently on Grandma's hunched back. Kim was almost as tall as Andy. I got the short straw. Grandma moved with slow, steady steps, dignified in a fifties-era outfit in a faded green. I wondered if she had sewed the wool skirt and jacket herself when she was a home economics teacher. A leaf brooch, shiny green stones framed in gold, and matching clip-on earrings enlivened the drab fabric. Her pale face was powdered, her lipstick a muted red, her flaxen hair coiffed. Kim wore one of her power suits, streamlined grey blazer and slacks, slimming her big-boned figure. More luxurious, shapely. More like Mom.

"Somebody says she was all ready but couldn't hear me knocking." Kim had a rueful smile. "I had to call her on my cell."

Andy laughed. I joined in with a desperate giddiness. Grandma seemed befuddled. I kissed her cheek. A woman about my age, in her late twenties, with long legs and charcoal hair, climbed the steps. "Carmela?" I said. "Carmela Gonzales?"

"Yeah. Oh. Hi Terri. I'm..." She blushed. "I'm really sorry about your Mom."

"Thanks." We stood on the steps for a second. Andy threw her butt into the hedge. I asked Carmela, "What are you doing here?"

"I'm a court clerk."

She went to elementary school with me. She was the best high jumper. Mom taught her how to swim, she taught everyone in the neighbourhood before she went back to school. Nobody knew me when I moved to the eastern edge of the prairies. I felt visible with Carmela. I'd forgotten what that was like, but it was okay, having her there. She knew me. She knew Mom. She would listen to every word.

We sat in the second row of wooden benches and waited for the preliminary hearing to begin. The lawyers appeared. We stood as the judge walked in. A guard escorted him in and led him to the prisoner's box. We had seen him once before at his first court appearance.

> He's plain.
> He's plump.
> He's wide.
> He's grey.

He doesn't say anything.
He looks around.
He's weird.

Kim had a leather-bound journal with the college's logo. Grandma brought a tiny book with a brown cover and yellowed pages inside. It looked older than her jam. I had a coil notebook from the drugstore and a pit in my gut. Andy had her hands to clench.

"I went to church last evening," Grandma said loudly. "I spoke with Dr. Malcolm and his wife, whose six-month-old baby was just christened. I told them I once had a little baby like that whose name was Althea."

Andy and I exchanged a glance.

The gun is a 45-calibre Colt semi-automatic handgun. (See Exhibit A.)

The constable takes dried blood off the weapon. See container holding small flakes of blood. (D.) How blond and boyish he is. Constable James.

A young girl and her father find the bullet up the street. (Photo 11. Young girl and her father.)

The floral-patterned shirt is torn badly.

See the constable use scissors to cut the bags.

Grandma kept leaning towards Kim, scanning her notes, before returning to her little book. She tugged my arm. "What did that man say?" she whispered.

"They found her purse on the pavement in a..." I hesitate. "In a pool of blood."

Grandma stiffened.

"Where's your hearing aid?"

She patted her purse. "I don't know how it works."

At the morning recess she pulled her hearing aid and the instruction pamphlet out of her purse. There were notes and underlined sections throughout the pamphlet and scribbles on the inside top cover of the velvet box. Kim read through the pamphlet and had Grandma try her aid.

"Testing, testing, one, two, three," she said.

"What?" she said.

Andy turned it up. "Testing, testing, Mars to Jupiter."

"Oh!" She pulled the aid out.

Andy said, "Guess that's too loud."

Mom lies in the fetal position on her right side. In the crosswalk. Outside the café. On the west side of the road. Corporal McLarney knows. He gets the call at 12:27. He's the first officer there. Mom's right arm outstretched, her skin "ghostly pale." She has a chest wound. Her eyes and mouth are open. Blood trickles from her mouth. Under her arms, inches from her chest, the gun lies jammed. The corporal knows because he moves it to make room for the ambulance workers. He handles it with surgical gloves. Empties it. Beside him stands a stocky man in a trench coat and a salt-and-pepper beard. "He was very polite."

A Grey Man. Average. Non-threatening. Hiding in plain sight.

The ID squad officer found no suitable prints on the gun or casing. Andy turned to me, wide-eyed. "That's bad."

I shook my head. "There's lots of other evidence."

She didn't seem convinced.

Grandma looked over. "What was that?" Her hearing aid was on her lap.

A retired RCMP officer drives home, his car windows open. Why not, the spring afternoon is glorious. He notices two people on the sidewalk at the corner, talking. A woman in a bright shirt. A man. Blink. The woman walks away. Mom. Blink. She steps into the crosswalk. Blink again. The man raises his arm. There's a loud bang. Flames leap out. Mom slumps. The ex-cop pulls over about two hundred feet past. Calls the 9-1-1 operator on his cell phone. And watches from his rear-view mirror. The man with the weapon looks around. Grey hair. Grey slacks. He walks to the body, gun in hand, and bends down. He stands up. He steps out into the street. He appears to be waving at vehicles. Directing traffic.

At afternoon break, the freckled corporal told us, "Your mother was probably dead before she hit the ground."

> Admissions of fact from the baggy-pants prosecutor.
> The day is sunny.
> Grey Man walks his little dog a lot.
> The woman on the road is my mother.
> Paramedics arrive at 1:33 p.m.
> She's at the hospital at 1:44.
> She's officially dead at 2:05.
> She's locked in a crypt overnight, in the hospital where she gave birth to me.
> She's cut open the next day.
> The bullet passes through her heart, diaphragm, stomach, and spleen. Death is rapid due to hemorrhage in left chest cavity.

I needed to go for a ride and Andy didn't want to go back to Mom's alone. We had the windows down as we passed the grain elevators where a boy in high school lost his dad in an accident, the walls of blackberries across from the rail line. The distillery and its gardens where our parents took us on Christmas runs to see the pretty lights and buy overproof rum for eggnog. Up the mountain road past the college where Kim worked in finance and back down again. Past Dad's new condo. Andy and I didn't say much. I didn't feel like talking and I guess neither did she. The breeze was soothing.

That evening I braved one-lane bridge traffic on the way to the long outdoor pool, the largest in the city, facing out onto the bay and the mountains. The salt water was cool. My arms ached when I climbed out. In the change rooms a mother dressed her fat-cheeked child who looked about two, the same age as Millie. I felt naked without her.

I wondered what passed before Mom's eyes as she fell. The trip to Paris with her fiancé. The dahlias she was ready to plant. Her daughters, her grandchild. Or careening down the hill on her bicycle half a century ago, arms stretched wide, hair and streamers flying in the wind.

I'm returning to my "starter home" but it's gone upscale. Instead of gravel and boulders it has a lawn. I have to check my garden. It's erupted since I've been gone, sweet peas ten feet high with monster blooms. I see my baby, only eight weeks old. She still wants to breastfeed. We crawl into the house together, me, my husband and baby, using a miniature door. It's like being in Alice in Wonderland. *We're too big and the door's too small. Mom never got to see this house. Well, she wouldn't have fit!*

I was awake by five-thirty in Mom's bed, tossing and turning and nervous as hell. I put on my housecoat, then dug out my blue cotton dress and ironed it, which I rarely do. Making coffee, I started at a noise outside and dumped it all over myself, even my underwear. I swore and got changed and wrote my dream down before I lost it.

Andy got up and made more coffee. I described my sleep sojourn to her at the kitchen table.

"I dream too," she said. "Mom visits like everything is normal. The last one, I'm a little kid. It's one of those winter mornings all rainy and bleak, you know you'll be soaked before you get to school. I can't drag myself out of bed. I smell waffles. I jump up and run to the kitchen. Mom's there just like always. She butters my waffles. Cuts them up for me. Pours the syrup all over so it really soaks in. I eat my warm waffles slathered in melted butter. Its normal and it's warm and I'm so happy, Ter. I wake up with this energy glow buzzing around my entire body."

I smiled so I wouldn't cry.

"I feel good after those dreams."

I nodded.

Mister Spencer is in construction. He's solid in the witness box, hands on hips, short and tough and balding. Husky voice. Says "okay" and "you know." He sees the crowd pointing as he's driving. Someone waving their arms. Thinks car accident, maybe a pedestrian. He pulls over, gets out. Someone lying on the street. Gentleman stooped over in a raincoat. He asks to help. Grey Man says, "Heart attack." Mister Spencer sees a body and a gun, says to himself, "Well, this doesn't look like a heart attack to me."

"No, no," says Grey Man to his lawyer, "I thought *I* was having the heart attack."

"Then he says 'suicide' to me. Next thing, the cops are there." Mister Spencer knows the guy. "I seen him walk around the park with his little dog quite a few times."

The low-eared defence lawyer asks, "How many times?"

"I don't have enough fingers and toes." Mister Spencer's not friendly with Grey Man. He tried that once. "I said something to him and he seemed very snappy. Well, how would you feel if somebody told you to kiss your you know what? I'd avoid him, yes. I've had my days too. I don't know if he's a nutball or nothing."

The last two months Grey Man changes his walk. All of a sudden. He walks on and on. His dog's gone.

That's the saddest thing.

My sisters, Grandma, and I walked down the block to the White Spot for lunch. My husband prefers calling it the Brown Spot. When we went there after the funeral, Bal told me, "You never see brown people in there." Except when he's there. I said, "It's my culture." I grew up on Pirate Paks with hamburgers inside a cardboard ship. Mom would eat half our fries in the car on the way home.

Grandma ordered liver and onions. The rest of us had burgers, mine with mushrooms and Triple O sauce.

"It's as if the defence is painting him as some mental case packing a pistol who just couldn't help himself," Andy said.

"That's definitely their strategy," I said, "going for not criminally responsible."

"He had to recognize her. He was Mom's old client. That's what the police told us. That bastard knew exactly what he was doing," Kim said.

I wasn't so sure but I didn't say that out loud. "How's your lunch, Grandma?"

"Well, dear." She chewed slowly. "I'm not feeling very hungry." If my fingers touched her cheek, the skin would crackle and break.

> The handsome corporal with the square jaw testifies.
> Grey Man is handcuffed on the street.
> He tells the corporal it was an accident.
> It was an argument.
> It was such a lovely afternoon for something like this
>   to happen.
> Mom is loaded onto the stretcher.
> Grey Man wants to know, Can I look at the victim?
> Have you ever served in Vietnam?
> No, the corporal answers.
> Neither did I, says Grey Man. Neither did I.

Out of breath, my lungs exploding, I trailed along the seawall behind my father and his girlfriend, who motored along on their thin muscled legs. Jogging was my father's obsession. Even Andy, the most athletic of us sporty girls, resisted Dad's endless training runs, fun runs, the half-marathons, his advice for us all to jog before whatever physical activity we were enrolled in. I liked to move for reward, tramping through rolling hills covered in wildflowers, playing hockey in the winters. Out of numbness, probably, I agreed to Dad's offer to meet up after the day's court proceedings "for the tail-end, cool-down loop" of his run.

"Wait up, guys. Dad?!" They stopped as I caught up. "Can we just walk for a bit?"

Priscilla looked annoyed. Quick, intense, she was a criminal prosecutor, considerably younger than Dad. Her parents had emigrated from Hong Kong but unlike so many residents, she was born in this city.

"Out of shape, are we?" Dad poked my midriff.

"Why don't you two catch up while I finish my run. Honest to God it's been one of those weeks," Priscilla said.

"But our big news." Strangely keyed up, Dad gazed at Priscilla with adoring eyes. I didn't recall him doling that out for Mom. Maybe in the beginning.

"Oh, right, of course," Priscilla said.

"What news?" I said automatically, before realizing I didn't actually want any news.

"Well, let's at least walk," Priscilla said, "or I'll cramp up."

We switched direction, walking back towards the beach parking lot. I was in between them. Mixed with the salty sea air, Dad smelled of sweat and cologne, Priscilla of an almond shampoo she used, an expensive one she'd gifted me a bottle of. It was awkward trying to walk and talk in a lateral trio while other runners, roller skaters, skateboarders, and bikers meandered and hurtled towards us. It was awkward when Dad delivered their "news."

"Guess what? Hold on to your socks. Priscilla's having a baby." Dad had a grin like a circus clown. I always found clowns terrifying.

"Whose is it?" I blurted out. I didn't mean it to be sarcastic.

"Ours, of course," he said, with a baffled frown.

Someone bumped into me. Moving shapes blurred, people, rushing, crowding, birds, white ones, seagulls, crying. I was distantly aware that I had stopped moving. The air was fishy and raw. I felt nearly as dazed as Grey Man directing traffic.

Priscilla said, "Congratulations, Priscilla. I'm so happy for you," her sarcasm understated.

This was surreal. My father was having a baby younger than my baby. I was going to have a newborn sibling.

"I, yeah, that's, that's wild. When are you due to, to, have it come out...?" Words proved elusive. Someone asked us not very nicely to get off the seawall if we were going to stand in the way. A milky-white splat on the cement—a seagull barely missed shitting on me.

"Gareth, she's about to keel over."

"She's fine. Ter's a tough nut."

Priscilla wrapped her arm around my shoulder and guided me to a nearby bench. She had maternal urges. This boded well.

Like Mom's fiancé, Dad was a white man of a certain generation. Was Priscilla ready for my father? Maybe, if she could squeeze enough of herself into his life without losing her fire, the way Mom hadn't been able to do. He might not ever love Priscilla or the baby as much as running or fly-fishing or the fact that he still had viable sperm. But it might be enough. Should I tell her? Did she already know?

Priscilla ducked into the public bathroom next to the concession. We waited outside.

"Dad. Don't forget about Priscilla. Make yourself do fun things with her, things that she cares about, even if you don't want to." Bal was trying. He and Millie cheered me on in hockey although he hated the game. Maybe I wasn't trying hard enough.

My father laughed my lecture off.

"Dad, I'm serious."

He finally asked, "How is the hearing going?"

"It's pretty rough."

"Right." His eyes were downcast.

I should have stopped there. "There were lots of witnesses in cars and on the sidewalk. Somebody talked about..." It was impossible to cushion it. "About him trying to fire another shot and the gun jamming."

"Good God." He looked away. He wiped his eyes. "Okay then. Okay." He patted my back. It felt good, like something a father was supposed to do.

Their final years together had been turbulent. Andy, still in high school, got the worst of it. Afterwards Mom would get in a fluff seeing his car outside her place dropping one of us off, that's how much he got her going. Even the last time I brought Millie and Bal back, at Christmas, I asked Dad to stop down the street when he drove us back to Mom's.

"Althea was a good gal," Dad told me after the funeral. "You don't spend twenty years with a gal and just stop, you know."

I knew what he was trying to say.

I'm at my school desk surrounded by people. Oh no not back in high school please. My head's on the desk. I'm shaking. My mother's standing near me. "How are you doing?" I ask her. She barely answers. It's so obvious. She's in pain like me.

The next morning I watched Grey Man sit in court, shifting, glancing around, his bulk dwarfing his lawyer's skinny head. The police had told us that Mom was his caseworker a few years back when she worked in income assistance. They knew each other. Mom used to say most of the clients were the salt of the earth, people with bad breaks, there but for the grace of God. But one or two scared her to death. Was Grey Man one of those?

> He comes to Emergency, six weeks before.
> He sees a Doctor Leary.
> Grey Man explains to Doctor Leary.
> He hurt his shoulder on the docks.
> He's been five years in a coma.
> How much does a guy have to fork over to get surgery
>   around here?
> He's blown up a dock.
> Murdered lots of people.
> He's on the floor screaming.
> He grabs Doctor Leary, pulls his legs out from under him.
> It's "fairly obvious" to the doctor he has
>   psychiatric problems.
> Paranoid tendencies.
> Personality disorder.
> The doctor says he is not committable.
> At this point in time.
> The cops take him.
> Find the knife hidden in his back brace.
> And let him go.

The judge ruled that there's sufficient evidence for Grey Man to stand trial. The hearing adjourned before three. The day was glorious.

Hugging the shoreline, we paddled up the scenic fjord surrounded by the steep coastal mountains. Kim had her own kayak and I rented one in the shop in the cove.

Kim's powerful bare arms were muscled. I marvelled as she unloaded her kayak from the top of her car, grabbed the rim of the cockpit with her hand, and packed it to the dock like it was a beach bag. She had to help me carry mine down from the back of the shop, each of us holding a carry handle at either end.

Kim was the firstborn who excelled in school and didn't talk back or skip out. No smoking in the courtyard, smoking up in the trails, or riding in the back of pickup trucks to bush parties up the intake road like me and Andy. To Mom's delight Kim was a competitive swimmer, before her shoulder went out in high school and she got chunky and flabby and then dangerously thin. I would hear her throwing up in the bathroom late at night. See her bloodshot eyes. We were two years apart, far enough. I struggled on the fringes of my year's in-crowd. She and her small group of misfit friends didn't care about being popular. Which of course meant, I knew now, that Kim's crowd was cool beyond cool.

We paddled past the luxury homes to forested shorelines. Kim pulled up next to me. "Hold us together, I've got a surprise."

I grabbed hold of her cockpit. There was a light chop, rocking us gently. "My last surprise was a new baby sibling. I almost got shat on by seagulls while I stood in shock on the seawall."

"That's a good story. You can work with that."

"Did you know about Priscilla being preggo?"

"They made me promise not to say anything."

"Traitor!" I whined loudly.

"They wanted to tell you in person." Kim reached into her front hatch. "This is a good surprise." She unfolded a small tray and a mesh bag. Out of it came clear drinking cups, lime wedges, a bottle.

"Tequila, seriously?"

Kim poured two generous shots and passed one over with a crescent of lime. She'd even salt-rimmed the plastic cup.

"Down the hatch, as Mom would say." Kim downed hers and bit into her lime. I did the same.

"This is maybe not Red Cross water safe," I pointed out. "Drinking and boating."

"That's what life jackets are for." She gestured for my cup. I complied. She poured for us again.

"Mom's estate is a gong show. She has four lines of credit."

"Good consumer capitalist." I could feel the second shot warming my veins.

I'd never been out on the water like this with my big sister. We used to do everything together. Forts in the woods. Playing tricks on the boys down the street. Endless games of Monopoly on rainy days. Then she was in high school, moody, somehow unreachable. Later both of us moved away to different universities, different cities, with me staying away.

She'd visited soon after Millie was born, but then with her new job hadn't made her way back. Kim and her wife didn't want kids of their own.

"I haven't been there for you," I blurted out. Maybe the tequila was talking.

"What the hell, Ter. You have a baby."

"I wasn't there for you. In high school."

"That's not your job. You were my kid sister for godsake."

"I knew. That you ate a lot and then... had an eating disorder."

"Yeah. Well. I wasn't there for you either," Kim said. "Things happened to you too."

Did Kim know about that? Pulled into the truck's back seat, locked in, held down, mouth covered, hands reeking of gasoline, a part-time gas station attendant, a "good kid." At a bush party. Before cell phone videos went viral, social media, thank God. Not before consent and gossip and the worst thing you could call a girl. Slut.

Kim poured us one more shot "for good luck."

Out here in salt foam her face was relaxed. She looked drunk and happy.

Grandma's house was musty, fusty browns and beige, the odour of apple dumplings and spilt jam and fresh-cut flowers. Grandpa, who had died shortly before Millie was born, lingered in his potting shed and the vegetable garden across the street next to the railway tracks.

That evening we had tea and cookies in the dining room. Grandma wanted to talk about her horses. Grandma and her sisters grew up on a farm in Saskatchewan.

"Minnie and Daisy were the nice horses. We would take them, the buggy, and the wagon loaded with sixty bushels of wheat, the four miles to the grain elevator. Daisy drove us to our music lessons on Saturdays. She was a dear. She would let us comb her mane or the hair of her tail, the coarse hair, and you could walk underneath, one side to the other, she'd never kick or bite us."

Grandma set her cup down. "Poor thing, she, in the thrashing season one year, she was at my Uncle Edward's. There were some other strange horses that were put in the barn for the same night. Daisy and another horse were in a double stall. I guess the horse on the other side of the stall got angry and started to kick Daisy. It kept kicking till it knocked down the barrier and killed her.

"The other horse wasn't a fast runner. She was more nervous and jumpy. She wasn't a dray horse. She was more of a trotter. She wasn't quiet-natured like Daisy."

She described it like it was yesterday.

I took a sip of milky tea. "That's sad."

"Well, I suppose it was." She raised herself with effort and looked out at the back garden with its peach and apple trees full of Grandpa's grafted-on branches, the rickety greenhouse, and rows of broken pots next to the fence. Her shoulders seemed to wilt. "I can't keep up with the garden, dear."

I stood beside her and looked at the clutter. A good granddaughter would stay and help.

Millie's crying for me. She wants to nurse. I'm all dried up. And anyways, I'm busy. I'm driving down the main road past the rec centre, the café, and Mom's office towards the hospital. I hear the siren and pull over. The ambulance swerves in front of me. A dishevelled man like a street drunk stands by the curb, shaking all over. We're gawking in our cars. He sees us staring and makes pig noises. I pull the car back out. They're behind me, my mom and my sisters, waving and yelling to get my attention. They want me to take something with me but I won't. I have to get out of there fast. I keep driving away from the mountains down to the sea feeling guilty, leaving them behind.

On my last evening Mom's snazzy car sputtered and died on the way to our special cove. I'd read the wrong gauge all week. As I trudged back from the gas station with two bucks of gas in a red jerry can, I smelled pizza from a café, and roses. The first time I ran out of gas I was sixteen, driving Mom's VW Rabbit with the stiff standard gearshift on the highway near the bridge into the city. I pulled to the shoulder and found a phone, probably at the motel where we teens tried to buy off-sales. Dad came to the rescue in our old station wagon and helped me fill up. This new car wasn't really Mom. It smelled clean and synthetic, not of spilled coffee and cigarette smoke. The perfume she'd dab behind her ears.

I walked down the steep path to the sandy beach bookended by boulders. It was dusk and mostly cloudy. Two freighters with their lights on floated across the inlet. The sky was peach-pink to the southwest near shapes I knew were mountains. A young couple sat on a blanket while their toddler played in the sand with an older woman, probably the child's grandmother.

Every summer our family drove out here in the evenings. Dad, my sisters, and I rode the logs into shore. Our old mutt, before Snookie, dog-paddled out as far as we could hurl sticks for him. Mom always got cold in the ocean. Instead, she'd spread out our blanket, serve up potato salad and roast chicken, then settle into her portable lawn chair with a glass of wine. Later I came to drink. On my graduation weekend the cops showed and I dropped a full bottle of Kahlúa. It smashed and at that moment, I was shattered.

I sat in the sand, my back propped on a log. It was strange how two of my girlfriends ended up with guys from high school. How Andy and I were getting along. Kim saw more inside me than I realized. And a new life was growing in Priscilla's belly.

I didn't feel like packing. I bought prosciutto, cherries, and snow peas at the market by the inlet. From Mom's bathroom I took her favourite perfume. From her closet an unwashed blouse still smelling of her.

The sweet pea had no flowers left. The runner beans caved in under last night's rain.

The child clutching her sand bucket reminded me of small hands and baby skin. Millie would not grow up knowing my mom, her grandmother. My flight left in thirteen hours. I got up, turned from the sea, and began my climb.

Acknowledgements

I am deeply grateful to many people and organizations who supported me on my journey to create this book.

I first found my way into fiction supported by Writers-in-Residence at the Whitehorse Public Library. Patricia Robertson in particular became a valued teacher and mentor over many years, publishing my first short story in the Yukon anthology *Writing North*. Wayne Grady also generously shared wisdom with me as a Writer-in-Residence, while Gary Geddes's enthusiasm at one of my first public readings meant the world.

I appreciated the guidance of inspiring professor Linda Svendsen during exhilarating fiction workshops in the MFA Program in Creative Writing at the University of British Columbia, alongside insights from talented fellow students including Kevin Chong, Ian Cockfield, Marilyn Dumont, Lee Henderson, Melanie Little, Kevin Patterson, Miranda Pearson, Calvin Wharton, and others.

Storytelling dates back millennia in the Yukon. A vibrant literary, theatre and oral storytelling community helped keep me going through a long, often lonely journey to bring this collection to life, in between being a journalist, theatre artist, soccer coach, and mother. Writing group members ebbed and flowed over the years; all nurtured me. Miche Genest, Laurel Parry, and Al Pope regaled me with their brilliant, often hilarious stories and cheered mine early on. Eve D'Aeth, Dean Eyre, Erling Friis-Baastad, Leslie Hamson, and Carol Pettigrew were part of my early writing community.

More recently, Ellen Bielawksi, Lily Gontard, and Joanna Lilley, along with Patricia, encouraged me to keep working on my manuscript and patiently, enthusiastically reviewed rounds of rewrites. It has been a privilege to teach other writers at what's now Yukon University, including with Patricia, and in high schools.

I am grateful for financial support from the Yukon Advanced Artist Award for this book. Thank you to Diane Schoemperlen, who was instrumental in finetuning this collection with her astute editing eye. I first met Marilyn Biderman on a café patio at the Atlin Lit Up festival in northern B.C. Marilyn offered sage advice and helped me to seek a home with Inanna for this collection.

To the late Luciana Ricciutelli, past Editor-in-Chief at Inanna, I am forever grateful for her belief in my words and her decades of fearless commitment to women's voices and experiences. My gratitude also to the dedicated Inanna team including Renée Knapp and Brenda Cranney, and editors Ashley Rayner, Kaitlin Littlechild, and Kimmy Beach. To Bob Michek of South Hill Graphics, thank you for being the most kind and patient web designer imaginable.

I began writing seriously during my undergraduate degree at the University of B.C. I'm indebted to the eclectic gang at and around *The Ubyssey* student newspaper. Here I found a community of young people who tried to make sense of the world and cared about trying to make it better. I found friends, a home, my first writing community, and names for my values, as a feminist, as someone who believes in justice and equity and self-determination for all people. Thank you to Keith Baldrey, Robert Beynon, Kelley Jo Burke, Charles Campbell, Nancy Campbell, Franka Cordua Von-Specht, Sarah Cox, Muriel Draaisma, Eric Eggertson, Charlie Fidelman, Karen Gram, Tom Hawthorn, Arnold Hedstrom, Debbie Lo, Mark Leiren-Young, Neil Lucente, Verne McDonald, Michael Nicoll Yahgulanaas (Yaku), Lise Magee, Rod Mickleburgh, Gordon Miller, Erin Mullan, Ros Oberlyn, Glen Sanford, Deborah Wilson, Stephen Wisenthal, Chris Wong, and many other old hacks and true originals.

Deep thanks to other friends and creative colleagues, too many to name, who have both challenged me and believed in me and my writing over decades, including Reneltta Arluk, the late Virginia Bawlf, the late Majdi Bou-Mata, Wren Brian, Michael Clark, Dawn Davies, Kathleen Flaherty, C.E. Gatchalian, Marjolène Gauthier, David Geary, Christine Genier, Anne Gibson, Sherrill Grace, Sara Graefe, Penny Gummerson, Ruth Hall, Sarah Hunter, Sheila James, DD Kugler, Brenda Leadlay, Kim McCaw, Hope McIntyre, Natalie Meisner, Mitch Miyagawa, Lillian Nakamura Maguire, Yvette Nolan, Lisa O'Connell, Michelle Olson, Pam Patel, Clare Preuss, Brian Quirt, Denise Relke, Teresa Robitaille, Judith Rudakoff, Elaine Schiman, Jan Selman, Melaina Sheldon, Sharon Shorty, Vicki Stroich, Vinetta Strombergs, Colleen Subasic, Heidi Taylor, Peggy Thompson, the late Bryan Wade, Bob White, Marcus Youseff, the late Svetlana Zylin.

Much love to my parents Verne Flather and Julia Murrell, who surrounded me with books and let me roam their shelves freely as a child, who raised me to ask questions about the world, to find and use my own voice. My late father passed away far too soon. My mother's honest feedback has helped to strengthen this collection. My stepfather Ric Murrell's love is limitless.

Thank you to my extended Gwich'in family who have embraced me without question as an uninvited anglo-settler. My strong daughters Erin and Sophia continue to teach me how to live in a truly ethical way. Finally, haii choo, an immeasurable thank you, to my husband Leonard Linklater who has shared suggestions on various drafts whenever called upon, and offered unwavering, unconditional support in all ways.